The Heart Hitch

by

Laurie Woodford

The Wild Rose Press, Inc.
PO Box 708
Adams Basin, NY 14410-0708
Visit us at www.thewildrosepress.com

Publishing History
First Edition, 2025
Trade Paperback Print ISBN 978-1-5092-6349-3
Digital ISBN 978-1-5092-6350-9

Published in the United States of America

Dedication

To Gloria, with love, admiration, and joy

Chapter One

"Wow. It really is small." My best friend, Jules, stands in the doorway of the twenty-four-foot trailer in Nearly Heaven RV Park that, as of today, is my new home.

I look around at my RV's stained bench cushions, greasy three-burner stovetop, moldy bathroom linoleum, saggy queen bed and bite my bottom lip to hold off tears. I've lost my job, my luxury town house, and now live in a kitchen, living room, and bedroom combo the size of a Shetland pony stall.

Jules looks like she's about to cry, too, so I force a smile, wave her indoors, and say in a look-at-the-bright-side tone, "There are advantages to living in a trailer, you know." I pat my tabletop. "With the push of a lever and repositioning of cushions, this dinette converts into a guest bed."

She slides a moving box aside then sits across from me on the padded bench at my dinette table. Swiveling her head from one end of my trailer to the other, she says, "I could shoot a spit wad from your front door to the back wall of your bedroom."

I tug an elastic tie from my wrist and pull my hair into a messy topknot. "Just because you *can*, doesn't mean you *should*." I palm my forehead and groan. "You're right. This aluminum bitch on wheels is cramped."

Jules sighs, her heart-shaped face all dewy and blue eyes sad. "Ramona, this just kills me. If our house weren't a remodeling construction zone right now, you'd be staying with us."

My heart goes soft. "I know. Listen, it's fine."

She crosses her arms on the table. "It's not fine. Girlfriend, we need to get you back in your town house."

The mention of my town house practically makes me swoon. I bought it a year after I was hired at Sawyer Pickens University to teach philosophy. Located on Bluebonnet Lane in downtown Jackalope, my town house charmed me with its granite kitchen countertops, hickory hardwoods, French doors to a cantilevered balcony, and, most of all, the illusion that I'd made something of myself.

Feet clomp up the outdoor metal steps. Jules and I turn toward the open doorway as her sons, Wyatt and Boone, step inside. "Mom, these are the last two boxes in the truck. We put the others on the patio," Boone says. They pile the boxes on the stack that leans like the Tower of Pisa against my small square of vinyl countertop, brush their hands together, then say in unison, "Where's lunch?"

Jules eyes her twelve-year-old twins, from their curly mops of red hair to their baggy gym shorts and sneakers, then arches an eyebrow. "I don't know. Maybe the Lunch Fairy forgot to pull egg salad sandwiches out of her butt this morning."

They half-frown. "Mom—"

Jules grins softly. "Backseat of the truck. Bag of turkey sandwiches and thermos of lemonade. There's a picnic table out back."

I wink at the boys. "Thanks for your help. You two

are so sweet."

Their freckled faces blush beet red before they head for the door. Jules clears her throat. "Gentlemen?"

Wyatt blinks then glances my way. "You're welcome."

Jules fires The Mom look, and Boone adds, "Ma'am."

They dart outside, and I cringe at Jules. "Please don't make them call me ma'am. It's so weird."

Jules leans forward, and her breasts bubble out of the neckline of her scalloped tee. She's a full-bodied Texan beauty with honey-blonde hair, light blue eyes, and a smile as broad as the San Gabriel River. "You wanna hear weird? Last night I made corn casserole, and those boys picked out the corn. Every damn kernel." I chuckle. "They inhale five pounds of deli meat a day but act like they'll die if they eat one little vegetable." I laugh, and Jules reaches over to pat my hand. "Now, about my girl living in this trailer."

I slump back against the bench, any energy I had left draining by the second. This move from my two-bedroom town house to a two-hundred-eighty-eight-square-foot trailer has depleted me, heart and soul. I blink at Jules. "You know the worst part? After all those years working my ass off to get a Ph.D. in philosophy to become Professor Ramona Sadler living in a trendy town house near campus, I'm right back where I started." I grew up in a trailer in Snap Peas, New York, and here I am, right back in a home on wheels in Texas Hill Country.

I try to swallow the sour taste in my mouth. Somehow, I always knew that no matter how hard I worked or what I accomplished, it could all be peeled off, like a clean bandage over a messy wound. Then it happened. Five months ago, on the last day of fall semester, Dean Bender announced their new college strategic plan. Six teaching positions were cut. Mine was one of them.

Jules shakes her head. "You're not back where you started. No one can ever take away your education or your five years' experience as a professor. You know I hate that my best friend on the planet lost her job and town house, but it's a temporary setback." She forces a grin. "And you're still a teacher."

I snort a laugh. I'm a K-12 substitute teacher at Liberty Trail School District where the kids call me Miss Mona. "I'm not sure breaking up mashed potato wars in the middle school cafeteria counts as teaching." I nod at Jules. "But you're right. It is temporary. As soon as Martin gets me my job back—"

Martin is my boyfriend. Dr. Martin Smallwood, renowned psychology professor at Sawyer Pickens University.

Jules drums her fingers on the table, and I swear I see steam coming out her ears at the mention of Martin. "Now that you brought up the M word," she says, sucking air through her teeth. "You and Martin have dated for two years. *Two years*. Then you get canned at work, have to sell your home, and he doesn't invite you to move into that big-ass house of his on Lantana Lane? I mean, what the hell?"

I wipe my sweaty palms on my khaki shorts. "It's complicated. You know he's a mama's boy. His mother equates pre-marital sex with the sign of the devil. If I moved in, it would tip her off that we've been playing *Rub the Ribeye*." I raise an eyebrow. "You know, bone in."

Jules huffs. "Martin's mother. The Hellstorm from Houston. Can't believe you haven't met her yet."

I straighten, sitting tall. "I've smelled her. After her weekend visits, Martin's house has this freaky odor of lilac perfume, winter salami, and, I don't know, toe jam. She loads his freezer with plastic containers of sauerkraut soup, and tripe stew."

Jules crinkles her nose. "Uck!"

"Martin loves it. Calls her visits 'comfort care.' He keeps a pair of her house slippers near the front door."

Jules slaps the table. "Let me guess, size ten."

I cough a laugh. "Yeah, they're more like house *boats* than house *slippers*. And hideous with embroidered red flowers and a matted, crusty fleece interior."

"God, if her feet are that crusty, imagine what her Southern Hemisphere is like. Just one more reason to ditch Martin, like yesterday. You really want *that* for a mother-in-law?"

"Mother-in-law?" I rub my neck. "You know we never talked marriage."

Jules shoots me a look like, *gotcha*. "Exactly. Two years and not a single mention of marriage."

I scratch my neck.

She leans toward me and squints. "Knew it. Hives. Happens any time the words 'Martin' and 'marriage' are spoken in the same sentence. You know that's not normal, right?"

I drop my hands into my lap.

Jules's eyes turn warm. "Ramona, you deserve more. So much more. Like a man you're head over heels about."

I wince. "That's a tall order. What couple, besides you and Chase, are head over heels?" Jules and Chase fell in love when they were freshmen in college, got married in a park gazebo the following year, and have reeked of soulmate ever since, in a good way. I shrug. "According to my parents, the key to a successful marriage is low expectations. That and bowling together."

Wyatt pokes his head in the doorway. "Mom, did you pack potato chips?"

Jules flicks her wrist. "Nope. And even if I did, it's not even noon."

She turns to me and tilts her head. "Ramona, about Martin—"

"Listen, I know he's on your shit list ever since he no-showed for my birthday party."

Her voice is tight. "He skipped your thirtieth birthday party for his stupid-ass hobby." Martin is a Ships in Bottles hobbyist. Jules purses her lips. "The man stood you up to stuff *Queen Anne's Revenge* into a wine bottle."

I sigh. "I know that should have been the last straw, but—"

There's a hard rap on the doorframe. Jules shakes her head. "Okay, boys, you wore me down. There's beef jerky in the truck glove box."

I startle at the sound of a deep male voice. "Thank you, ma'am."

Jules jerks her head toward the door, and I turn to see a stout, cheerful-looking guy in the doorway wearing a T-shirt that reads, *I Brake for Bacon.*

Bacon guy grins. "But we wouldn't want to spoil our lunch."

A skinny guy in a baseball cap and checkered shirt pokes his head and shoulders in. "Just wanted to stop by and welcome you to the neighborhood." He elbows Bacon. "This here is Joe. Lot thirty-eight." He tips his cap. "And I'm Ugly Jim. Lot forty-two."

I bury a chuckle. "Nice to meet you both."

He nods. "We won't keep y'all. Just want you to know we do groundskeeping here, so if you get pests—"

Bacon Joe pipes up, "You got your slugs, your ticks, your scorpions, your moles."

Ugly Jim smiles. "We gotcha covered."

As they wave and head off, Jules grins. "Meeting neighbors already. Sweet."

"Yep. This morning, Frank, the retired guy with a comb-over and three-legged schnauzer, gave me quarters for the RV park laundromat."

She smiles, then eyes me. "So, let's get back to it. You were talking about Martin and last straws."

I bite my lip. "I know Martin can be difficult. I get that he's high maintenance and self-centered, and a one-trick pony in bed—"

She throws her hands up. "Exactly. So dump him already."

I stare up at the low ceiling. "But I grew up in Snap Peas, population of eight hundred sixty-four if you count the family of woodchucks living underneath my parents' shed. Dinner conversations never went deeper than tractor engine pistons and whether to pronounce the 'o' in opossum."

Jules chuckles. "And what does that have to do with Martin?"

"Martin and I talk about film and literature and

current events, and, I don't know, stuff besides opossums." I raise my eyebrows. "Plus, he's going to a committee meeting today. Says his number one priority is to get my job back."

She knits her brow. "On a Saturday?"

"Emergency meeting in the dean's office at three o'clock. Apparently, the college bigwigs realized their firing spree left them short-staffed. Now they need to rehire some of us for fall semester."

Jules snorts. "That's college administrators, for ya. They gave the axe to a bunch of professors to—" She feigns a finger down her throat. "—fund student success program initiatives." She straightens, then crosses her arms. "You know that shit would never fly in Maintenance. The dean would end up with a monkey wrench up his ass." Jules works at Sawyer Pickens University as Foreman of Operations Maintenance. She wears gray khakis, a matching shirt with embroidered name tag, and a baseball cap that reads, *Keepin Pickens Clean.* "I hope Martin comes through for you. I really do. But if he doesn't, remember: you might have grown up in Snap Peas, New York, but you live in Texas now." She flashes a smile. "You can dump Martin and jump a cowboy."

I chuckle. "Oh, you love your cowboy." Chase runs their family ranch, *Cowboy Crest Quarter Horses.*

She winks. "I'll tell ya, a good cowboy's the way to go. My Chase is one of four boys raised by a strict mama. He's a man of few words, smells like leather, and in the bedroom he never giddyups before I'm satisfied by his sit trot."

I burst a laugh. "Chase is great, but some men of few words are just, I don't know, saddle burs."

She arches an eyebrow. "Like who?"

"Like that doctor at the hospital who does our volunteer schedules." I'm on the Patient Panda volunteer team at Cassidy Memorial Hospital.

I've been a volunteer for the past two years, ever since my mom had a heart attack and open-heart surgery. Helping patients in Texas makes me feel, in some weird way, like I'm helping my mom in New York, too. Or maybe it just makes me feel less guilty about not visiting her more often.

I huff. "Dr. Lonnie. I don't think he's even a real doctor anymore." I nibble my knuckle, suddenly aware of the racket my heart is making inside my chest. *What the heck? Why is my heart beating so fast? I know it's not because I like the guy or anything. I guess just saying his name—Lonnie—gets me so worked up with annoyance that my chest starts pounding.* I purse my lips. "He strides onto Ward Four wearing jeans and a ridiculously tight T-shirt, finds some stupid reason to take a red pen to my patient paperwork, then strolls off."

"Dr. Lonnie. Sounds familiar." Jules winks. "Tight T-shirt, huh?"

I roll my eyes, my face growing warm. "He's the guy who wrote me up because I changed out a bad light bulb in Mrs. Hernandez's room."

"Changed a light bulb? What was wrong with that?"

"According to Dr. Lonnie, it was out of my scope of practice. But the hospital tech was busy, there were light bulbs in the supply room, and I didn't want poor Mrs. Hernandez straining her eyes to do her crossword puzzles. Lonnie told me I would have known that was a violation of my volunteer duties if I'd read page seventy-six of the Patient Panda Handbook." I blow air through my cheeks. "*He* wrote the handbook."

Jules leans back. "Oh, yeah, *that* guy."

"Yeah, and that was the same day I got fired from the university, remember?"

"Yep, it's all coming back to me." Something must catch Jules's eye, because she cranes her neck to look out the doorway. "Talk about a bad day."

I nod, willing my heart to stop racing, then say, "Talk about a pain in the butt doctor."

Jules stands slowly, peering outside.

I stretch my neck. "What do you see?" Then I stand.

Stepping to the doorway, she squints into the distance then turns to me and smiles. "It ain't Ugly Jim, that's for sure."

We move out onto the patio to get a better look at the shirtless man in jeans and cowboy hat jogging from the far corner of the RV park headed this way. I grasp Jules's wrist. "Good God. I can see his abdominal six-pack from here."

She leans forward. "I'm a happily married woman, so I'll deny ever having said this, but it looks like he's got a quarter keg in his pants."

I watch the man stride toward the wooded trails adjacent to my lot. "But it's kind of strange, right? I mean, why's the guy jogging in jeans, a hat, and boots?"

Jules shoots me a puzzled look. "The question you should be asking is: Where exactly does this Godsend from Planet Hot live so I can show up wearing nothing but a frilly apron and offer him a neighborly cup of sugar?"

I roll my eyes, even though she's right about that guy. He's hotter than a branding iron searing the backside of a bull.

"I'm telling you, that cowboy is exactly what you need. He may not be wearing spurs, but I'll bet he's got one stiff saddle horn."

I hold up a hand. "I'm dating someone, remember?"

Jules groans. "Let's review Martin Smallwood's fine qualities, shall we? He stood you up on your thirtieth birthday, has the dumbest hobby ever, and talks about his feelings ad nauseum."

I shrug. "He's a psychologist. And he did write the book." Martin's book, *So, the Feeling Wheelhouse Turns*, has sold over one hundred thousand copies worldwide.

"I'll say it again. Dump Martin and jump that shirtless cowboy."

I watch the man disappear into the woods then face Jules. "I know you're just being a good friend." I search her eyes. "But I've lost my job and my town house. Please don't make me lose my boyfriend, too, even if he can be a dickwad. Not today."

Her eyes melt. "Okay, not today." She lifts her chin, looking around. "Besides, guess your cowboy's jogged off into the sunset."

I drag two lawn chairs over.

Jules glances at her watch and sighs. "I'd love to stay, but we need to hit the road." She walks to the rear of the patio and calls out, "Boys! Truck, now! There's beef jerky in the glove box." She turns to me. "Chase is bringing a new horse back from auction. Don't want to miss watching him work a wild pony on the lunge line."

I smile.

"Plus, I have to go into work later. Got a text this morning that there's a slow water leak in campus Building Eight. Never a dull moment."

I press my lips together, suddenly verklempt. "Thank you for helping me move and, you know, for being you." I stretch out my arms to give her a hug, then get distracted as the man suddenly emerges from the woods. I turn toward him, my jaw dropping. There, cradled against his rock-hard bare chest, is a lamb.

"Holy moly lamb of God," Jules mutters.

I shake my head. "Talk about all creatures great and small." Then I narrow my eyes. "Wait a minute, that guy looks familiar."

The man glances over, does a double take my way, and I swear I blush from head to toe. *Well, shit. There goes my heart, making a racket again.*

Jules nudges my elbow. "You know him?"

I hold my breath. He lifts his chin, his face registering awkward recognition, then frowns and quickly tips his hat. My face heats, reddening two shades darker. Then, his boots crunching on gravel, he trots off toward the farm next door.

I rub my sweaty brow. "I've never seen him in a hat before. But I'd know that saddle bur anywhere."

Chapter Two

Five minutes later, Jules and the boys are gone and I'm sitting in my trailer on my unmade bed, dragging a hand over my face. Dr. Lonnie Acres is my neighbor. He lives right next door to Nearly Heaven RV Park on the property with the big barn and acres of pastureland filled with the white, woolly bovids I count jumping over fences at night when I can't sleep. Things were already awkward between us, with his scowling at my Patient Panda paperwork and writing me up for changing a light bulb, and now I've seen him shirtless. Holding a lamb.

I hold a hand to my fluttering chest, remembering that woolly lamb all snuggled against Lonnie's rock-hard... I shake my head. *Holy moly, Ramona. What on earth is wrong with your ticker today?*

I let out a laborious exhale. The worst part? Lonnie's seen me, his hospital volunteer, on the day I moved into my twenty-four-foot trailer with the rusty front steps and power awning that no longer powers. My cheeks burn and stomach sinks, the same plummeting sensation I had as a kid when the school bus, filled with classmates from town who lived in two-story houses with big garages and manicured lawns, dropped me off at Eight Oaks Trailer Park. On a good day, kids just snickered and elbowed one another as I walked up the bus aisle to exit. On a bad day, after the doors swooshed closed and the bus driver shifted into "drive," the older kids yelled, "Trailer trash!"

through open windows at the rear of the bus. *Trailer trash*. At the sound of those two words, I swear the beating of my heart had slowed to a crawl, or maybe even stopped all together.

My parents always said, "Kids can be mean." I knew that well. I also knew that those kids who called me names were just sad bullies not worth one hurt feeling. But the truth is, it had hurt. It still hurts. It made me feel low, like people didn't see *me*. They didn't see *Ramona*, the girl who loved to read books and climb trees. The girl with a big heart for animals, who would have given anything to have a horse with a white blaze, and long, black mane blowing in the wind as she galloped through fields feeling utterly free. They didn't see the girl who aspired, who had real fucking ambitions, that would take her far beyond the sad little township of Snap Peas, New York. They didn't see *me*. They'd seen some kid in hand-me-downs living in a single-wide trailer.

I stare at the bare walls in my tiny bedroom, and my hands fall limply into my lap. I thought I'd shown them all. At seventeen, I graduated from high school and left Snap Peas behind for good. I went off to college in Minnesota, grad school in Idaho, then landed an academic job here in Texas. Trailer trash, my ass. For five years I was Ramona Sadler, *Professor* of Philosophy.

And now I'm...embarrassed. God, I'm so embarrassed.

I rub my forehead, feeling guilt-ridden over my embarrassment because I know, deep down, there's nothing wrong with living in a trailer. I've met good folks here at Nearly Heaven, like Prisha Chatterjee from Ohio, living in her motor home here in Texas to be near her granddaughter. I've met sweet parents homeschooling their kids in their thirty-two-foot fifth wheel so they can travel the country for a year. Then there's retired Frank, with the three-legged schnauzer, living in his Outback Travel Trailer and touring national parks whenever the urge strikes him. There are others, like me, who seem to be here because it's what they can afford. Like the unemployed young man living in a teardrop trailer who kayaks every chance he gets, and the middle-aged woman living in a truck camper, who waitresses part-time at the Road Runner Café. Bacon Joe and Ugly Jim live in small trailers like mine, and I see nothing for *them* to be embarrassed about. They're doing their best, making ends meet, lending a helping hand to neighbors. I bring my hand to my tightening chest, unable to shake the feeling that I spent years earning a Ph.D. and working my darndest in the Philosophy Department at Sawyer Pickens University only to end up just like my parents. And sadly, I've spent a lifetime feeling embarrassed by them.

I bite my lip, a sarcastic chuckle escaping my mouth. Then, on moving day, when I'm still getting my head around the downward spiral my life has taken and feeling at my most vulnerable, Dr. Lonnie Acres just happens to stroll by in his low-hanging jeans, showing off his ridiculously muscular arms and chest while cradling the cutest farm animal on the face of this planet.

Sitting up straight, I shake out my hands, trying to stir myself out of my funk. Okay, so Lonnie knows I live in a trailer. Big deal. It's temporary. Martin's going to the meeting today, and if anyone can talk Dean Bender into giving me my job back, it's Dr. Martin Smallwood. It'll all be okay. Life can't be that unfair. There's no way

I worked this hard for that long to be right back where I started for good.

I eye the row of unpacked boxes, open the flap of a box labeled "Linens," and start stacking towels and washcloths in the narrow closet outside the bathroom. Next, I stretch a cotton sheet over my mattress and slip my pillows into cases. I pull out the last item in the box, hold it up, and burst out laughing at the blue apron my mom gave me for Christmas a few years back.

Even though my parents didn't have much money, we always had plenty of food around. Our cupboards were stocked with canned soups, jars of peanut butter and grape jelly, loaves of white bread, and boxes of sugary cereals. Our refrigerator shelves were lined with cartons of milk, orange juice, and eggs, and packets of baloney and American cheese. My mom wasn't into cooking. We fried up slabs of cube steak or slid frozen chicken pot pies into the oven, which suited me just fine until I went off to college and felt like I was the only student there who'd never heard of chicken parmesan. I vowed to take a cooking class someday. When I got my job here in Jackalope, I signed up for Dishes of Tuscany. When Mom heard I actually paid someone to teach me how to cook pappardelle with wild boar ragù, she practically laughed her ass off. That Christmas, Mom sent me this apron. Smiling, I run my finger over the bold, white lettering: *This Bitch Can Cook.*

I look at my watch. Twelve-o-five on a Saturday. Draping the apron over my lap, I pick up my phone and dial.

Mom answers on the fourth ring. "Ramona? It's not Sunday."

I call my mom every other Sunday evening at 6:45,

after she's out of the bathtub, but before her favorite sitcom starts. "I know, Mom. I was just thinking about you and—"

"And it sure as hell isn't six forty-five."

"Just wanted to call to see how you're doing." I raise my voice over the blare of a TV game show on her end. "So, how are you?"

"Well, I just ate a tuna fish sandwich and listened to your father burp the alphabet, so just dandy."

I chuckle. "Did he make it all the way to Z?"

"Only to R. He's losing his edge." She coughs a few times. "What's happening in Texas?"

"I moved into the RV today."

"No more town house?"

I shake my head even though she can't see me. "No more town house."

She slowly inhales then exhales a few wheezy breaths into the phone. "Well, think of all the money you'll save on utilities."

"Yep. Silver lining." I chew my lip. "So, how are you feeling?"

"Saw Dr. Patel last week. On the way home, your father and I stopped at Bunny's Burgers. You know, Big Jonny warned us that Bunny was getting stingy with the fries."

Jonny, a family friend, owns Big Jonny's Tires and Lube where my parents worked for years before retiring.

"He wasn't kidding. There were eight fries on my plate. Count 'em. Eight."

"What did Dr. Patel say?" I try.

"Same old stuff: get fresh air, eat more vegetables, blah, blah, blah. Did I tell you Ricky bowled a two-seventy-six last week? His team got second place."

Ricky, my big brother, also works at Big Jonny's. In my parents' double-wide, there's a photo of them and Ricky wearing their blue work T-shirts that read, *Unstick Your Parts at Big Jonny's Tires and Lube*.

"That's great, Mom. Did Dr. Patel—?"

"I told him I have vegetables up the wazoo. Last week Tina brought me a batch of corn fritters and fried pickles."

Tina, Ricky's wife and the cafeteria lady at Snap Peas Elementary, brings Mom school lunch leftovers. "I'm not sure fried pickles is what Dr. Patel had in mind. Do you have any appointments this week?"

"Your father has a horseshoes tournament at the Legion on Friday. I'll probably go to root for the old bastard." Then Mom ends the phone call with her usual, "Okay, I'll let you go. Glad you're still breathing."

"Oh, uh, bye, Mom. I lov—" Before I can get the words out, she's gone.

****

I'm tossing the apron back in the box, when my phone rings. I frown at the screen: Cassidy Memorial Hospital. "Hello?"

A low rumble of throat clearing then, "I'd like to speak with Ramona Sadler, Patient Panda volunteer on Orthopedic Ward Four." The voice, of an elderly man, is vaguely familiar.

I knit my brow. "This is she…uh, wait. Is this Butch?" Butch Zimmerman, a seventy-four-year-old retired surgeon, was admitted to Ward Four after taking a bad fall off a high ladder. He's stubborn, cantankerous, and the kind of patient we refer to as "heavy on the call button." He's also my favorite patient ever.

I hear a smile in Butch's voice as he says, "The one

and only."

I mock groan. "How'd you get my cell phone number?"

"You jotted it down in a weak moment of pity."

"Did not."

"Okay, I got it from the Volunteer-from-Hell who refused to clip my toenails. What kind of Patient Panda is that? Refused. Can you believe it?"

"Well, yeah. Definitely out of our scope of practice. Not to mention disgusting."

He grumbles. "You Pandas stick together. Listen, I'm calling to see if you're coming in this afternoon."

"I'm not scheduled until tomorrow."

"Oh, all right. I was just hoping maybe you could…" His voice trails off.

"Butch, is something wrong?"

"Not exactly wrong."

Then I remember who I'm talking to. "What gives?"

"I need a favor."

I snicker. "I don't do toenails."

"Do you do chocolate?"

"What?"

He sounds sheepish. "Earlier, I scored some bite-sized candy from the hospital clown."

I snort. "You mean you *stole* bite-sized candy from the hospital clown?"

Butch's voice goes high. "He left his candy sack unattended, and I just took one. Or maybe two. Or seven. Either way, now I have a hankering."

I cringe. "I'm not sure which is more terrifying. The clown or his candy sack."

Butch huffs. "Welcome to my world. I'm a sad, hospitalized old man who just needs a little chocolate to get through his lonely day of wound care and pain meds that constipate. I haven't *gone* since I arrived here."

I bury a laugh. "Thanks for talking bowels before lunch."

"The state of my bowels is nothing compared to my feet. Thanks to the Volunteer-from-Hell, I'll be able to slice a French baguette with my toenails by the time I get out of this place."

I sigh. "And me bringing you candy is going to solve your problems?"

"They'll offer an infirmed old man a ray of chocolatey sunshine in this dank hellhole called Ward Four."

I roll my eyes, trying to keep my heart from melting for the poor old guy. Then a sobering reality creeps into my mind. Going to the hospital ups my chances of running into Lonnie again, and I don't need another awkward encounter with The Shirtless Sheep Whisperer. I look around at unpacked boxes and whine, "Butch, I have a lot to do today."

He gulps a lump down his throat. "I understand. Sorry to bother you."

I wince at the disappointment in his voice. Chances are, Lonnie's not at work. He's probably still in his barn. Cradling lambs. All shirtless and shit. "Listen, Butch, you'll need to drink a big cup of prune juice before you get the candy."

A gasp of glee comes through the line. "Deal."

"And one more thing," I tell him. "Keep your socks on."

Chapter Three

I step through the sliding glass doors of Cassidy Memorial Hospital carrying a canvas tote weighed down with candy bars, rolled-up puzzle books, and a thirty-two-ounce bottle of prune juice.

The lobby is busy, as usual. Scrub-clad professionals bustle at a fast clip toward the elevators. An elderly man clomps his walker toward a chair in the waiting area. At the reception desk, a young woman bounces a toddler on her hip while filling out paperwork. I dart my gaze from one end of the cavernous space to the other and nod relief. No Lonnie Acres in sight.

I head for the elevators, breathing in the aroma of Tex Mex wafting from the cafeteria, and carefully weave my way past a man hobbling on crutches, and feel my shoulders soften. I may be just one little Patient Panda volunteer in a hospital full of medical professionals, but there's something about this place that makes me feel like I belong.

On Ward Four, Luciana looks up from the nurse's station and beams. "Ramona. Didn't see you on the schedule today."

I lift my tote. "Special delivery for the grouchy old man in Room Ten." I sign my name on the volunteer roster.

She blows air through her cheeks. "Just in time. Your favorite patient has been heavy on the call button."

She swipes at a rogue strand of hair escaping from her banana clip. "I thought my toddler was demanding, but he makes her bloodcurdling screams for cookies seem like nothing."

James comes striding down the corridor, his hands in the pockets of his blue scrubs. He slides into a chair at the edge of the nurse's station, then waves me over, his dark brown eyes suddenly flashing concern. "You're all moved in?"

"Yep. Jules and her boys helped me move this morning."

He runs a hand over his shiny, black braids and groans. "So Martin didn't—"

I shoot him a sheepish look. "He was, you know, busy."

James sucks in his cheeks.

Thanks to our Friday night happy hours at The Yello Armadillo, James and his husband, Miguel, know way more about Martin's less-than-savory side than they probably should. I scramble to change the subject. "Hey, you haven't seen Acres around, have you?"

He arches an eyebrow. "Dr. Hottie? I mean, Dr. Lonnie? No. Want me to page him?"

I jerk my head back. "God, no. Want to avoid him." I swallow hard, thinking back to the moment Lonnie and I locked eyes this morning. It was so awkward. Me standing there in front of my crappy trailer. Him walking past, practically half naked. I wipe my hands, that are suddenly all hot and sweaty, on my T-shirt.

James cocks his head. "Because—?"

I cringe. "A little secret?"

He widens his eyes. "With the disclaimer that I am The King of Gossip? Absolutely."

I look around. "Lonnie and I are neighbors."

"Stop. It."

I nod. "He lives on the farm next door to my RV park. Trotted by my trailer this morning. Shirtless."

James feigns a swoon. "No."

I raise my eyebrows. "Carrying a lamb."

He swivels his head. "Just checking for the Punked You crew."

I loud-whisper, "I think he has a nipple piercing."

James gasps. "You're killing me."

I flash an evil smile. "Okay, that last one was a lie." I rub my temple. "God, it was so embarrassing seeing Lonnie. It felt like that Saturday morning I went to Buckeroo Grocers all hungover and ran into Dean Bender in the checkout line. I hadn't showered or brushed my teeth. I was wearing pink pajama pants and my *I Eat Asbestos* T-shirt."

James frowns. "Awkward, but what does that have to do with seeing Dr. Lonnie?"

I whisper, "He knows I live in a trailer just like Dean Bender knows I get drunk and eat asbestos."

He lowers his chin. "Ramona, there is nothing wrong with living in a trailer."

"Yeah, tell that to all the Snap Peas middle schoolers who called me 'trailer trash.' " James's eyes go sad, and I hold up my hand. "I know what you're saying, but it's not like I'm living in my trailer because I woke up one day and wanted to simplify my life and *go tiny*. I'm there because it's what I can afford on my substitute teacher's pay. Then, on move-in day when I'm still grieving the loss of my sweet town house in downtown Jackalope, there's Supervisor Lonnie all bare chested and tan and smug."

"Bad timing, I'll give you that." He frowns at the flashing call light on the large square phone on the nurse's desk and mutters, "Room Ten. Again."

I stand, then hike the handle of my tote up my shoulder. "Looks like duty calls."

From the doorway, I clear my throat, and Butch looks up from the dog-eared page of his thick Churchill book and says, "Your badge is on upside down."

I step inside. "Your eyesight's not bad for—"

He sets the book on his nightstand. "For an old guy?"

I walk to his bedside and toss one of the puzzle books onto his tray table. "Your words, not mine." I lower my tote to the floor and pull out the plastic bottle.

Butch frowns. "That's a hell of a lot of prune juice."

"We made a deal." I twist off the cap, grab a cup, and give a good pour. "Drink up. I hear Nurse Meany has a long hose and big bucket with your name on it."

Butch downs the juice in three gulps then grins. "Ah!"

I go into Patient Panda mode, checking his room for loose cables or other tripping hazards, looking around to see if something he might need later—like his water bottle or box of tissues—is within easy reach. Then I pull up a chair. "What's your pain level today?" If Lonnie overheard that, he'd probably write me up for asking a question that's out of my scope of practice. My job is to check for room hazards, put straws in water cups, wheel around a snack cart with crackers, apple sauce, and pudding cups, and make sunshiny chitchat. I look at Butch's tired, gray-stubbled face and bury a sigh. Considering the poor guy's in a hospital gown with a foot-long incision sutured along his right knee, his pain level seems like a reasonable conversation starter.

Butch wriggles his fingers at me. "I answer for chocolate."

I pull the bag of miniature candy bars from my tote then watch Butch tear it open with his teeth and dump a pile on his tray. I hold up a finger. "Hey, one candy bar per answer."

He pops chocolate into his mouth and points at the orange, grimacing face on the laminated pain level chart near his bed.

"Hmm. Level Seven. I can let a nurse know, if you'd like."

Butch reaches for more candy. "Don't bother. Nurse James says no meds for another two hours." He unwraps a chocolate. "But these are exactly what the doctor ordered."

I can't help but smile. There's no getting around the fact that Butch can be a real pain in the butt. But just two weeks ago, he was going about his daily life on his fifty-acre ranch, then climbed a ladder to change a flood light, lost his balance, and dropped twelve feet onto patio brick. In his younger days, he probably did chores like that without a hitch. Physically, he may score an orange grimace on the pain chart, but his pride would most likely score the agonized red face.

Butch cocks his head. "I probably don't say this often enough, but…thanks."

I jerk back. "Often enough? You never say thanks. Like never."

He slides candy my way. "What can I say? I'm a doctor. We're the worst patients."

"Tell me about it." I unwrap a candy bar. "What kind of doctor were you again?"

"Orthopedic surgeon in the Army for twenty-five years. Then when I retired with a good pension and zero tolerance for sitting on my ass, I went to podiatry school."

"You're a *podiatrist*?" I snort a laugh. "With those toenails?"

"Hey, don't mock my toes. Or podiatry. There's good money in bunions. Especially here in Texas."

Sucking on chocolate, I shoot him a confused look.

"Sandal season eight months out of the year."

"God, how did you stand it? Seeing all those feet? Heel spurs. Hammer toes."

He holds up a hand. "Don't forget flat feet, toe fungus, and Haglund's deformity."

"Uck!"

Butch chuckles. "I loved my profession. And feeling useful. Now I can't even change a light bulb without ending up on Ward Four."

I study his defeated expression and sigh. "Sorry."

He waves a hand. "Ah, it was a crap knee before the fall. Would've had to have it replaced in a year or two anyway."

I grin. "Well, look at you being all sunny-side up."

There's a knock followed by James's low, cheerful voice. "Good afternoon, Mr. Butch."

Butch rakes the candy and wrappers back into the bag and passes it to me.

"Nurse James here for an incision check."

I tuck the bag back into my tote as James pulls vinyl gloves from a box near the door then stretches them onto his hands. He shoots me a quizzical look.

"You know, Ramona. Since our little talk a few minutes ago, it occurred to me that it's Saturday. Why are you here *working* instead of *playing* with Martin?"

Butch looks over at me. "Who's Martin?"

James approaches Butch's bedside. "Martin's her—" He feigns a cough, sarcastically, into the crook of his arm. "—boyfriend."

I roll my eyes then look at Butch. "James is not Martin's biggest fan."

James slides the blanket off Butch's leg then studies the incision site. "The guy stood her up on her birthday to put a ship in a whiskey bottle."

Butch furrows his brow. "I'd rather put whiskey in a glass."

James presses his gloved fingers to Butch's leg, checking for swelling. "Right?"

I slump in my chair. "What can I say? Relationships are hard."

James pulls the sheet back over Butch's knee. "True. Last night I overheard Miguel telling his sister that I'm high maintenance." He gives me a look like, *Can you believe that?* "Me. High maintenance."

Butch shakes his head. "I hear ya. My girlfriend isn't talking to me. Again."

I cough. "Girlfriend?"

Butch side-eyes me. "Don't look so surprised. Old people get dates, too."

I wink. "Yeah, but usually the ones with good personalities."

Butch grins. "You got a point. It was my glowing personality that put me in the doghouse." He runs a hand through his thick gray hair. "And with my girlfriend royally ticked off and my son too busy with some beekeeping class, I don't have anyone to take me to church tomorrow."

I wrinkle my nose. "Church? Tomorrow? Aren't you, no offense, too lame to leave the hospital?"

James chuckles. "Guess he's on the mend. His physician cleared him for a supervised outing." He pats Butch's shoulder. "Incision looks good. No redness or swelling or foul-smelling discharge like the poor patient down the hall."

I wince. "That super sweet lady with chronic, explosive flatulence?"

James nods. "That's the one. I heard someone put an air freshener in her room." Tossing his gloves into the trash, James heads out the door, calling over his shoulder, "I'll be back later with your pain meds."

Butch blinks at me. "Favor?"

I throw up my hands. "I'm here. On my day off. Delivering you chocolate. What more could you want?"

He bites his lip. "Could you take me to church tomorrow? It's just three miles down the road."

I squint at him. "Church? Somehow, I figured you for more of a garlic-around-your-neck than a rosary-around-your-wrist kind of guy."

"Full of surprises. It's all part of my charm." I pinch my bottom lip, and Butch continues, "Church starts at ten, but I like to get there by nine forty-five to nab cookies in the narthex before the service." He lowers his chin and gives me a pathetic look. "Please?"

I rub my chin. It's kind of a big request and definitely out of my scope of practice. But if Butch's doctor cleared him for a supervised outing, it must be okay. And it sounds like his girlfriend and son won't take him. My chest suddenly feels heavy. What if my mom hadn't had the support of her family when she was in the hospital? Grasping the straps of my tote, I stand and give a curt nod. "What time should I be here?"

He throws a victory fist in the air. "Nine-thirty sharp. I'll be in my Sunday best."

Heading toward the nurse's station, I realize just how much my mood has brightened. A few hours ago, I was in my trailer feeling depressed about the nosedive my life had taken, and embarrassed that Lonnie saw the site where I crashed and burned. Then Butch calls, and the next thing I know, I'm chatting with Luciana and James and cheering up a patient's day with chocolate and prune juice, and I feel…good. Really good.

I slowly navigate around an older lady in a hospital gown inching her way down the corridor. My throat thickens. She reminds me of my mom, after her surgery, looking so frail shuffling along the halls of Mercy Upstate Hospital. Back then, being around patients made me nervous. I bristled at the sight of IVs and foley bags, at the smell of rubbing alcohol and warm urine. I looked at my mom's pale face and felt scared; I had no idea what to do, how to help her. So, after a few days I packed up and left. I couldn't wait to get on a plane back to Texas and leave all that infirmity behind. But the guilt of not staying longer to help my mom followed me onto that plane and eventually gnawed at me so hard that I signed up to volunteer here at Cassidy Memorial. I wasn't helping my mom, but at least I was helping someone, right?

What surprised me is that I liked it here: the chatter at the nurse's station, the med techs buzzing around the ward, the way Klem, the cafeteria server, jovially warns patients away from yesterday's meatloaf. After a long workday in the stuffy philosophy department at Sawyer Pickens University where the Ivy League tenured professors devalued me, I looked forward to volunteering at Cassidy Memorial where I felt like I made the tiniest bit of a difference in patients' lives.

I turn the corner toward the nurse's station and grin at James, seated in front of his computer. Then my face falls at the sight of Lonnie standing there in his ridiculously tight T-shirt, running a finger along the volunteer sign-in sheet. He has my Patient Panda Volunteer Handbook, the one I decorated with panda bear stickers and accidentally, or maybe not so accidentally, left behind in the volunteer lounge.

Lonnie glances up as I approach, then points to my name printed on the handbook that, after two glasses of wine one evening, I bedazzled with red glitter. I feel the hair on the back of my neck prickle as he squints at me and says, "Looks like someone found her glitter gun and lost her handbook."

Before I can stop myself, I shoot back, "Looks like someone found his shirt and lost his lamb." I freeze, then blink wide-eyed at James who brings a hand to his mouth trying to cover his positively gleeful expression.

Lonnie clears his throat, and I watch his neck flush red. "I earmarked sections of the handbook you might want to brush up on." He sets it on the counter. "For example, Section fifty-six: tripping hazards."

I write my name on the sign-out sheet. "Tripping hazards?"

"Yes, I received notice of a handbag on the floor near the patient's bedside in Room Twelve. You were the volunteer on duty."

My head jerks back. "I didn't—"

James raises his hand. "Mine. Manbag. Set it down for one hot minute while I helped Mr. Yakamoto onto his bedpan. He'd ordered the cafeteria jalapeno poppers for lunch. Let's just say things were poppin'."

Lonnie scribbles a note on his clipboard. "Thank you for the clarification, James."

Then Lonnie looks at me, and I notice his neck flushing again like he's, I don't know, a little nervous being around me. I guess he's embarrassed about this morning, too. Or maybe he's embarrassed *for me* now that he's seen where I live.

He runs a hand through his hair and clears his throat. "Then there's Appendix Thirteen C. Unauthorized room deodorizers are strictly prohibited. Someone plugged a rose-scented air freshener in Room Fifteen. Again, you were on shift."

I shrug. "Wasn't me. I'm just on shift a lot these days." I started putting in extra volunteer hours after I was canned at the university. On days I'm not called in to substitute teach, being here gives me something to do. Now that I live in the RV park, being here gives me someplace to go.

Nodding, Lonnie slides the handbook toward me. "Okay, just remember. No air fresheners."

As I head toward the elevators, my volunteer handbook digs into the flesh of my arm. Just like Lonnie. The thing gets under my skin. Being around him just makes me so…agitated. His rules, his smugness, the way he writes me up for stupid infractions, the way his gorgeous green eyes seem to look right through me. Yep, the guy gets under my skin, all right.

I press the down button and wrinkle my nose. Maybe it's all the talk about air fresheners, but I smell something…off.

Then I hear, "Ramona Sadler?" and turn to see a

statuesque woman eyeing my name tag. She's wearing a white linen tunic, black stretch pants, and the largest thong sandals I've ever seen on a female.

I cock my head. "Yes, I'm Ramona."

Taking a step back, she sweeps her heavily shadowed eyes from the top of my head to my feet, and grins like a cat that just swallowed a carp. "I am Malvina. Mother of Martin."

Chapter Four

Martin must be the spitting image of his father because, as I stand in the elevator face-to-face with Mama Malvina, the only resemblance I can make out is that they're both six foot two.

I press the button for Lobby and force a grin. "This is such a...surprise."

Malvina licks her bottom lip. "That's what my Martin said. But it's pouring rain in Houston and sunny here in Hill Country, so here I am." She places a manicured hand on my wrist. "I'm so glad I'm here. When Martin told me the news, I couldn't wait to meet you. He called the hospital switch board, and when the receptionist said you'd signed in for a volunteer shift, I drove right over."

I furrow my brow. "Uh, the news—?"

The elevator doors open to the lobby, and Malvina links her elbow with mine. "So exciting, isn't it? Walk me to my car, then I want every detail tonight over dinner. I'm making Martin's favorite. Pork bone soup."

"I, uh—"

"Come early." She playfully nudges my elbow. "You can help me make sour cherry strudel for dessert."

I scramble to get a mental grip on why Martin's mother, a woman I haven't met in the two years that he and I have dated, has suddenly popped up unannounced all giddy and excited about some "news." It feels like a bad surprise party. Only instead of cake and ice cream, I get pork bone soup. Malvina stops in the middle of the lobby and twists to face me. "You are a very pretty girl for my very handsome Martin."

I chuckle nervously. "Thanks?"

She studies me. "Long, wavy auburn hair." She leans back slightly. "It will look perfect in a half-do."

I cock my head. "I'm more of a ponytail in a baseball cap type of gal."

She squints, eyeing me. "Beautiful hazel eyes with lashes a camel would kill for. You know a dark plum liner would really bring them out."

I step forward, giving her elbow a tug, and we walk toward the sliding glass doors. "I'm not really into makeup. A quick swipe of mascara and lip gloss and I'm on my way."

In the parking lot, Malvina points to a white SUV. "Why wait for dinner to talk details? Just say the word and I'll call Father Bakos. He's been my priest for years. You and Martin will adore him."

I jerk my head. "Father—?"

Malvina presses her key fob, and the SUV lights flash. "And I'd be happy to reserve the banquet room at The Copper Kettle." She opens the door and slides into the driver's seat.

I jut out my lower lip. "I'm sorry, I don't—"

Malvina closes the door then rolls down her window. "Don't worry about the short notice. I know people." Backing out of the parking space, she calls from the window, "You'll make such a beautiful bride!"

I make a beeline, or more like an angry hornet dash, toward my truck, jabbing my finger on my phone contacts. When Martin answers, I huff, "What. The.

Fuck?"

He scrambles. "Mama surprised me, too. Now, Ramona, I know—"

I weave through a row of vehicles, hiking my tote strap over my shoulder, then pressing my phone to my ear with one hand and scratching at my neck with the other. "Your mother thinks we're getting married!"

He sighs. "She saw your toothbrush and hair scrunchies in the bathroom then charged into the bedroom and sniffed out your panties in the laundry basket."

I cringe. "She sniffed out my… There are not enough emotions in your fucking Feeling Wheelhouse to describe what I'm experiencing right now."

"Mama assumed if a woman is staying over at my house, we must be engaged."

I shake my head. "And you said?"

"You know I can't bear my mother's disapproval. I told her a little white lie."

Heat rises in my throat. "You told her we're getting married?"

"I, uh…I just went with it. Listen, she leaves Monday. Just play along with it this weekend. Then after she goes home, we'll figure everything out."

I rub the angry patch of bumps on my neck. "This is a time-sensitive issue, Martin. Your mother's calling Father Bakos and booking The Copper Kettle."

"Ramona, I hear that you're upset, and I'll help you process your feelings later, but right now I need to check the pork bone broth. I promised Mama I'd keep it at a simmer."

I feel my jaw tighten. "Unbelievable."

"She invited you to dinner, right?"

"Oh, yeah. I'm supposed to show up early to help with the fucking strudel."

"Good. We'll talk about everything tonight."

I huff. "Martin, there is no way I'm sitting through this charade over pig dick soup."

He draws in a long breath, then responds in a measured tone. "That's unfortunate because, over dinner, I was planning to share details about the meeting today. I took on Dean Bender and fought tooth and nail for you."

I stop in my tracks. The meeting. How had I forgotten about the meeting to get my job back? To get my life back. "So, you have good news?"

His voice goes sing-songy. "Someone's sounding like an *impatient* panda."

"Martin—"

"See you at dinner, Ramona. Oh, and bring house slippers."

I slide into the driver's seat of my truck, plunk my tote on the passenger seat, and take a deep breath. Martin took on Bender. He said he fought tooth and nail to get my job back. He must have good news.

I'm about to put my key in the ignition when I glance through the windshield and see Lonnie, in his jeans and stupidly tight T-shirt, walking through the parking lot. There's a woman walking beside him, moving quickly in black stiletto pumps to keep up. She's wearing an open white lab coat over a navy, sheath dress that's perfectly tailored to her elegant figure. Her shiny black hair flows to the middle of her back. She's striking. Is that Lonnie's wife? Or girlfriend? I watch as they stop in front of a white pickup parked in the row in front of mine. They turn to face one another. Whoever she is, it looks like there's trouble in paradise. She jabs a finger in Lonnie's direction as she talks, and when he says something in return, she throws up her hands, shaking her head. Lonnie crosses his arms in front of his chest, turning his head away from her angry gaze. She talks for a while more, her posture becoming steadily less rigid and her demeanor gradually softer until Lonnie's arms fall to his sides, and he turns to face her again. Then she takes one of his hands in both of hers, and they stand there, their bodies appearing slumped with fatigue, for a few moments before she turns and walks away.

I lean forward in my seat. *I wonder what that was all about.* I watch Lonnie stand motionless for a moment, his head bowed, before reaching to open the door of the pickup. He looks like he's about to slide into the driver's seat, but pauses and slowly turns his head in my direction. *Oh, shit.* I duck down, but it's too late. His neck is craned and his eyes fixed. He's spotted me. *Oh, shit!* His face registers that same awkward recognition it did this morning when he walked past my trailer. I do the first thing that comes to mind: I wave. *Oh, fuck.* I wave. A giddy fangirl kind of wave. Because I'm busted. I sat in my truck watching Lonnie's drama play out with the woman in the lab coat and stilettos like I was watching a theatre screen with a bucket of popcorn. Lonnie jerks his head. I sit on my hands. Then he lifts his chin, nods, gets in his truck, and drives off.

I blow air through my cheeks. Could this day possibly get any worse? I'm about to start my truck when my phone rings.

Jules's voice spills through the line. "Ramona. Can you meet me at The Mangy Mule? I have a load of shit to tell you."

I check the time. Three forty-five. Plenty of room to have a beer with Jules and make it to Martin's for dinner. "Sounds good. I have a shitload to tell you, too. Like I met Martin's mother."

Jules's voice goes high. "What?"

"She thinks Martin and I are engaged. Invited me over for pork bone soup and cherry strudel."

I pull the phone from my ear as Jules screeches, "Cannot process! Have you talked with Martin?"

"Just for a minute to rip him a new one about the Mama Malvina fiasco. But then he told me he fought for me at the dean's meeting." I bite my lip. "I've got a good feeling there will be champagne at dinner tonight."

Jules sounds desperate. "Ramona, you need to listen to me. I was at that meeting."

I jerk my head. "Wait. You were invited to the meeting?"

"No. I showed up with a bucket of sawdust and told them Maintenance was called to clean up old carpet barf. I kept my baseball cap pulled down and wiped floorboards long enough to hear the whole thing."

"Martin didn't notice you?"

"Nope. No one pays attention to janitorial staff. We're fucking invisible. Anyway, when your name came up for rehire and the dean asked committee members to vote yes or no, two members said yes and two said no, which left one for the tiebreaker."

I feel my chest deflate. Jules does not sound happy. "And the tiebreaker was a no?"

Jules sighs. "Sorry. It was no. Even more sorry. It was Martin."

I palm my forehead, feeling suddenly light-headed. "What?"

"Martin said he wished he could vote affirmatively, but he cared too much about the reputation of Sawyer Pickens University to vote for a professor with a degree from some state school."

I stutter. "Some state school?" I stare out the windshield at parking lot asphalt. "So, my Ph.D. from Idaho State doesn't count because it's not Ivy League?"

Jules huffs. "According to Martin, who then reminded everyone about his prestigious degree."

My jaw tightens. "I can't believe this."

Jules's voice sounds shaky. "There's more. I'm not sure if I should even tell you this."

"Please. I need to know everything."

She sighs. "Martin said…you're not in their league."

I'm silent, listening to the sound of my chest pound as I clench my fists on the steering wheel. *Not in their league?* I swallow down the painful lump in my throat. I'm fucking *not in their league*?

"Ramona?"

"I'm going to be late at The Mangy Mule." I bolt straight, every muscle in my body feeling tight enough to snap. "I've got an emergency appointment to go see a psychologist."

Chapter Five

My truck tires screech to a halt at the curb in front
of Martin's three-story colonial on Lantana Lane. I grab
a Buckaroo Grocers bag from the backseat and head for
his house, my pulse racing.

Slamming the gate of his white picket fence behind
me, I take the stairs to his front porch two steps at a time.
I rap a quick warning knock on the mahogany door then
barge into the foyer, wrinkling my nose at the aroma of
pork and sauerkraut. "Martin?"

Not waiting for an answer, I stride through his living
room, past the Victorian sofa and settee, hearing the
distant clanging of pots and pans coming from the
kitchen, as I make my way to the library.

Martin's library. I clench my jaw at the memory of
being impressed by this room when I first met Martin. I
was downright dazzled by its walls of bookshelves,
crown molding, rolling ladder, and erudite appeal. I was
dazzled by Martin and his Ivy League degrees. Now,
standing in the doorway, my eyes narrowed at Martin
seated in a wing armchair holding a leatherbound book
in his lap, I feel zero dazzle. I study him in his pressed
slacks, sockless loafers, and buttoned-up white shirt with
starched collar stiff against his pale neck. Nothing. Not
even a razzle, let alone dazzle.

Strange, because Martin's an attractive man. He's
tall and lean with butter blond hair, walnut brown eyes,

and a chin cleft. He showers twice a day, dresses impeccably, and gets pedicures and nose hair waxes at Manny's Salon. Looking at him now, all I see is a self-centered, pompous ass that Jules and Chase and James have seen all along. I see a man who said he fought for me at the dean's meeting when he voted against me, a man who told the hiring committee I'm not in their league. I see the last straw.

Suddenly, it's all so clear to me now. Dr. Martin Smallwood never had a romantic hold on me. My heart never raced with excitement in anticipation of seeing him. My palms never sweat when he was nearby. My breath never caught when he walked into the room. All this time I liked the *idea* of Martin more than the man himself. Any wobbly knee sensation I had around Martin had little to do with him and everything to do with the shaky ground on which my self-esteem stood.

I clear my throat. "Martin."

He sits straight. "Ramona. You're early." Setting his book on the end table, he leans forward and clasps his hands on his lap. "Since Mama's in the kitchen, perhaps this is a good time for me to express my hurt and disappointment over your angry tone during our phone conversation earlier." He arches an eyebrow. "Me thinks some emotional de-escalation is in order."

I choke a sarcastic laugh. "And me thinks I'll pass on your fucking psycho-babble bullshit." I hold out my bag. "Just came to get my things."

He frowns. "I don't understand."

My voice is surprisingly measured. "I'm breaking up with you, Martin. I'm here to collect my stuff, walk out your door for the last time, then go about my life. A better life. Because you won't be in it."

He holds up a hand. "Let's keep things in perspective. Mama showed up unexpectedly, and I reacted with a little white lie. You know I'm not good with surprises." He glances at the door and lowers his voice. "Remember our one-year anniversary?"

I let out a long breath. How could I forget? That night in bed, I fired up an ecofriendly, remote controlled, vibrating love egg thinking it might be a fun way to celebrate. Martin burst into tears. "Oh, I remember. That's why for our two-year anniversary I gave you a bound collection of Sigmund Freud's works and a glass brain paperweight." I pinch my chin. "And what did you give me? Hmm...nothing."

He scrunches his face. "It was a busy week."

"Yet you had time that week to stuff the USS *Constitution* into a brandy bottle."

Martin stands and shoots me a bewildered look. "Ramona, let me get this straight. You're upset because I told my mother we're engaged?" He shrugs. "I'd always assumed that when I propose marriage, you'd jump at the chance."

My body jolts back because I just ran head-on into a brick wall of crazy. "What? I'd *jump* at the chance?" I scratch at my neck. "*When* you propose?"

He stands then takes a step toward me. "We've been together two years. Of course, when the timing's right for me, I'll propose. Why does that come as a surprise?"

I huff. "Uh, maybe because last week, when I dropped by your office for lunch and Dean Bender was there, you pretended I was a client."

"What am I supposed to do? Prance you around campus like my show pony? I have a professional reputation to uphold. You're not even tenured."

I shoot him a look like, *You are unbelievable*. I hold up a finger. "I shouldn't even waste my breath following you down this gopher hole, but if we were married, which let me make perfectly clear is *never* going to happen, the secret would be out of the bag."

He gives a sad little chuckle. "When we married, you wouldn't be Ramona Sadler anymore. You'd be Mrs. Dr. Martin Smallwood, wife of renowned psychologist and author of *So, The Feeling Wheelhouse Turns*. You'd take on my credentials and your professional track record would be obsolete. Win-win."

I clutch my chest laughing. "The only thing that's a win for me is that I'm done dating a dickwad."

Turning on my heels, I storm out of the room and head upstairs, starting with the bathroom. I open my bag and toss in my toothbrush, cotton swabs, mascara, and hairbrush. I pick up my econo-sized bottle of extra-strength pain relievers then set it back down. "Won't need this anymore. Goodbye, Martin. Goodbye, pounding headaches."

I hear the loud creaking of hardwood stairs, then Martin's voice, "Darling? I'm sure we can process and repair these negative feelings."

I bellow down the staircase, "Don't darling me. Bottom step. Now."

I head for the bedroom, empty the one dresser drawer Martin allotted me then fling socks, two T-shirts, a pair of shorts, yoga pants, sports bra, and the red silky nightgown that Martin barely noticed into my bag. Then I rifle through the laundry basket and reclaim my panties.

I stomp downstairs to find Martin and Malvina standing at the bottom of the staircase. Malvina fidgets with the hem of her tunic, looking utterly confused.

Martin frowns, his hands folded in front of his belt. His voice is laced with a tinge of desperation. "Let's all sit down and talk things through."

I hiss. "Not happening, Martin. I'm out of here." I glance at Malvina, whose jaw is dropped, and soften my tone. "I should explain. Sorry to be so blunt, Malvina, but your pencil-dick son lied." Their heads jerk in unison. "Martin and I are not engaged. Never have been. Never will be."

Malvina brings a hand to her mouth.

Martin bites his lip. "Mama, there's been a misunderstanding."

I toss my head back. "Ha!"

He throws his hands up. "Okay, so I lied. I'm sorry." He turns to his mother. "I didn't want to disappoint you." Then he turns back to me. "But that's no reason for us to break up for God's sake."

I nod. "Maybe not. But this is—" I narrow my eyes at Martin. "Remember the dean's meeting today?"

"Ah, yes, I planned to tell you everything over dinner."

I raise a hand. "No need. I heard all about it." Martin cocks his head, and I lock my gaze on his. "Do you remember when a maintenance person came into the meeting room?"

Martin knits his brow. "No."

I sigh. "To clean up carpet barf?"

Malvina cringes, and Martin nods and says, "Oh, yes. Gray uniform. Sawdust bucket."

I laser focus my gaze on him, my eyes feeling fiery. "That was Jules. She called me. Told me everything."

Martin's eyes flash panic. "Ramona—"

"In fact, Jules is waiting for me. She ordered a

pitcher of beer with my name on it, so—" I take a step down. "I'm out of here."

He scrambles. "I can explain."

Malvina turns to Martin and frowns. "What's happening here?"

I sigh. "What's happening is that your son went to a meeting today where he promised to try to get my job back for me, but instead, told the hiring committee that, because I have a state school degree, I'm not in their league."

Malvina gasps then stares down at the floor.

Martin takes a step forward. "Ramona, welcome to academia. I was merely stating the obvious. You're Idaho State. We're Ivy League. You grew up in public schools. We went to the best private schools money could buy. Let's face it and acknowledge the reality: you and I operate on different tiers."

"And your tier is—?"

"Higher, of course."

I storm down the stairs, through the foyer, then pause in front of the door and turn to face him. "That's classism, Martin. Pure and simple, and despicable."

He raises his eyebrows. "I'm just saying that there are differences between us, Ramona. That's simply a fact."

I snort a laugh. "Don't I know it. And here's another fact for you, Martin." I grip the brass knob and pull open the door. "We're over."

Chapter Six

It seemed like a good idea at the time: me and Jules, at The Mangy Mule, ordering a second round of Mexican margaritas after devouring a basket of hot wings and downing a pitcher of beer.

Now, the sun, streaming through my narrow bedroom window, slowly torments me awake, and I roll over with a groan and wipe my drooly cheek with the back of my hand. We should have stopped with the beer.

I palm my forehead and run my tongue along my woolly teeth, feeling a strong need for coffee. Then more coffee. Blinking open my eyes, I skim a hand across my thin blanket then grab my phone. Nine forty-two a.m. Not bad. I still have a full day ahead. A big stretch then I roll onto my side. I can unpack a few boxes, put up curtains, get this place in order, maybe even volunteer at the hospital later.

Hospital. I bolt upright. Butch. Pick up for church at nine-thirty sharp. Well, fuck me!

****

At ten-o-five a.m., after racing through the parking lot, then barreling through the lobby and Ward Four corridor, I stand in the doorway of Room Ten gasping for breath.

Butch doesn't look over. "Church started at ten o'clock."

I bring a hand to my chest. "I'm so sorry."

He frowns, glances over, then jerks his head back in surprise. In my frantic rush to get out the door, I threw on jeans and a crumpled T-shirt, brushed my teeth while speed peeing, then jumped into my truck. At a stoplight, I pulled my bedhead hair into a ponytail and wiped my smudged mascara with a licked finger. I look like shit.

Butch grips his walker, clunks to the doorway and out into the corridor.

I shuffle beside him, repeating, "I'm late. I know. So sorry."

On the way to church, in spite of my apologies, Butch treats me to a big-ass can of The Silent Treatment.

Nearly every pew is full inside the cavernous sanctuary of Sagebrush First Presbyterian. Butch parks his walker in the aisle outside the second-to-last row, and we slide into our seats.

I put on a sad face and blink over at him like a naughty puppy. "I said I'm sorry."

He ignores me.

Running my finger along the service program, I loud-whisper, "Look. We only missed hymn number two-eleven, joys and concerns—"

He shoots me a sour look. "And the sermon."

I tap my foot. "The sermon might've been on *forgiveness*. Ever think about that?"

He rolls his eyes.

"Now sit back and enjoy—" I point to the program. "—the Prayer for Illumination."

He huffs. "With the constipating pain meds I'm taking, I need the Prayer for *Elimination*."

Nudging his elbow, I grin. "Good one." I study Butch in his Sunday best: navy slacks, white shirt, dark gray blazer, and polished leather shoes. My chest deflates. I messed up, and he has every right to be mad.

The pianist strikes a series of thundering chords, and the congregation stands. Butch clutches the back of the pew in front of us, pulls himself up, then thumbs through the hymnal. I tilt my chin up at a large screen. "Lyrics on projector," I whisper. "High tech."

As a cacophony of voices belts out the hymn, Butch turns to me with a pinched expression. "Is that a human behind us clawing for those high notes? Or an alley cat in labor?"

I widen my eyes and bring a finger to my lips. *Shhh.*

He shakes his head. "All I'm saying is maybe someone should let the dogs out and end the suffering."

I bite my lip. I've never seen him so miserable. "Butch, I'll bring you to church next week, early enough for you to score all the cookies in the narthex your little heart desires."

Staring straight ahead, he mutters, "Next week won't count."

The song ends, we sit, and the pastor, in a long black gown, stands behind the communion table set with a challis, loaf of bread, round trays filled with tiny juice cups, and baskets of bread cubes.

I whisper to Butch, "What do you mean next week won't count?"

He shrugs. "Just won't count. That's all."

As the pastor reads scripture while pouring wine into the challis, I rub my aching head and sigh. I messed up, but I've apologized a gazillion times. I feel my jaw tighten. Butch is being impossible.

The pastor breaks the bread loaf in two and says to the congregation, "This is not a Presbyterian table; this is the Lord's table. Come one, come all."

Butch pulls himself to his feet, then limps into the aisle to join the line.

I'm right behind him. "Forgot something?" Butch ignores me. I tap his shoulder. "Your walker." He waves me off. "Butch, you can't risk a fall. Now, wait here. I'll get your walker."

Hobbling forward, he hisses over his shoulder, "Who died and left you boss?"

I cross my arms and loud-whisper, "The God of Patient Pandas."

A gray-haired woman raises her eyebrows at us. *Shhh.*

Butch turns and looks me in the eye for the first time this morning. "I will not clunk up to the Lord's table with that aluminum contraption when I can walk up with the perfectly good legs God gave me."

I snort. "Ever hear that pride cometh before the fall?"

Butch pffts. "Ever hear that punctuality is a virtue?"

My voice goes tight. "How many more times can I say I'm sorry?"

The woman wags a bony finger. *Shhh!*

Then it happens. I don't know if Butch's foot catches on the carpet or if his brand new titanium knee gives out, but in slow motion, it seems, Butch tumbles over like a fallen statue.

The sanctuary fills with a collective *Uhh!*

I bound forward, reaching for him, but he topples, landing with a thud. Not a thunk, or a splat, or a crash, or a crunch. But a thud, like a heavy book dropped on a low pile rug.

I rush over and kneel beside him. "Oh, my God. Butch, are you okay?" Placing a hand on his shoulder, I ask, "What's your pain level, one to ten?" I watch him roll to his side, then scramble to prop himself up. "Relax. Let's assess your situation before you try to stand."

Butch cranes his neck up at the crowd of concerned faces peering down at him. Then he locks his gray eyes onto mine. "I served in the U.S. Army for twenty-five years." Digging his palms into the carpet, he lifts his shoulders off the floor and scooches his lower half into a sitting position. "Obstacle courses. Hand-to-hand combat training. Twenty-mile night marches with fifty-pound ruck sacks." He glowers at me. "What's my pain level? I tripped over a piece of damn carpet. I'm fine. And I don't need you hovering over me like some mother hen."

The woman who shushed us earlier brings Butch's walker over, and the line slowly starts moving again. I take a deep breath. "Butch, I know this is frustrating. I'll help you up, then you take the walker—"

He waves me off. "I don't need that walker."

"Butch—"

"I said no."

I plead. "I'm just trying to help."

"Go help another one of your charity cases on Ward Four. I can do this myself."

I rub my pounding head, feeling completely drained. In the past twenty-four hours, I moved into my trailer, met Mama Malvina, broke up with Martin, and found out I'm not getting my job back. Then I drank too much, woke up bed heady and hungover, and now *this*. I stand up and stomp my sneaker against the carpet. "Fine! Be that way." My voice is much louder than intended and Butch jerks his head. I raise my eyebrows at him. "I'm getting in line for communion before the grape juice goes sour and the bread cubes get stale." I throw up my hands. "And you, Butch 'Dr. Stubborn' Zimmerman, can just sit on the floor all day if you want."

Suddenly, there's a low voice behind me. "Dad?"

I wheel around and notice his green eyes first because they're fixed on me intensely, like they're boring into my soul.

"Dad, are you okay?" Lonnie's lips are pursed, his face a storm cloud of emotion as he studies Butch—*his father?*—all helpless on the floor after his Patient Panda ripped him a new one in front of a church load of Presbyterians. "Does anything hurt?"

Butch grins up. "Just my pride, Son." He cocks his head. "Thought you were at some beekeeping class."

I rub my nose, feeling a bit light-headed. *Well, that explains the whiff of pine and honey.*

Lonnie shakes his head. "Knocked off early." Then he eyes me. "Good thing."

I cringe. "I was just…he fell and wouldn't use his walker and—" I grab the walker, position it next to Butch, then reach out my hand to help.

Lonnie waves me off. "From the look of things, your shift is officially over." He kneels beside Butch then twists his shoulders, looking up at me. "I'll take it from here."

Chapter Seven

At home, I take a long, hot shower, my elbows knocking against the walls of my cramped shower stall as I soap up and scrub hard, hoping all my guilt and anger from this morning will swirl down the drain.

I towel off, still pissed. Yes, I was late picking Butch up for church. But I was doing him a favor—a big favor—out of the goodness of my Patient Panda heart. I rub the towel briskly along my scalp. I do him favors all the time. Chocolate, puzzle books, prune juice, sunshiny chitchat. And it's not like I get paid for that shit. I wrap the towel around my chest, dart into the bedroom, and groan. What do I get in return on a Sunday morning when, instead of eating bagels and cream cheese in bed, I chauffeur an infirmed old man to church? A scolding from Dr. Stubborn and a big dollop of smugness from his son, The Lamb Whisperer.

Pulling on shorts and a T-shirt, I try to shake off the shocker that Lonnie is Butch's son. It seems like Lonnie is everywhere I turn these days. I smooth my hair into a damp pony, slump onto my bed, and curl my knees to my chest. The memory of Butch sprawled out on the sanctuary carpet flashes across my mind. I bring a hand to my nauseous stomach and sigh. I let Butch down. I agreed to pick him up at nine-thirty sharp, showed up *very* late, then when he fell and was at his most vulnerable, I went all Angry Panda on him. My face grows hot. I need to make things right and apologize to Butch. Glancing at the ceiling, I let out a long exhale. And I need to apologize to Lonnie for not being kinder to and gentler with his infirmed, elderly father when he took a tumble in the middle of Sagebrush First Presbyterian.

I go to the kitchen, pour a cup of black coffee, and sit at the dinette feeling an achiness in my heart that I can't put my finger on, a heartache that goes way beyond my morning trials with Butch and Lonnie. Taking a sip of rich, nutty brew, I stare down at one of the last boxes to be unpacked labeled, "Miscellaneous." I open the flaps and pull out a notebook, cube of Post-its, a plastic bag filled with spare chargers and earbuds, then smile at the well-worn paperbacks from my childhood. *Misty of Chincoteague, The Black Stallion, National Velvet*. I must have read these books a hundred times as a kid. They were my escape, the salve to my wounded heart. I'd get off the school bus, grab a snack, then climb my favorite tree carrying one of these books tucked in my waistband. Within moments of turning the pages, echoes of my schoolmates' snickering and name calling died down to nothing. I delved into the sights and sounds of racing hooves, blowing manes, and the children and horses whose hearts pounded with freedom and promise. The world that leapt off the pages felt so real that I felt free and filled with promise, too.

I run my fingers over the tattered cover of *National Velvet* and smile remembering my tenth birthday when I unwrapped a box containing socks, a butterfly yoyo, and this book. My mom, with an expression of pride and curiosity, watched me holding the book to my heart, and said, "Mrs. Percival tells me you're an advanced reader.

I figured with the way you're all goo-goo eyed over those horses down the road that maybe you'd like this story."

I feel my throat thicken at the memory. It's been a year since I traveled to Snap Peas. I flew up on a Thursday, spent two full days with my family, then couldn't get on a plane fast enough Sunday morning. I tell myself I keep my visits short for my parents' sake, that since I sleep on the sofa in their double-wide trailer, my backpack and stuff gets in their way. The truth is, I feel like *I* get in their way. Sometimes I feel guilty, but it's not like anyone in my family begs me to stay longer. Or asks me to visit more often. And none of them have ever gotten into a car or onto a plane to visit me.

I rub my arms, thinking back to my phone call with Mom yesterday. Her raspy voice. That cough. Her wheezing breaths. I take a big gulp of coffee, and a dark cloud of worry envelopes me.

Picking up my phone, I text my brother, Ricky. — *Just checking in. How's Mom?*—

I stare at the blank screen for the next minute, then draw in a quick breath at the three dancing dots.

—*Busting balls as usual. Why?*—

—*She was coughing on the phone yesterday.*—

—*She coughs like a pro. Said that's why she quit bowling. I think she was just a sore loser after throwing a gutter ball in the fifth frame.*—

I bring a hand to my lips. Mom didn't tell me she quit bowling, and she certainly didn't tell me she quit because of her coughing. Squeezing my eyes shut, I cross an arm over my stomach, a wave of nausea hitting me hard. Mom had a heart attack two years ago, and I planned to spend this summer helping patients on Ward Four. The pang of guilt doubles me in half.

My finger trembles as I type. —*I'm coming to Snap Peas.*—

—*Okay. When?*—

I stare at the question. Classes at Liberty Trail School District end this week, so my chances of getting called in to substitute teach are slim to none.

—*Very soon.*—

—*Staying a couple days?*—

I chew the inside of my lip. Martin and I are over, and summers for Jules are crazy busy with her kids home twenty-four/seven, so my social calendar is practically nonexistent. I stand, and the sound of Mom's coughing echoes in my brain as I pace my living space. Then it hits me: I have a pickup truck and a home on wheels.

Taking a deep breath, I type. —*Towing my trailer up. Staying for a while.*—

—*Roger that. I'll tell Mom. Bring some Texas beer.*—

For a minute, I don't breathe, a shiver of panic running up my spine. Ricky's probably already on the phone with Mom. Looks like it's settled. I'm towing my trailer to Snap Peas to visit my family for the summer. I slump back onto the bench, my mind scrolling through the long list of tasks I need to complete before hitting the road.

But, first, I need to make things right with Butch.

****

Butch is sitting up in bed when I arrive, his skin pale against his light blue hospital gown. I give a courtesy knock on his doorframe, then head to his bedside, feeling sheepish. "I'm here to sincerely apologize. I showed up late. Then got all impatient. I'm very, very sorry." I shake a box of chocolate-covered caramels at him.

"Peace offering?"

His lips curl into a wide grin. "How did you know those are some of my favorites?"

I slide the box onto his tray table. "Knew I couldn't go wrong with chocolaty chewy goodness."

He points to the chair beside his bed then frowns. "I'm the one who needs to apologize." He opens the box. "You were doing me a favor, and I acted like a grumpy, old coot."

A woman's voice calls from the doorway, "More like a grumpy old bean goose."

I turn to see a barely five-foot-tall elderly woman in white skinny jeans and bright aqua blouse, her shoulder-length jet black hair teased to the size of a lampshade. She strides over in red cowgirl boots and holds out her hand for me to shake. "Huang Mingzhu. Pleased to meet you." I shake her hand then pull over another chair.

Sucking on a mouthful of candy, Butch mumbles, "She goes by Ming." He furrows his brow. "Bean goose?"

Ming arches an eyebrow. "That's right. Taiga Bean Goose. Breeds in Siberia and winters in northwest China." She squints at Butch. "It's a cold, cold duck."

He cocks his head. "Thought you said goose."

Ming side-glances me. "See what I have to deal with?" Then she eyes Butch. "In case you're wondering, I'm still mad at you. I brought you socks." She tosses them onto the bed. "As a favor to the staff so there's something between them and those toenails." Butch holds out the candy, and Ming plucks two from the box. "The nurse called and told me you fell. I'm calling a temporary truce."

Butch's face softens. "Well, I appreciate that."

Ming pivots in her chair, straightens my badge, then squints at me. "Pretty face, rockin` figure."

I feel my neck flush.

She touches her chin. "It's still the weekend. Shouldn't you be with some hot guy instead of at the hospital doling out candy to this old bean goose?"

Butch throws up his hands. "Just tell me what I did, and I'll apologize."

She wags her finger at him. "You know what you did. Apology not accepted."

I lean over to Ming and whisper, "What did he do?"

She cups her hand in front of her mouth. "I'm seventy-one years old. I don't remember."

I chuckle then look at Butch who's eyeing the doorway and sliding the box of candy underneath his bedsheet. "Hey, Son. Don't just stand there. Come on in."

My stomach drops. I slowly turn my head toward Lonnie who's wearing faded jeans, a navy tee, and an expression that says he'd rather do prostate exams than step foot inside this room.

Lonnie runs a hand through his hair and moves at an efficient clip to Butch's bedside. "Just stopping by to take a look at your incision."

Butch waves toward me and Ming. "Lonnie. Manners? You can't squeak out a hello to Ming and Ramona?"

Lonnie nods in our direction. "Ming. Ramona. Hello." He looks at Butch. "I'm not ten, Dad. I was going to get around to it." He moves the bedsheet aside, frowns down at the incision site then side-eyes me. "No tenderness from the fall earlier?"

Butch smiles at Lonnie. "Feeling great. My knee is

on the mend, Ming brought me socks, and Ramona brought me an undeserved, heartfelt apology."

Biting my lip, I look over at Lonnie. "I owe you an apology, too."

Lonnie raises an eyebrow. "For publicly flogging my infirmed father as he lay on the floor a stone's throw from the Lord's table?"

I study him for a second and swear he's burying a grin. And his neck is slightly flushed, the way it was yesterday when he was reciting rules from my Patient Panda Handbook. "Yes, that. Sorry."

Lonnie blinks my way. "It happens. If I had a dollar for every time—" Then he tilts his head. "And you made up for it by bringing him socks."

I shake my head. "Nope. That was Ming. I brought him chocolate."

Lonnie's head jerks. "You brought him candy?"

"Sixteen-ounce box." I wriggle my fingers. "Hey, Butch. Share much? Hand 'em over."

Butch goes all sheepish, then slides the box from beneath the sheet.

Lonnie rubs his forehead and huffs. "I can just see the headline now: *Panda Kills Patient One Chocolate at a Time*."

I crinkle my nose. "What?"

Lonnie throws out his hands. "He's diabetic."

Butch holds up a finger. "*Borderline* diabetic."

I widen my eyes at Butch. "You told me you have no dietary restrictions."

He shrugs. "I don't. I eat anything I want."

I shoot Lonnie an apologetic look and sigh. "Go ahead. Write me up. But in my defense, it's kind of our thing. Butch gets annoying. I get impatient. Then I bring him chocolate, and it's like everything's right with the world again. It's kind of like giving a whiny two-year-old a box of animal crackers to shut him up."

Butch's jaw drops. "Hey!"

Lonnie crosses his arms over his chest. "No wonder his A1C has been through the roof. You know section twenty-five B in the volunteer handbook warns about this very thing."

Ming stretches her hands out. "Don't write her up, Lonnie. Your father can be a manipulative old rat snake. How do you think I ended up dating him?"

A weird silence falls across the room like the calm before a Texas hailstorm. I watch Lonnie's jaw tighten, his eyes blinking slowly like he's trying very hard not to say something he might regret later. He pulls the bedsheet over Butch's leg. "Incision looks fine. You'll have a good chance at being discharged tomorrow if—"

Butch slumps with a groan. "If the prune juice kicks in?"

Ming shakes her head at Butch. "You still haven't pooped?"

Butch grimaces. "No, and after the Prayer for Elimination and everything."

Chuckling, I look at Butch. "You're getting discharged?"

He nods. "Hopefully, tomorrow afternoon. Do you have a morning shift?"

My chest deflates. My trip to Snap Peas is a three-day drive. Everything I own is in my trailer, so there's nothing stopping me from leaving tomorrow. For some reason, I feel kind of anxious to go see my mom sooner rather than later. I guess for me and Butch, this will be goodbye. "Actually, I'm heading off to New York to visit my family. I'd like to get on the road early." I glance over at Lonnie. "Oops. Sorry about the short notice. I'll be off the volunteer roster for a while."

Lonnie sighs. "Section forty-eight C. Volunteers should give two weeks' notice."

Ming sits straight. "Wait, Ramona. You're driving? From here to New York? How far is it?"

"About eighteen-hundred miles. The internet says it's a twenty-eight-hour drive. I'm towing my trailer, so I'll stay over a couple of nights at campgrounds along the way."

Butch taps his fingers against his cheek. "You've towed a trailer before?"

I cock my head. "No."

Butch whistles. "That's an awfully long way for a young lady to tow a trailer all by herself."

I snort a laugh. "This young lady has been driving a big, old pickup truck for years, you know."

Butch rolls his eyes. "I'm just saying it's a big undertaking for someone who's never done it before."

Ming raises her hand. "Agreed."

Lonnie squints at me. "Have you ever disconnected and connected the water?"

I shrug. "No."

He bites his lip. "The sewer? The electric?"

I shake my head. "Nope."

Lonnie knits his brow. "Then how—?"

I arch an eyebrow. "I guess that's what how-to videos are for."

Butch coughs. "Ramona, not to be an old protective geezer or anything, but I'm worried about you heading off eighteen-hundred miles on your own when you've never towed a trailer, let alone connected the utilities."

I smile. "Aw, that's sweet, but—"

Butch grumbles. "I'm not sweet. I'm worried. Big difference."

Ming looks at her watch and frowns. "I'm worried, too. And I'm also late. I promised to meet cousin Cheong to help him choose fabric for his wingchairs. The guy wouldn't know a decent color pattern if it was floating in his miso soup."

Lonnie glances at his watch. "And I need to get back to my office."

Ming leans over to kiss Butch's forehead and whispers loudly, "You know there's no way Ramona should be towing an RV all the way up to New York all by herself, right?"

As Lonnie and Ming head toward the door, I step to Butch's bedside and tell him, "Good luck going home tomorrow. Make sure you watch out for tripping hazards. You know, area rugs, electric cords—"

Butch blinks up at me. "That's sweet, but—"

I feel my throat thicken. This is it. Butch is being discharged. I'll probably never see him again. I clear my throat. "I'm not sweet. I'm worried. Big difference."

He looks at me then knits his brow. "Well, I guess this is…goodbye."

For a moment, I don't know what to do. I want to hug him, but that might be weird. Not to mention, probably against Patient Panda protocol. "Well, goodbye."

I hold up my hand to wave, and Butch surprises me by taking my hand in his. "Bye, kid."

My voice comes out small. "Bye, Butch."

Then he gives a loud whistle toward the doorway and yells out, "Ming?"

I hear the clicking of bootheels then see Ming's head in the doorway.

Butch gives a decisive nod. "That thing you said about pandas and RV's earlier? I'll get it all sorted out."

Chapter Eight

Butch and Ming must have slathered a guilt trip on Lonnie so thick that it was less painful for him to agree to accompany me on my eighteen-hundred-mile road trip to Snap Peas than to stay here in Hill Country and deal with those two disapproving septuagenarians.

I could hear the coercion in Lonnie's voice when he called yesterday afternoon. "Here's the thing," he began. "My dad's worried about you hauling a trailer that far by yourself."

I tried to protest, but he kept talking.

"Listen, I know it's sexist. If you were some male accountant who didn't even know how to start a hand mower, Dad probably wouldn't think twice about it."

My voice came out a tinge indignant. "So, what am I supposed to do? Not drive to Snap Peas?"

"It's not what *you're* supposed to do. It's what *I'm* supposed to do."

"Which is?"

He drew in an audible breath. "Help you drive, connect and disconnect your trailer utilities, and assist with any road emergencies that might occur."

I was silent for a moment, trying to wrap my head around his offer. I wasn't nervous about hauling my trailer that far, but I did have a trepidation or two. For instance, what if I got a flat tire on the highway? Or what if I did have trouble connecting the electric? I knew I'd figure it all out. It wasn't like I needed a big, strong, shirtless man to handle things for me. But there was something reassuring about having another person around if things got dicey. I felt my shoulders ease for a moment, then tense up again at the thought of Lonnie— that big, strong, shirtless man—handling things on the road. *What if I ended up wanting him to manhandle me?* I coughed into the phone. "That's really nice, but—"

Lonnie cleared his throat. "But? I'm not sure you understand the pressure I'm under. My dad's bad enough, but he's banded together with Ming."

I snorted. "You're afraid of a seventy-year-old woman who's five feet tall in lifts?"

He huffed. "Hell, yeah. On tiptoes, Ming's tall enough to reach kitchen knives. She told me there's a hair sweater reserved for me in purgatory if I don't accompany you on this trip. Something about campground trolls preying on pretty, single women who drive pickups." He sucked in a quick breath. "Her words, not mine."

I felt my breath catch. *Pretty* and *single* might have been Ming's words for me, but Lonnie repeated them. Did he know I was single? Did he think I was pretty? I stifled a groan. *What was I thinking? Lonnie didn't even like me.* With my mind heading in the wrong direction, a road trip together would be a very bad idea. "That's sweet, but you can tell Ming that I've slayed plenty a troll. Besides, your dad is being discharged from the hospital. I'm sure he'll need help at home."

Lonnie's voice was insistent. "Dad assures me he has nurse's aides, meal delivery, and physical therapists up the wazoo. Not to mention Ming, at least until he pisses her off again."

I pinched my chin. "Wait. Don't you have to work?"

"In case you haven't noticed, my Patient Panda gig is part-time. Put my schedule together early. I can answer emails or phone calls on the road. They don't need me back in the office until the end of the week."

"What about your farm?" Then I winced. My question implied that I assumed he lived alone. For all I knew, that gorgeous woman in the white lab coat who grabbed his hand in the parking lot was his wife or girlfriend or friend with benefits, including farm sitting.

"Did my homework before calling you. I have an animal sitter lined up."

I bit my lip, feeling touched, not to mention surprised as hell, by the magnitude of his generosity. After months of Dr. Lonnie Acres being on my case about Patient Panda protocol, he was offering up a bear-sized favor. Maybe he didn't dislike me as much as I thought he did. I brought a hand to my pounding chest. It would be nice to have a companion during the long trip. I'd just need to keep my mind from taking detours. I drew in a breath. "Well, I mean, how would this work?"

"Like I said, did my homework. Wheatland Airport is twenty miles west of Snap Peas. I'll drive up with you, then fly back home."

My face went warm. "Um, that's a lot to ask."

His voice sounded...kind. "You're not asking. I'm offering."

I exhaled, suddenly aware of just how tight my muscles had been over the past few hours from gearing up for my solo trip. After I left Butch at the hospital, I set to work filling the gas tank, checking the oil, securing items in the trailer that could shift while being towed, researching how to disconnect and connect the water, sewer, and electric. With Lonnie's offer, knowing that I wouldn't be making the trip alone, the muscles in my shoulders, neck—hell, even that pesky knot in my lower back—softened like a stick of butter in a ray of sunshine. "Hey, Lonnie...uh, thank you."

He paused. "No problem. Hair sweaters are not a good look on me."

****

At six fifty-eight a.m., I'm sitting on a patio chair listening to warblers chirp from oak branches and Prisha, two lots down, sing showtunes while watering her hydrangea. Lonnie arrives wearing khaki shorts and a T-shirt, a big green backpack, and a sleepy frown.

I wave, willing my gaze to focus from his neck up rather than doing a slow scroll over his muscular chest. "Ready to roll?"

Lonnie knits his brow then walks around to the front of the trailer, inspects the hitch connection, then turns to me. "You disconnected the electric, water, and sewer?"

"Yes, sir." Last night, I watched how-to videos on the ins and outs of disconnecting and hooking up RV's. This morning, I woke up before five and got busy. I pull my shoulders back. "Safely disconnected fifty-amp shore power. Donned PPE, dumped black water tank, emptied gray tank. Flushed with freshwater and disconnected sewer hose." I cringe. "Then burned PPE gloves."

Lonnie nods, a grin sweeping across his face. "Truck unlocked?"

I stand, fold up the patio chair, then slide it into the bed of the truck underneath the cargo net with the other chair, folding table, and large cooler. Reaching into my jeans pocket, I grab my keys and toss them his way. Then my gut flip-flops. My truck is kind of my baby. I walk toward the passenger door then pause and look over at Lonnie. "No pressure or anything, but I love my truck."

Lonnie tosses his pack into the backseat, then slides into the driver's seat. I climb into the passenger's seat, pushing the canvas tote, that I'd filled with bottled waters and granola bars, aside with my foot. I watch him adjust the mirrors then I pat the dashboard and tell him, "I'm just saying. Please be nice to her."

He turns the windshield wipers on and off, presses buttons for a/c and fan control, pushes the radio knob and seek arrows, and connects his phone to wireless technology. "Will do." Glancing at the rearview mirror, he draws in a deep breath, turns the key in the ignition, shifts into "drive," then slowly drives my truck forward.

And I do mean *slowly*.

As in, a tortoise recovering from foot surgery could outrun my truck as we inch out of my driveway then along the gravel loop of Nearly Heaven RV Park.

At the speed bump halfway to the RV park exit, Lonnie brings the truck to a full stop before gingerly tapping the gas pedal and creeping over the bump. I cock my head. "Is everything…okay?"

He rechecks the rearview mirror. "Just getting to know your vehicle."

I side-eye him. "At this rate, it feels like you're growing old together."

He huffs. "Safety first. I took an oath to do no harm, remember?"

I purse my lips. "No harm in driving over five miles per hour."

With an exaggerated eye roll, he creeps the truck out onto Salt Lick Trail then gradually accelerates to a cruising speed of thirty-five miles per hour. With Lonnie focusing on the road with eagle-eyed intensity, conversational chitchat is out of the question. I might as well get comfortable.

I gaze out the passenger window at the stretch of tall grass and sage. It's the end of May, and Texas Hill Country landscape is spotted green with live oaks, juniper, and mountain laurels, and grays and browns from expanses of sun-scorched meadows, limestone, cacti, and yuccas. After growing up in upstate New York, I had a tough time making friends with this landscape. At first, I missed the lush, rolling fields, and dense forests in Snap Peas. But then March hit and the wildflowers bloomed, and my heart opened to Texas's natural beauty.

Lonnie flicks the turn signal then merges onto I-35 North, and I lean back, my eyes skimming the brown fields that, two months earlier, were carpeted with the brilliant blue of Texas bluebonnets. Every March, I print a photo of bluebonnet fields in bloom and send it to my mom. She's never said anything about the photos, but I think she likes them. Looking out at the brown fields where the blue used to be, I sigh. They've all gone to seed now. I guess nothing lasts forever.

When we're comfortably cruising along on I-35, I jab the radio knob and tune to a Top 40 station. When that goes staticky, I tune to Classic Rock. Then Regional Mexican. R&B. Texas Country. Then Oldies. When I can no longer escape the static, I turn off the radio. Then I turn to Lonnie, aware of the taunting reality that I could easily reach over and touch him. I clear my throat. "Radio reception sucks. We have a twenty-seven-hour drive ahead. Wanna talk?"

He frowns. "About?"

"I don't know, basic stuff. Like do you have brothers or sisters?"

"Nope."

I blink. "Nope as in you're vetoing the topic? Or nope to siblings?"

"Only child."

"Interesting. How did you feel about that?"

"Fine."

I sigh. By the end of our phone call yesterday, I somehow actually believed that Lonnie wanted to help me drive all the way to New York. Now, with his one-word answers to my questions, it's clear that Lonnie's only accompanying me on this road trip to avoid being driven mad on Butch's and Ming's guilt trip. The only reason he's sitting in my truck is to get his father off his back. I shrug. "Sorry. We can go back to listening to static." I cross my arms in front of my chest, my disappointment turning to annoyance. "I forgot you hate me."

Lonnie's head jerks. "I don't hate you."

I pfft. "Okay, I said *hate* for dramatic affect. But ever since you met me, you've scowled at my patient paperwork and threatened to write me up."

He snorts, and I notice that his neck has flushed red again. "Yeah. Because I hate my job." He side-eyes me. "You try supervising volunteers. It's like trying to herd a pack of prairie dogs."

My jaw drops. "Prairie dogs?"

"Yep. The cheerful little rodents are all excited to volunteer, then as soon as I impose rules, they disappear down their little sand holes, flipping their middle fingers and calling over their furry shoulders, *What are you going to do? Fire me?"*

I give him a look like, *Wow.* "Prairie dogs don't have middle fingers."

He's not amused.

I hold up a hand. "Hey, wait a minute. *I'm* not a prairie dog."

He pffts at me. "Aren't you?"

I snap my head his way.

He goes on, "Wasn't it just yesterday that you said, 'Oops, leaving tomorrow so just take me off the schedule'? You didn't say it out loud, but I heard you thinking, *I'm a volunteer. What are you going to? Fire me?"*

I chew a fingernail. "Okay, you've got a point. But if you hate supervising volunteers so much, why do it?"

"I caved. There was a sudden vacancy. I'd just left my former hospital position, and HR called and begged me to take the volunteer coordinator job. It's only part-time, so I figured how bad can it be?" He groans. "Turns out, it can be bad. Really bad."

I jut out my bottom lip. "Looks like we have something in common. I hate my job, too. I used to teach Philosophy at Sawyer Pickens University. Then last fall, my position was cut. Now I'm a K-12 substitute teacher."

He sucks air in through his teeth. "Ooh, tough gig."

I nod. "Yeah. Kids in groups will turn on you. I have a recurring nightmare that I'm teaching second-grade art class and things go very badly after I dole out the round-tipped scissors."

Lonnie chuckles. Then he glances at me, his eyes smiling, and I damn near want to giggle.

Does he actually...like me? I mean, as a friend, of

course. I may realize that Dr. Lonnie Acres is hot as hell, but I've seen the kind of women he spends time with. That woman in the parking lot radiated professional accomplishment, impeccable style, and high-end, well, everything. I grin over at him as he runs a hand through his wavy brown hair that, even this early in the summer, has enough pure honey highlights to attract every bear within a hundred-mile radius. I ask, "So, you've been a doctor for how long?"

"Ten years."

"Do you like it?"

"Mixed bag."

"Meaning?"

Lonnie shrugs. "Meaning…work is not my favorite topic these days."

"All right. I hear ya."

"Thank you."

With work being a sensitive subject for him, my mind quickly scrambles for the next question. "Favorite meal?"

He shoots me a look like, *lame,* then answers, "Omelets."

"Omelets. Really?"

"Got chickens. Fresh eggs."

"Favorite…color?"

He sighs. "You can do better."

I bite my lip then grin. "You're right. I can. What I'd really like to know is…what's your issue with Ming?"

Lonnie glances over at me with an incredulous expression. "I don't have an issue with Ming."

I throw up my hands. "Ha! Yesterday at the hospital, I could have cut the tension with a putty knife. I mean, every time Ming talked, all the muscles in your jaw tightened."

"Really? I had no idea you found my face that interesting."

My cheeks flush. *Gotta admit, I do find his face interesting. And his muscular arms, for that matter. And his hard abs...* I sit straight. "What I found interesting was your reaction to her. It's like you're allergic to red cowgirl boots."

He grips the steering wheel. "Okay, so Ming and I are not best friends."

"Because?"

"Because...it's complicated, okay?"

I slump in my seat. "Okay."

Lonnie blows air through his cheeks. "My turn. Siblings?"

I sit straight, trying to bury a smile. "Older brother named Ricky."

"What does Ricky do?"

"He's a technician at Big Jonny's Tires and Lube."

He nods. "Married?"

I stifle a groan. "Yep. To Tina. She and Ricky started dating in eighth grade, so I've known her, like, forever."

"What does Tina do?"

"Besides annoy me?"

He chuckles. "Uh-huh."

"She's the cafeteria lady at Snap Peas Elementary."

Lonnie cocks his head. "And she's annoying because—?"

I pinch my chin. "She's superficial. I blame it on her looks."

He glances over. "Go on."

"Besides her long blonde hair and doe-brown eyes, her body is, well, ridiculous." I huff. "And she doesn't even work out. Never goes to the gym. Which especially weird since all she ever wears is yoga pants and a cropped sports tee." I look over at Lonnie to confirm his focus on the road before saying, "Tina's very proud of her ass. It's like she's got a matched set of perfectly round basketballs in her yoga pants. And she's never stepped foot on an exercise machine. It's the kind of ass celebrities take out insurance on." I snort. "You know, Tina told me once that if she and Ricky ever wanted kids, they'd adopt because she doesn't want to mess with *the spacing*."

He scrunches his face. "The spacing of—"

"Her ass cheeks!"

He shrugs. "So that's what annoys you about her? Her basketball ass?"

"Did you not hear the part that she won't give birth in order to preserve the spacing of said basketball ass?"

He side-eyes me. "I can never *un*hear that."

"Plus, she's, like, obsessed with cafeteria food."

"Didn't you say—?"

"Yes, okay, that she's the cafeteria lady." I shrug. "She's just annoying. Exaggerates every little ache and pain. Like when she stubbed her toe, she walked around on crutches for two days. Oh, and during my last visit, she complained about how *terribly uncomfortable* her routine pap smear was."

He chuckles. "Maybe your brother the lube technician could help her out next time."

I burst out laughing. "Wish I'd thought of that one. I told her to grow a pair. Of ovaries." Lonnie smiles, and I notice, for the first time, that he has a dimple on his right cheek. "It's just annoying. I mean, there Tina is griping about a stubbed toe and my mother—" I stop myself.

Lonnie glances over. "Your mother?"

I bite my lip. "Nothing."

He exhales a steady breath. "Ramona, what about your mother?"

I peer out the passenger window, at the dry, brown fields where the once brilliant bluebonnets have faded to nothingness. "It's complicated, okay?"

Chapter Nine

Four hours later we've navigated the loopy maze of heavy Fort Worth traffic and are cruising past a string of chain restaurants and fast-food joints in a stretch of big city suburbia.

I have to pee. Pressing my knees together, I squirm in my seat. "Please, I'm begging you. Take the next exit." Earlier, I pointed to a gas station off Exit 283 and asked Lonnie to make a quick detour. He suggested we get past city traffic before stopping. It made sense at the time, but now, fifteen miles later, my bladder feels like a water balloon. "You know, I'm not a guy. I can't just dangle it out the window and let 'er rip."

Lonnie stares straight ahead at the interstate. "I *am* a guy. Never done that."

"The point is, it's always an option for you. Just like on hikes in the woods. Every tree for you is an opportunity to relieve the call of nature, while I end up squatting in a ring of shrubs then scratching the poison sumac rash on my butt for the next two weeks."

"Sorry that biology sucks for you. Happy scratching. And for the record, I asked if you wanted to stop at the service station at Mile Marker 332 near Waco and you said, 'No.' "

"I didn't have to go *then*." I point at an upcoming exit. "Gas station and a Fast 'n' Hotdogs. Not one but two bathrooms!"

He cranes his neck toward the exit. "I, uh—"

I gasp as he passes the off-ramp. "What the hell?"

He winces. "Ach. I'm sorry. Here's the thing: there's a nice service station just six miles up ahead. Clean restrooms. Vending. Gas station. Hell, there's even a cafeteria and picnic tables."

I cross my arms over my chest. "Six miles. Great. I'll just cross my legs and think about dry things."

He lets out a very long sigh. "I have a confession."

"I'm listening."

"I very carefully mapped out the trip and highlighted gas stations and rest stops that have pull-through parking spaces for trailers."

"How's *that* a confession?" I shake my head. "Telling me you spiked your Boy Scout leader's canteen with laxatives before The Eager Beaver Canoe trip is a confession." I throw up my hands. "Admitting you planted a wad of chewed bubblegum on your cousin's chair before his valedictorian's speech…confession."

He glances over with a sour look. "Note to self: Cover canteen before canoeing, and check chair before sitting."

"So, you mapped out the trip. Not a confession."

"No, but this is: I mapped out the trip because I can't back this thing up. No reverse. Drive only."

"You can't back up my truck? Because?"

"I can't back up your truck with your trailer hitched to it because I tried something like that once and failed miserably. Only that time I wasn't towing a twenty-four-foot RV with your monstrosity of a pickup. I was driving a station wagon with a four-by-eight-foot cargo trailer attached, and I couldn't do it to save my life."

I study him as he shudders at the memory. "Good

God. You have post-traumatic stress from backing up a station wagon?"

He rolls his eyes. "That day I tried to back up, I was moving out of student housing. I'd pulled into a parking space outside my dorm, then proceeded to stuff every inch of the cargo trailer full of my worldly possessions."

"You could fit your life into a four-by-eight-foot cargo trailer?"

He shrugs. "I was a twenty-two-year-old med student. I owned a shitload of textbooks, scrubs, booze, and a beanbag chair."

I chuckle. "What? No lava lamp and porn?"

"The textbooks were my porn. I mean, please. *Snell's Clinical Examination by Regions*?"

I burst a laugh, and Lonnie grins over at me, causing a warm wave of happiness to surge through me from head to toe. *I think he really does like me.*

He rubs his temple. "That day, all I needed to do was back my car and little cargo box out of the parking space and drive it to my new apartment building."

"And?"

"Tried for over an hour. Ended up backing it out halfway at an angle with nowhere to go. I blocked two cars and an SUV in the process. Let's just say, people were not happy with me."

I bring a hand to my face. "Don't make me laugh. I'm not wearing adult diapers."

"Had to call the trailer company service desk. They sent out two eighteen-year-olds who took one look at what I'd done and practically peed their own pants laughing." He shoots me a nervous look. "God, don't tell my father."

"Don't tell your father? What are you? Twelve?"

"I never told him what happened. The man could parallel park an Army tank on a city street without using his mirrors. Now, promise me." He grins. "That is, if you want me to take this exit."

I look up to see the service station off-ramp and clap my hands as Lonnie clicks on the turn signal. "My lips are sealed."

Fifteen minutes later I'm sitting at a shaded picnic table on a patch of lawn outside the Stop and Go Comfort Station. Lonnie joins me, sets a bulging paper bag on the table, then glances my way. "You look comfortable."

"I stopped. I peed. I conquered." He pulls two wrapped sandwiches, bags of chips, and cans of soda from the bag. I pull my phone from my jeans pocket, set it on the table, and open a banking app. "Thanks. How much do I owe you?"

Popping the tabs of our soda cans, he slides one across the table. "Nothing."

I take a too-big swig of soda and crinkle my nose from the bubbles. "You don't need to buy me lunch."

"I know, but—"

I raise a hand. "Actually, I need to reimburse you for lunch *and* for filling my truck with gas."

He tears open a chip bag. "Listen, I know you're perfectly capable of paying for these things. But it's just lunch and gas." He crunches on a chip. "I need to pay."

I knit my brow. "No, you don't."

"Do so. I was raised by Butch. I have a deep-seated gentleman complex."

I snort a laugh. "Gentleman? Wasn't it you who held my bladder hostage for miles? And compared me to a prairie dog with a hair-trigger middle finger?"

"Okay, so my gentleman complex is…complex. But

you packed a big cooler full of food for dinners, so it all evens out." He peels the wrapper off his sandwich. "Hope you like falafel."

I unwrap my sandwich "Falafel? From the Stop and Go Comfort Station?"

Lonnie nods. "Thought we'd have to settle for slabs of American cheese on white bread, but it turns out Chef Khalil does a nice little business here."

I bite into the perfectly spiced falafel on a buttery brioche bun, close my eyes, and moan, "Mmm. This is so good." I blink open my eyes to see Lonnie watching me, then he quickly averts his gaze. Something in my belly flutters. *Get a grip, Ramona. It's one thing to feel all giggly because you think the guy likes you as a friend. It's another to start feeling…Oh, God. There goes that fluttering again.*

He clears his throat. "So, the plan is to make it to Thunderbird, Tennessee today. I mapped out four acceptable rest stops between here and Lightning Duck RV Park."

I chuckle. "Lightning Duck?"

"It's got a pond." He eyes a straw next to the stack of napkins and picks it up. "And apparently a lightning-fast swimmer." Tearing the paper, he taps the straw against the tabletop until the tip is exposed and says, "Reserved a pull-through." He reaches across the table, grasps my soda can, then slides the straw into the opening. "With full hookup."

I swallow hard, feeling breathless. Exposed tip. Fast swimmer. All Lonnie's talk about pull-throughs and full hookups while he's sliding a long, stiff object into the opening of my can. Well, shit. That earlier flutter in my belly has definitely migrated south. I dab my sweaty upper lip with a napkin. "Sounds great. What's the address? I'll look up directions."

He pulls his phone from his T-shirt pocket and scrolls. "Two forty-two West Coneflower Road, Thunderbird, Tennessee." He squints at the screen. "Uh, lot number…sixty-nine."

Chapter Ten

It's nearly six o'clock when we turn into Lightning Duck then follow the narrow, paved road toward the huge pond and tree-lined RV spot with a square sign screaming: *Lot Sixty-nine*.

Lonnie slowly pulls the truck and RV into the lot driveway and parks. Then we step out into warm, thick air.

I tug at the back of my damp T-shirt and say to Lonnie, "Thank God for the stiff breeze." *Stiff* breeze. *Really? Get your mind out of the gutter, Ramona.* Resisting the urge to drag my hand over my face, I breathe in the sweet scent of flowering dogwoods and add, "Beautiful place."

Lonnie nods toward the pond. "Water view."

We stand facing one another, and I sense he's feeling as awkward right about now as I am. This is our first night together in my tiny-ass trailer. If we were dating, it would be romantic. If we were good friends, it would be fun. But we're not dating. And we're only friend*ly*. Yet we'll be sharing a living space the size of a wardrobe box with one tiny bathroom where I'll be peeing…and maybe worse! Just thinking about that makes me wish I really were a prairie dog so I could dive into my sand hole.

Lonnie's gaze darts around the RV site then he gives a decisive nod. "Well, time to set up camp." He busies himself hooking up the electric, water, and sewer.

I head for the truck, pull out the chairs, folding table, and cooler, then set them up near the rear of the trailer, and unlatch the pull-out grill. By the time I've hooked the propane to the grill, Lonnie's stacking wood in the nearby fire pit. I point to the cooler. "Which will it be tonight? Veggie burgers or tofu dogs?" I open the lid and rummage through containers and ice packs. "Salads include kale strawberry, summer couscous, and Mediterranean chickpea." Holding up a giant candy bar, I smile. "And pure chocolate for dessert."

He joins me at the cooler, wiping his hands along the sides of his shorts. "Everything sounds great. I vote for veggie burgers." He bites his bottom lip. "So, you're vegetarian?"

Closing the lid, I turn to face him. "No. But you are so—"

"I'm…vegetarian…?" He asks that slowly. "Based on…what, exactly?"

My mouth feels dry. "Well, for starters, falafel burgers."

Lonnie cocks an eyebrow. "But you packed all this vegetarian food before I bought the falafel burgers."

I scramble. "Well, you have sheep and chickens, and I figured you for a person who doesn't eat his pets."

"You're right. I only eat my chicken's eggs. And if I get goats, I'll only drink their milk. But that doesn't mean I'm vegetarian."

I toss up my hands. "Okay, I've seen you in the hospital cafeteria eating some leafy, seedy, tofuy, salady thing."

Lonnie tries, unsuccessfully, to bury a shit-eating grin. "So, at the hospital, you watch me eat?"

I feel my ears burn, then swallow hard at the memory of watching Lonnie's strong jaw clenching and releasing as he chewed on that damn salad. "No. I definitely do not watch you eat."

He clasps his hands and taps his thumbs together. "Yet you watched me long enough to give a pretty specific description of my tofuy salady thing."

"Well, I...so, you're not vegetarian?"

He shakes his head, and a thick strand of wavy hair bounces against his strong cheekbone. "I love a good steak. And pork chops. And *real* burgers."

I blow air through my cheeks. "Well, I guess I shouldn't have packed the Not Really Bacon and Faux Sausage links for breakfast."

His ridiculous green eyes flash a smile, and I'm aware of that darn fluttering in my belly again. "It'll be fine," he reassures me. "Nothing like eating one hundred percent plant food first thing in the morning. Breakfast of champions."

I chuckle, realizing that, in spite of the awkwardness of this being our first night together in my tiny trailer and me just getting busted for watching him eat a big bowl of ruffage in the hospital cafeteria, I somehow feel comfortable with him now. It's like all the tension I felt over his comments about Patient Panda violations has melted away. I guess laughing in the truck and chatting over lunch did the trick. "Speaking of eating, we should talk about sleeping arrangements." Well, shit. That did not come out the way I wanted. I just dove back into a deep pool of awkward. Lonnie blinks, and I stammer, "The table is a, uh, bed."

"You have a table bed?"

I nod. "The backs of the dining bench pull out and

attach to the table. There's a six-inch-thick trifold mattress that goes on top." I ramble on nervously, trying to ignore the bemused look on Lonnie's face. "I have sheets and a blanket, and I brought decent pillows for the, uh, table bed. There's a real bed that's, well, in the bedroom. I figure maybe we can flip a coin or arm wrestle for it?"

Lonnie shakes his head slowly. "Ramona." His voice is firm. "When it comes to the bed in the bedroom, there will be no flipping or wrestling." He winces, and I notice his neck flush red. "I'll sleep on the table bed."

"You're sure, because—?"

"I'm sure. Actually, I'd planned on sleeping in the truck, so this is a big step up."

I jerk my head back. "You were going to sleep in my truck?"

"Gentleman complex, remember?" He raises his chin. "Well, I'm going to wash up before dinner." He grabs his backpack from the truck, slings it over his shoulder, then nods toward the walking path. "According to the map, and the RV park manager who I spoke with yesterday, there are restrooms and showers that way."

I bury a smile. Guess Lonnie doesn't want to pee— or worse—near me either.

"Right past the playground and general store."

I watch him head off toward the trail, counting the seconds until he's out of earshot. Then I grab my phone.

Jules answers on the first ring. Before I can say hello, she blurts, "I've been thinking about you all day. How's the trip with The Lamb Whisperer?"

I chuckle. "Surprisingly well. Turns out he doesn't hate me. He just hates supervising volunteers. We actually talked about shit, had a few laughs. It's been…nice."

"Of course he doesn't hate you. The guy never would have agreed to go on this road trip with you if he didn't *like* you."

"Well, his father and Ming laid a guilt trip on him."

She snorts. "He's a grown man who could have said no." Her voice goes all sing-songy. "He likes you."

I pace in front of the trailer. "We're at a campsite in Tennessee. Get this: Lot number *sixty-nine*."

Jules gasps. "Ooh, the universe is definitely telling you something."

"I don't know if it's because I'm suddenly single again or because I've been sitting an arm's length away from Lonnie's ripped chest in a tight T-shirt and muscular man legs in khaki shorts all day. But I have to admit, it's crossed my mind more than once."

"Uh, it's because you're human. Where is he now?"

"Taking a shower before dinner."

"So, as we speak, Lonnie's all naked and dangling his soap on a rope in your little shower?"

"He's in the RV park shower house. When he gets back, we're going to eat kale salads and veggie burgers."

"That sounds awful. Why don't you skip those sad little burgers and just go for the buns."

I bite a thumbnail. "God, don't get me thinking about his buns. Tonight, he's going to sleep on my table bed."

"You don't stand a chance. I've seen Lonnie. He'll be sprawled out on your table just yards away from you in your queen-size bed. Just sleepwalk into the kitchen and eat him up with a spoon."

I snort a laugh. "But wouldn't that be, you know, bad? I just broke up with Martin two days ago."

"Ha! Doesn't matter. You should have broken up with Martin two *years* ago."

I bite my lip. "For all I know, Lonnie's seeing someone. I saw him talking with a gorgeous woman in the hospital parking lot."

"Ramona, there's no way a girlfriend would have approved this road trip. Believe me, he's single."

"He's also hard to read. He told me he planned on sleeping in my truck tonight. Said he's got a gentleman complex."

"Oh, please. You're a beautiful woman. He's a man with a penis. Just say the word, and he'll be all over you like a feral hog on candy corn."

I rub my bare forearms, suddenly feeling my stomach roil, the way it did so often when I was a kid. "You know, he probably mentioned the whole gentleman thing to make sure I don't get any wrong ideas. I mean, what am I thinking? He's a doctor, from a family of surgeons, who could moonlight as a rock-hard-abs model."

Jules's voice is stern. "Ramona."

I ignore her. "And I'm a substitute teacher, from a family of tire and lube technicians, living in a trailer—"

Jules coughs into the phone. "Nope. Not listening. Next time you're on the highway, toss that low self-esteem bullshit out your truck window. Now, listen carefully. You are a ravishing, intelligent, incredible woman. Super model Dr. Lonnie would be lucky to eat your candy corn."

I burst a laugh, then look over to see Lonnie, with his backpack slung over one shoulder and towel around his neck, walking toward the campsite. "He's coming back. Gotta run."

"Okay, but remember you're an amazing, finally single, red-blooded woman about to spend the night with a man who volunteered to drive you eighteen-hundred miles. If you get shy at the campfire tonight, don't be afraid to crack out the booze."

Chapter Eleven

Lonnie and I sit in front of the campfire, paper plates heaped with veggie burgers and salads balanced on our laps, as the wood pops and crackles against the flames. It's humid here in Tennessee, but the fire keeps mosquitoes at bay.

I've changed out of my jeans and into khaki shorts. Lonnie's traded his sneakers in for sandals, and I can't help but notice that the guy has good feet. They don't look flat, crazy-wide, or freakishly soft. There are no crater gaps between his toes. They're just a nice pair of man feet.

I glance down at my sneakers. My feet haven't seen a professional pedicure since last fall, back when I was Professor Sadler and dressed in blouses, creased slacks, and strappy sandals. Ever since becoming Miss Mona, the substitute teacher, I've worn rubber-soled, closed-toe shoes in case I'm trampled by a pack of first graders or have to dodge paper airplanes during sixth grade detention. Just as well. Pedicures are no longer in my budget anyway.

I sip kombucha from a plastic cup, then glance at Lonnie taking a big bite of salad. The flickering firelight illuminates his square jaw and makes his eyes appear smoldering. The evening air is still warm, yet a shiver runs up between my shoulder blades. I raise my cup. "We made it all the way to Thunderbird, Tennessee without a flat tire, overheated engine or warning light flashing on the dash. Cheers." He smiles, and I bite into my burger, then lick ketchup from the corner of my mouth. A twinge of excitement runs through me when I catch Lonnie watching me. *Hmm, maybe I'm not the only one whose body parts are fluttering.* Then my stomach gets that sinking feeling again as I remember that impeccable woman in the parking lot, taking Lonnie's hands in hers. It's everything I can do to fight off the voice in my head telling me that I'm not in her league.

He swallows hard. "You'll be visiting your family for how long?"

I slump back in my chair. "For the summer."

He raises his eyebrows. "That long? Guess I'm down a Patient Panda for a while."

"Yeah, I really am sorry about going all prairie dog on you."

He grins warmly. "Confession time. I know I'm hard on you at work, but you're no prairie dog. I expect more from you because I've read your volunteer file and you're the best Panda on record."

My jaw drops into a smile. "Really?"

"Yep. Most of my volunteers just go through the motions. They show up for their shifts and turn in their paperwork to pad their medical or nursing school applications. But you really care. The patients and nurses on staff tell me that all the time. You're a model volunteer." He winks, and my heart starts making a racket inside my chest just like the day I spotted him cradling a lamb against his bare chest. He adds, "You'll really be off the schedule all summer?"

"Believe me, I'm as surprised as you are. I usually only stay in Snap Peas for a few days." I finish my burger and toss my paper plate into the fire. "But I haven't seen my family in a while, and with my summer teaching break and having a trailer to stay in while I'm there, I figure what the hell."

He chuckles. "Having your own space will make a difference. If I stayed under the same roof with my dad for the summer, we'd have to hide the kitchen knives."

I laugh.

"When was the last time you visited Snap Peas?"

"It's been a year." I clasp my hands in my lap. "I know I should visit more often."

He shrugs. "I'm not judging."

"No, but I am. I should, especially now that—"

He leans forward. "Now that what?"

A pang of guilt tightens my chest. Do I tell him the sad truth? That when my mom had a major heart attack two years ago, I dropped in for three days with a grocery store bouquet of carnations, then couldn't get on my plane back to Texas fast enough?

I glance at my phone. "Hey, it's only eight o'clock. Would you be interested in meeting my friend, Jack?"

Lonnie knits his brow then his jaw muscles tighten. "Jack?" he asks, a slight edge to his voice.

Wait a minute. Does he think I'm talking about a real guy? Is he...jealous? Biting my bottom lip, I reach down beside my chair, lift the lid on the cooler, pull out two plastic cups, then a bottle of Tennessee's finest whiskey.

He lets out a long exhale and smiles my way. "Jack and I have met before. But it never hurts to catch up on old times."

I pour, then set the whiskey bottle on the ground between our chairs.

Lonnie takes a drink and swallows fast. "When I was in med school and came home for a visit after living on my own, I was nervous about it. You know, all those family dynamics."

I lift the cup to my lips, wrinkling my nose as the alcohol burns my throat. "Honestly, spending the summer with my family scares the hell out of me."

He tilts his head. "Now things are getting interesting. Tell me and Jack all about it."

I draw in a deep breath. "I love my family, but I've never fit in. Even as a kid, I remember sitting at the dinner table listening to my parents and brother bicker about whether three bowling strikes in a row are called a turkey or three-bagger and thinking, *Who the hell are these people*? It's like I hatched from an egg." Lonnie bursts out laughing, and I splash more whiskey into our cups. "On my last visit, they got into a heated debate about what brand of oil is best for wheel bearings. I wanted to join the conversation, but it was like, I've got nothin'."

Lonnie leans back. "I get that. My dad and I might both have medical backgrounds, but other than that—" He shakes his head. "—let's just say it's tough finding common ground."

"Yeah, you and Butch do seem really different. Which is probably why I never made the connection that you're father and son."

"Plus, I bear a much stronger resemblance to the Acres side of the family."

I bring a finger to my chin. "Wait. That's right. You have different last names."

"Yep, Butch Zimmerman married Priscilla Acres, my mom, who was way ahead of her time. She insisted on hyphenating my last name."

I smile. "You're Lonnie Acres-Zimmerman?"

"I was. Until I turned thirty and decided to make my life easier with a name change."

"And you went with your mom's last name."

He nods. "Otherwise, I would be Lonnie Burnell Zimmerman III."

I chuckle. "Burnell?"

"Now you know why he goes by Butch." Lonnie sips his whiskey. "After decades of writing Lonnie Acres-Zimmerman, I decided the shorter the better."

"Is your mom happy that you went for Acres?"

"I think she was." He folds his hands in his lap. "She's gone now. Cancer."

I bring a hand to my mouth. "Oh, I'm so sorry."

His lips curve into a sad grin. "Thank you. Me, too. She was a special person. Smart. Funny. Strong when she needed to be, but also sweet and affectionate."

"She sounds wonderful."

He nods. "She was and we were close. And, of course, I love my dad, but we just don't get each other. You know?"

"Yeah, I do. There are so many things I don't get about my family."

"Like—?"

"Like now that my parents are retired, they all eat dinner at four-thirty sharp."

"Talk about early bird special."

"Right? Last visit, when I made dinner and didn't have it ready until four forty-five, Mom, Earl, and Ricky were literally pacing in front of the kitchen table."

Chuckling, he shoots me a quizzical look. "Ricky's your brother, but *Earl*?"

"Earl's our father."

"Stepfather?"

"Nope."

Lonnie cocks his head.

I explain, "When Ricky and I were little, Earl insisted we be on a first-name basis."

Lonnie snorts a laugh. "Seriously?"

I chuckle. "One Saturday morning, little Ricky and I were snarfing our bowls of cereal and I asked *Dad* to pass the cheese toast. He looked at us and said, 'I have a name you know. It can be burped out in one syllable.' Then he swallowed air and belched, Earrrl."

Lonnie doubles over laughing.

Smiling, I hold up a hand. "It gets better. Then Earl told us, 'Don't expect much.' "

Lonnie covers his mouth trying to stifle his laughter while looking sympathetic. "Oh, God. And—?"

"We didn't. And Earl delivered."

Lonnie shakes his head and sips his whiskey.

I gaze into the campfire, savoring my whiskey. A tingly warmth radiates through my body. In part, from the booze. Also because it feels really nice talking and laughing with Lonnie about my weird family and listening to him talk about issues in his family, too. Whenever I tried to talk with Martin about my family, the conversation turned into a big, fucking Feeling Wheelhouse marathon with Martin labeling my feelings for me then giving an in-depth critique of my family dynamics. With Lonnie, there's no labeling or judging. There's just…sharing.

I shift in my chair, crossing my bare legs. When Lonnie's gaze darts to them, my breath catches. "So, what was it like growing up with Butch?"

He draws in a deep breath. "He worked very long hours. You know, between surgery and military life. But he tried to be an involved parent. He coached my Little League team one year and made it to my science fairs most of the time. He came to a few of my band concerts."

"Band. What did you play?"

"Tuba."

I cough a laugh so hard that whiskey sprays from my mouth.

He holds up a hand, smiling. "Hey, tuba's a big deal on military posts. I was lead tuba in marching band."

I laugh harder. "Lead tuba? There was more than one?"

Lonnie laughs. "Me and Lionel Fallicka. He had a mouthful of braces, so he never really committed to the high notes. I had lead tuba in the bag for years." He sets his cup on the ground. "What about you? Any instruments?"

"Made it through half a year of flutophone then called it quits. My parents, Ricky and our dog, Rex, were thrilled." I wriggle my fingers at Lonnie. "Come on, more about Butch."

"Dad was big on rules. You know, wake up early, make your bed, do your chores." He grins. "He cared about our family legacy. His father was a surgeon. My grandparents on both sides were physicians. Dad had high expectations for me academically and career-wise. It was assumed that I'd follow in his footsteps, go to med school then become a surgeon." His grin dissolves. "When I left surgery, he was devastated."

I frown. "How long ago was that?"

"I quit a year ago. It drives Dad nuts that I'm at the hospital part-time. And that I spend most of my time in the barn taking care of my sheep and chickens while trying to figure out what I want to do professionally. He's not a fan of what he calls my lack of ambition."

I jerk back. "Wow, that's kind of harsh."

"Dad can be hard on people. But, in fairness, he's just as hard on himself."

I scratch my cheek. "I can see that."

"You know, it's funny. He's usually very slow to warm up to people, but he really likes you."

I feel my face flush. "Well, I like him, too." I chuckle. "Butch and I just kind of hit it off. The first day I met him, he kept pushing his call button and complaining that the nurses weren't arriving at his bedside fast enough. I told him, 'You know, you're not the only infirmed person on Ward Four, so maybe stop being *so heavy on the call light.*' I think he liked that I didn't take his shit."

Lonnie laughs. "Sounds like my dad."

I tilt my head at him. "Doesn't sound like Ming takes his shit either."

He shakes his head. "That's for sure. And you were right: I do have issues with Ming. Not so much with her, but with her dating my father."

"It's awkward for you?"

He stares into the fire. "More difficult than awkward."

"Because?"

"Because my mom—" He swallows hard. "She died a year ago."

I softly gasp. "Oh, that recent."

He blinks slowly. "Yeah, and now there's Ming who, by the way, I've known for years."

"You have?"

"Ming was my mom's best friend."

I bite my lip. "Oh."

Lonnie shrugs. "It's not what you think. Dad was devoted to Mom, and I don't believe for one minute that he was unfaithful to her." He draws in a breath. "It's just that it happened so fast. One Saturday morning, six months after Mom died, I stopped over at Dad's ranch with fresh eggs. Ming was there in a negligee and cowgirl boots. Things have been weird ever since."

I groan. "That would be difficult."

"On Sunday, when you saw me interacting with Ming in Dad's hospital room, I was feeling pretty raw. It was the one-year anniversary of my mom's death."

I bring a hand to my chest. "Sunday?"

"Yeah, that's why dad was hell-bent on going to church. Mom went every Sunday. Dad doesn't usually go to church, but he wanted to be there on the anniversary."

My stomach falls. "Oh, God. And I was so—"

Lonnie waves a hand. "It's okay. I should have been the one taking him to church. You were doing him a big favor then you had to deal with his stubbornness and me swooping in getting all pissy." He shakes his head. "Sorry about that. I wasn't exactly my best self."

I give a warm grin. "That morning, none of us were our best selves." I shake my head. "Then I stop by the hospital with, like, a gallon of candy."

He laughs. "And I tell you to reread section five thousand and eight of the Patient Panda Volunteer Handbook."

I chuckle, then sit quietly for a while, staring into the flames.

Lonnie turns to me. "You told me a little about Earl.

What about your mom? Close?"

Something catches in my throat, and I swallow hard. "I mean, she's my mom." I take a sip of whiskey. "When I was a kid, she packed our school lunches, made sure we had clean clothes, took us to the playground and swimming lessons and doctors' appointments. She always worked. Odd jobs like picking grapes and washing dishes when I was little. Then full-time, as a receptionist at Big Jonny's, once I was in school. But she was our family engine, the one who made everything run. It was like, even when she was at work, she was somehow always there, too. You know?"

Lonnie slowly nods.

I touch my chin. "But now? Close? I don't know. It's hard to know what to talk about. It feels like after I went away to college, we didn't have much to say anymore. To be honest, I kind of dread the visits. I feel awful saying that, especially now that—"

Lonnie leans forward, his eyes searching mine.

I sigh. "Two years ago, Mom had a major heart attack."

His eyes muddy with sadness. "How's she doing?"

"The bypass surgery was successful. Her recovery was slow." I force a grin. "But she says she's too much of a big grouch to kick the bucket." I fidget with the hem of my T-shirt. "She's had some issues since then. Dizziness, shortness of breath. It seems like she's always at some doctor's appointment."

His gaze feels like a warm hug. "And how are *you* doing?"

"I'm doing—" The truth is, ever since my mom's heart attack, I've felt like my own heart needs a jump-start. That fist-sized organ beating inside my chest feels like a big, blubbery, bleeding mess. I want to be there for her. I want to help her. But I have no idea how to make a meaningful connection with her. How to bridge that gap between her heart and mine. I finish my whiskey in one gulp. "I'm doing just fine."

Chapter Twelve

The sexual tension I felt from Lonnie's stolen glances and my fluttering belly at the campsite in Thunderbird, Tennessee dissolved mighty quick after our conversation about my ailing mom in Snap Peas, New York.

We put away the whiskey, feigned surprise about the time—*Can you believe it's nine o'clock already?*—and talked about our early morning ahead. Then I snuffed out the campfire, packed up the cooler, and Lonnie curled up on his table bed while I quietly closed my bedroom door behind me.

****

At six thirty-five a.m. we sit outside my trailer eating breakfast to the calls and whistles of blue jays and cowbirds from nearby tree branches. I'm freshly showered, sipping a cup of black instant coffee, and feeling surprisingly well-rested. I bite into a piece of vegan bacon, wipe the corner of my mouth with my thumb, and nod at Lonnie. "I'll drive today."

His brow furrowed, he spoons scrambled eggs onto toast. "You sure? I don't mind driving again."

"After my visit, I'll be hauling this thing back to Texas on my own. Figure I might as well practice while I have a copilot to unwrap my candy bars and pop the tabs on my soda cans for me."

He arches an eyebrow. "And write you a

prescription for hyperglycemia."

I grin. "That too."

At first, it feels strange pulling a twenty-four-foot trailer behind my truck. I drive ten miles under the speed limit, check my mirrors constantly, and notice every little clunk of tires on uneven pavement. Then it starts to feel like second nature—from years of riding passenger in Earl's old pickup when he towed stuff on a flat trailer— as I steady the steering wheel, take wide turns at intersections, and gauge distance in the rearview mirror before clicking on my turn signal and changing lanes.

We're driving along Interstate 40 headed toward Nashville, past distant rolling hills and clusters of red oaks. I glance over at Lonnie. "So, what's your favorite book?"

He draws in a breath. "*Crime and Punishment*."

"I see your literary tastes are light and airy. Favorite…sea creature?"

From the corner of my eye, I see his head jerk. "Vampire squid."

I wrinkle my nose. "Sounds scary."

"Perfectly harmless. Doesn't eat live prey, only organic dead material." He holds up a finger. "And poop and snot."

"Thanks for those juicy tidbits. Hope my vegan bacon stays down." I drum my fingers on the steering wheel. "Mine is the beluga whale. They have these big-ass, flexible foreheads called 'melons' that help them make expressions and sounds, like whistles and chirps and clicks. They can live up to fifty years old." I glance over. "Too much?"

"It was a lot." He turns toward me. "Favorite movie?"

"*National Velvet* and *Seabiscuit*."

"Just one."

"Can't."

He huffs. "Okay...favorite sports team?"

I raise my eyebrows. "Shirtless pro tennis players."

"They're not a *team*."

"Don't care."

Lonnie sighs. "Hmm. Greatest life mystery?"

I narrow my eyes, concentrating. "People who read magazines while sitting on the toilet. I don't get it. Eat more leafy greens and legumes then go about your life until the urge strikes. It's really not that complicated. Earl used to hole up in our one bathroom for, like, an hour with a tabloid magazine. And the man farts all the time."

Lonnie clears his throat. "Back to favorites. Music?"

"Rhythm and Blues."

"Holiday?"

"Valentine's Day."

He cocks his head. "Interesting."

I feel my face heat into a full-on blush. "Okay, call me mushy, but I love Valentine's Day. It's all hearts and chocolate and cute little cards asking, *Will you be mine?* When I was a kid, I'd daydream about someday getting one of those big, heart-shaped boxes of candy tied with a bow like the ones I saw on aisle seventeen-B of Wheatland's Grocers."

He chuckles. "You still remember the aisle."

"Yep. Still remember every decorative box of candy and the ginormous chocolate hearts."

"Along those lines, favorite food?"

"Sugar."

"Favorite...patient?"

"Butch." I jerk my hand up, fast, and cover my mouth. "Oh my God. Please don't tell him."

He chuckles. "Deal. I won't tell him he's your favorite patient. And you won't tell him about the time I jack-knifed the cargo trailer in the student housing parking lot." I flick on the turn signal, and Lonnie jerks his head in my direction. "What are you...? Exit 278 isn't one of my mapped-out stops."

"The service station you mapped out is another twenty miles down the road. I drank too much coffee this morning. I need to pee like a racehorse, and there's a gas station right over there."

He leans forward. "Looks congested. Parking's going to be tricky."

I take the exit. "Got a strategy."

"Hope it's a good one."

Turning into the station lot, I pull my truck and trailer through to a gas pump, shift into "Park," then turn to Lonnie. "While we fill up the tank, we take turns doing restroom and snack runs. No parking spot needed."

Lonnie opens the passenger door, walks to the pump, and waves me toward the station. "Racehorses first."

I clasp my hands in front of my chest. "Seabiscuit thanks you."

Five minutes later, carrying two bags of salted peanuts, I'm back at my truck.

Lonnie nods. "Filled up this tank. Time to empty mine. Be right back."

I stand outside the driver's seat stretching my legs and looking around. While I was inside, the parking lot became busy. Two vehicles are circling, waiting for an available gas pump. I internally cringe. Any other time,

I'd pull out of the way, so other drivers wouldn't have to wait. But I'm towing a trailer. I'm sure people understand.

Then I hear a voice from behind me. "Ma'am," a man says. "Can you kindly park so we can use the pump?"

I shoot him an apologetic smile. "Oh, uh…yes." My mind scrambles for options. Lonnie should be back any minute. I just need to stall. I pat my pockets like I'm looking for my truck keys. "Just need to find my—"

The man clears his throat. "Your keys are in your hand, ma'am. Right between your thumb and that bag of peanuts."

I wince then glance over at the service station doors. No Lonnie yet. I face the man. He's wearing an *Ew, People* T-shirt. I plaster on my sweetest grin. "The thing is, I'd rather not park, you know, with the trailer." He rolls his eyes like, *women drivers*. "And my, uh, friend will be right out."

He points to two SUV's behind him, his voice more insistent. "There's a line, ma'am."

"But—"

He eyes a free parking spot straight ahead. "And plenty of room for you to park right there."

My gaze darts to the station doors again. Still no Lonnie. "Okay, thanks."

Sliding into the driver's seat, I consider a Plan B. I could circle around the lot until Lonnie comes out, but with the long gas lines there wouldn't be enough clearance room. I'd end up having to back up anyway. I stare ahead at the vacant spot between an SUV and minivan. Taking a deep breath, I shift into "Drive" and slowly pull straight into the space. All I have to do when

Lonnie returns is pull back out as straight as I pulled in. Easy peasy.

Then I glance in my side mirrors. The *Ew, People* man, now pumping gas, pulled so far forward that there's no way I'll have room to back out straight. I groan, suddenly aware of my racing pulse, and wipe sweat from my upper lip with the back of my hand. Then I hear Lonnie huff.

I turn my head to see him standing outside my open window holding two cans of soda and waving an imaginary banner that screams: *I told you so!*

His voice is flat. "I've seen this movie." He walks around the truck's hood then slides into the passenger seat. "It has a long, drawn out ending that *sucks*."

I throw up my hands. "There were cars waiting in line for the pump."

"Why didn't you stall for time?"

"Tried that. But the guy got all, ma'am, you need to park this thing now, ma'am."

Lonnie blows air through his cheeks. "Seen how this unfolds. Worst movie ever."

My stomach flips with nerves, but I go on the offensive. "Well, maybe your movie was poorly casted."

Lonnie snorts. "And *this* movie?"

I glance down at the keychain dangling from the ignition that my mom gave me when I first moved to Texas and bought my pickup. It's a metal keychain of a big-ass pickup truck. I pull my shoulders straight. "My movie stars Ramona Big-ass Truck Sadler." Shifting into "Reverse," I inch my truck back, keeping the wheel completely straight so that I don't scrape the SUV next to me.

Lonnie clears his throat. "I'm thinking you should

turn the wheel slightly to the left to make room for—"

I snap my head his way. "And I'm thinking maybe you should play a supporting role. Now step outside and flag me in the right direction, so I don't crush the bumper of that car at the pump."

He opens his door. "I'll give it my best shot, but we both know I'm not exactly a pro at this."

He wasn't kidding. Lonnie stands behind the trailer flailing his arms in one direction, then the other as I try to make sense of which way I'm supposed to turn the wheels and how far. I blow out a breath. It's my truck and trailer, and I got us into this jam. I need to get us out of it. Tapping the gas pedal, I creep back until a vehicle somewhere behind my trailer lays on the horn. I see Lonnie in the mirror again, frantically waving his arms. I'll just have to use instinct and trust that Lonnie will alert vehicles in harm's way. Checking my mirrors, then gently pressing the gas pedal, I turn the wheel slowly to the right, then straighten, then a bit more to the right. There's another beep from behind, and Lonnie's flapping hands in the mirror, so I push the brake and wait while a sports car turns around and heads out the other way. Then I continue backing up, checking mirrors, turning then straightening the wheels then inching forward to give a bit more room. Finally, I'm officially out of the parking spot with a straight shot ahead to the road.

Lonnie slides into the passenger seat and looks at me wide-eyed. "You did it. Un-fucking believable. I mean, really. Fucking well done." He pops the soda tab and places the can in my cup holder. "Sorry about the F-bombs. I'm just…impressed as fuck."

I bite my lip to keep from beaming. "Couldn't have done it without you. That sports car would have been toast if it weren't for your crazy jazz hands out there." Lonnie bursts a loud laugh, and I smile over at him. Then I shift into "Drive." "Let's hit the road."

Chapter Thirteen

We head toward Louisville on Interstate 65 cruising past strip malls and signs for Hangry Burgers and Cluck's Chicken Wings. Lonnie reaches for his soda, and I catch a whiff of his tingly scent of pine, leather, and bee balm. You can take the man out of Texas Hill Country, but not the country out of the man. I breathe in. Dang, country smells good.

The ringing of my cell phone blares through the truck speakers.

I glance at Lonnie. "I'm feeling mighty good about my driving skills right now, but not good enough to poke around on the dashboard screen to answer my phone."

Lonnie reaches toward the dash. "I'll get it for you. It's from Smallwood?"

I hear myself gasp. "Oh, don't—"

Too late.

"Ramona?" Martin's voice sounds pleased. "I knew you'd answer."

Lonnie whispers, "Sorry."

"Martin, I'm driving. Can't talk right now."

"I'll make this brief. With my mother back in Houston, I'd like to schedule a de-escalation session."

I huff. "What?"

"Now, Ramona, we've been over this countless times." He sighs impatiently. "We can't heal the wounds without de-escalating the anger first."

I mime a figure down my throat. "Not interested."

"Nonsense. There's not a feeling in The Wheelhouse that can't be processed."

I cringe over at Lonnie who looks confused.

Martin goes on, "So come over on Saturday."

I jerk my shoulders back. "No. I'm not coming to your house, Martin."

"We need to talk. *Plus*, I have some of your things. A pink loofah. Shiny Mane Conditioner. And I found a little round thing in your nightstand. Weird, it lights up and vibrates—"

I drag a hand down my face. "Consider them yours, Martin. Your hair could use a good conditioner, and, for the round thing, I suggest using setting number six. Can't go wrong with a pulsating flicker."

From the corner of my eye, I see Lonnie's shoulders shake with laughter.

Martin sounds utterly confused. "Pulsating…what?"

I roll my eyes. "Listen, I have to go."

A desperate edge creeps into Martin's voice. "Please. Come over for dinner. I'll make that sausage casserole you rave over, and we'll talk things through."

"Not gonna happen."

"Ramona—"

"And by the way, Martin, I've never raved over your sausage."

Lonnie laughs then covers his mouth.

Martin coughs. "Who's that?"

I flash Lonnie an apologetic look. "A man called Lonnie. You're on speaker."

Lonnie clears his throat. "Sorry to eavesdrop, man. But it's kind of unavoidable here in the passenger seat."

Martin's voice is tight. "Ramona, where are you going with this Lonnie fellow?"

I sigh. "Not that it's any of your business, but he's helping me haul my trailer to Snap Peas. I'm staying there for the summer."

Martin huffs. "Well, that throws a monkey wrench into dinner plans."

I roll my eyes. "Frees you up for hobby time. Enjoy shoving *The Sea Cloud* into a port bottle."

"But—"

I glance at Lonnie, who looks even more confused now, and cue him—by dragging a finger across my throat—to kill the call. "I'm signing off now, Martin. Need to focus on dotted yellow lines."

"Ramona—"

Lonnie presses End Call.

I'm silent for a few moments, my gut twisting. Then I burst out, "That was my ex, Martin Smallwood. He's a psychologist and author of *So, The Feeling Wheelhouse Turns*."

Lonnie nods. "Ah, that explains that."

"And he's a ships in bottles enthusiast. He no-showed for my thirtieth birthday party for hobby time."

He slowly nods his head. "And that explains *that*. *The Sea Cloud*. Nice touch."

I grin. "Thanks. Anyway, recent breakup."

"Figured as much."

"The night before I took Butch to church, I was at Martin's house grabbing my toothbrush and picking my dirty panties out of his laundry basket."

Lonnie twists toward me. "Sounds like Martin thinks you'll be back with clean panties."

"He'd be wrong. I told him loud and clear that night

that we're over."

He sighs. "Sometimes people hear what they want to hear."

"Yes, they do. Sorry you had to hear all that. Talk about airing dirty laundry." I groan. "So embarrassing."

He leans back in his seat. "There's no need to be embarrassed. We all have dirty laundry."

I wriggle my fingers at him. "You're right. Time for you to hang yours out on the line, too."

"You sure? Skid marks and all?"

I cough. "You just had a front row seat to The Sadler and Small*wood* Show. I want skid marks, pit stains, and collar grime."

He chuckles, then blurts out, "I was engaged to Ming's niece."

I jerk back. "Oh."

"Shi-Yun Wang. She's a surgeon at Cassidy Memorial." He turns toward me. "Actually, that day in the hospital parking lot—"

I wince. "White lab coat. Long black hair. That was Shi-Yun?" My stomach sinks. He was engaged to a drop-dead gorgeous surgeon. I had told Jules that Lonnie was hot enough to date any woman he wanted.

"Yeah. We were engaged for almost a year, then…" His voice trails off. "Well, a lot of stuff happened. I told her I couldn't marry her, that I was calling off the wedding. Spent a day on the phone cancelling the florist, the caterer, the pastor—"

"And?"

"And instead of hearing, 'We're over,' Shi-Yun heard something like, 'He'll come to his senses.' " He shakes his head. "She still sends me screenshots of wedding arbors and heart-shaped luminaries."

My chest drops, as I remember the day I saw them in the parking lot. At first it looked like they were arguing. But later, Shi-Yun was holding Lonnie's hands in hers. "Sounds like Shi-Yun thinks you two are still engaged."

He sighs. "We're not. I was clear about that. But I guess—"

I swallow hard. "She heard what she wanted to hear?"

"You got it."

Chapter Fourteen

Things got weirdly quiet in the truck after our big ex reveals, so when Lonnie suggested stopping for food somewhere near Spirit Ash, Ohio, I couldn't flick my truck blinker on fast enough.

Lonnie directs me to turn onto one country road after another.

I squint. "Where is this place?"

He points out his window. "Right up there."

I shake my head. "All I see are signs for Save a Bunch and Winkley's Five and Dime."

"Yep. Turn into that parking lot. It's right between the two."

I pull my truck and trailer into the nearly empty lot then cock my head at the sign over the door of the restaurant: *Dim Sum and Some More.*

The inside of Dim Sum and Some More is small and sparsely decorated. A handful of red paper lanterns hang from the white ceiling. The walls are mostly bare except for a few framed photos of Chinese dragon art and the menu. There are six small tables and, oddly, one padded booth beneath a wall air conditioning unit.

I grin at Lonnie, from across the booth, as I dip another pork dumpling in soy sauce. "The food here is amazing."

He nods. "I may have issues with Ming, but she gave a great recommendation. She says this is the best Chinese food in all of Ohio."

I set my chopsticks down and drink some tea. "So, about Ming. She was your mom's best friend, and now she's dating your dad. Guess I'm still trying to get my head around the situation."

"You and me both." He bites into a duck wing then frowns in concentration. "The worst part is that she and I never talk about Mom. When it's just me and Dad, we talk about Mom all the time. You know, little things like we'll be in his yard near the rose bushes and mention that they were Mom's favorite flowers. Or we'll point to the bird feeders and recall how excited Mom was the first time she saw a painted bunting. It's just natural." I nod. "But when Ming's around, it feels like a taboo subject. She comes over, and it's like Mom never existed."

I slump back. "Ouch."

He holds up a sparerib with his chopsticks. "But Ming knows her Dim Sum."

I smile. "And Some More." Biting into a spring roll, I study Lonnie. His hair is tousled, and there's thick brown stubble on his jaw. "How long have you known Ming?"

"Since I was a little kid. She and her late husband lived in Army officers' housing in Fort Gordon when we were there. Eventually, we were all stationed in Texas and became close. Ming likes to remind me that she's known me since my Coopy the Chicken phase."

I snort a laugh. "Aw, Coopy Chicken, huh?"

"I was obsessed. I wore Coopy pajamas, used bath towels as wings, and started roosting in a tree in our backyard."

I lean back and smile, picturing little Lonnie in chicken pajama pants. "That's so cute."

"It was fun until I decided I could fly down from the tree with my 'wings.' "

"Oh, no."

"Had one of my 'wings' in a splint for three weeks."

I turn my head toward the rumble of the dim sum cart being wheeled to our table by a big, stocky redheaded man.

He smiles, his fair cheeks flushing. "Hey, guys. I'm Henry, one of the co-owners here." He gestures to the cart. "Dim sum?"

I point to the middle tray. "I'll try the turnip cake."

His boyishly freckled face takes on an impish expression. "Some more?"

I chuckle.

Lonnie smiles. "I'll have an egg tart."

As Henry slides a small plate in front of me, two voices—a man's and a woman's—conversing loudly in Chinese echo from the kitchen. Henry clears his throat as their voices grow louder. He grins our way. "I hope you're enjoying your meal."

Then the man and woman, an older couple, each with short black hair and round rim glasses, step out of the kitchen and gesture to Henry, yelling something to him in Chinese.

Henry wheels around and yells, "*Hǎo de! Wǒ shuōguò wǒ huì chǔlǐ de!*" Lonnie and I look at one another wide-eyed. The couple march back into the kitchen, and Henry looks at us, rolls his eyes, and laments, "Parents." Then he pushes the cart away.

Lonnie bites his lip. "Didn't see that one coming."

We both burst a laugh then I say, "Families come in all different shapes, colors, and sizes."

He tilts his head. "So, what about little Ramona? Let

me guess. Plunky the big blue porcupine?"

I cough. "Please, I was way too sophisticated for Plunky." I wink, and Lonnie's ridiculous green eyes flash a smile, and my insides go all fluttery. "I spent a lot of time running around outside. Jumping rope, riding my bike, climbing trees." I shake my head. "When I got older, I spent hours in trees, reading and just, I don't know, imagining things."

"What did you read?"

"Any horse book I could get my hands on."

"That's right. *National Velvet* and *Seabiscuit*."

"And *Misty of Chincoteague, The Black Stallion*—"

His voice sounds warm. "What did you love about them?"

I cradle my chin in my hands. "Oh, I love horses, their athletic beauty, their connection with nature…the way they bond with their trusted person. In the stories, it was like the horse and human were soulmates, you know?"

He grins, and his soft gaze seems to reach into my own soul. "Yeah, I do know."

I sip tea. "I guess I always craved that kind of closeness. My parents raised me and my brother to work hard, to know right from wrong, to help our neighbor, that sort of thing. But they aren't exactly deep wells of emotion. At least, they've never let on to be. I mean, I know they love me, but they don't express it in words."

Lonnie glances down at the table for a brief second, then searches my eyes. "Ever?"

I shake my head. "Nope. It's not their thing. What about your parents?"

His grin is sad. "My mom told me she loved me all the time." He glances at the ceiling. "And Dad tells me on occasion. He says it like a public service announcement." I shoot him a confused look, and Lonnie sits straight, crosses his arms, and looks intensely into my eyes. "Son, you should know, that I love you."

I burst a laugh. "That sounds like Butch, but it's nice."

"It is. I mean, the old guy could work on his delivery, but—" Lonnie winks at me.

My breath catches, and I feel all light-headed, in a good way. How does he do that to me with one little wink of an eye?

He smiles. "So, what did little Ramona imagine while she was sitting up in the tree reading her horse books?"

Drawing in a deep breath, I lift my chin. As my lips curl into a wide grin, my eyes shine from the memory. "I imagined…possibilities…freedom. Jumping on a horse and galloping off. Just riding and riding until I was…somewhere else. Until I was someone else." I look at Lonnie and see his eyes turn sad.

He leans forward and opens his mouth to say something.

I nod toward the wall clock. "Speaking of riding off. Ready to hit the road?"

Chapter Fifteen

Twenty miles south of Cleveland, we exit Interstate 71 then wind along County Road 9 until Lonnie points out his passenger window. "Up there. Next right."

I lean forward at the wheel, squinting at the sign up ahead. "Squirrels n Nuts RV Park?"

"It was either that or Berry Nice Campsites."

I turn into the park entrance and drive slowly past shiny motor homes parked in tidy lots and pitched tents on spacious sites. Then I ease the truck and trailer into lot ninety-six.

Stepping from the truck, I breathe in the sheer beauty of our private campsite surrounded by maples, pine, and oaks. In the distance, I spot a glimmer of tall lemony-green grasses and rippling blue water. "This is so beautiful." I turn to face him, catch his eye and give a little wink. "Our campsite is berry, berry nice."

Lonnie runs a hand through his hair, his gaze darting quickly up and down my body, then he clears his throat and smiles. "They promised a pond view. And delivered."

My heart fluttering, I feel suddenly verklempt. I search his eyes. "Thank you."

His head jerks slightly. "For what?"

"For mapping out rest stops and reserving RV parks with clean restrooms and lovely views." My throat thickens, but I don't have to worry about tearing up.

People in my family don't cry. I didn't cry when I got called "trailer trash." Or when I waved goodbye to my parents before boarding a bus to head off to Minnesota for college. I didn't cry when I lost my job. Or my town house. And I certainly didn't cry when I broke up with Martin. I tilt my chin up at Lonnie. "And thank you for helping me drive, and for filling the truck with gas, and hooking up utilities." I grin. "And for slaying campground trolls."

His dark green eyes lighten. "Actually, it's been nice." He flashes a smile and leans forward. "Berry, berry nice." A breeze picks up. Goose bumps arise on my bare arms from the cool air. I rub them, and Lonnie pulls off the long-sleeved shirt he's layered over a T-shirt and slides it over my shoulders. I pull the soft fabric against my skin, closing my eyes as I breathe in the piney, leathery, salty aroma of country.

****

That night, I spread a thick blanket on the ground next to the campfire and sit cross-legged eating Mediterranean salad and sipping hot tea as Lonnie devours a tofu hot dog. I've changed into sweatpants and hoodie. Lonnie's in jeans and long-sleeved shirt. I raise my mug. "To another successful day on the road. No burnt-out brake lights or transmission fluid leaks. And we're less than seven hours from Snap Peas."

Lonnie clinks his mug to mine, his expression turning thoughtful. "We could take our time in the morning. Get on the road around nine or ten?"

I bring a hand to the tingling hairs at the nape of my neck. *Take our time in the morning.* I realize I just broke up with Martin and that I'll be in Snap Peas all summer. But, God, there's nothing I'd love more than to take my time with Lonnie.

He bites his lip. "Unless you need to, you know, get to your parents' house earlier."

I stare down at the blanket. My parents' *house*. They live in the double-wide trailer we moved into when I was twelve. It was a big step up from our single-wide in Eight Oaks Trailer Park. My parents scrimped and saved to buy a few acres and that brand new double-wide. We were all thrilled to move out of the crowded trailer park and into our new home. But now, that home is eighteen years old. It's not like one of the nice contemporary modular homes you see nowadays. Theirs is a plain-old, aluminum-sided trailer with a ten-year-old front deck that Earl and Ricky built. I look up at Lonnie and blurt out, "It's not a house. It's a trailer. A double-wide on a three-acre lot."

Lonnie eats a forkful of salad then licks his lip. "Three acres? Nice."

My shoulders soften with relief. "Yeah, as a kid, I loved having a big outdoor space to run around in. And, yes, a leisurely morning sounds perfect." *A leisurely morning with Lonnie.* My mouth waters as I squeeze ketchup onto my tofu dog. "You know, we never really talked about this part of the trip. Once we get to Snap Peas."

He nods. "I booked Motel Sky near the airport for tomorrow night and a morning flight for Thursday."

My heart sinks, and I stifle a groan. He booked a motel room for himself instead of staying in my trailer—with me. Of course he did. Mr. Gentleman Complex who'd planned on sleeping in my truck until I offered him the table bed. "Motel Sky. Good choice."

He chuckles. "Only choice."

119

"Yeah, Wheatland Airport isn't exactly a hub." I look down at my plate, feeling a tinge of panic. Tomorrow is goodbye. For the whole summer. When we started this road trip, I never expected to enjoy Lonnie's company this much. But I *really* enjoy his company. A shiver runs up my body even though I am not cold. And I really enjoy his handsome face…and strong neck. I swallow hard. And his ripped chest and rock-hard abs, and the way his tight ass flexes in his khaki shorts. *Good God, Ramona. Get a grip.* I clear my throat. "So, if we're on the road at nine-thirty, we'll get to my parents' place just in time for cube steak and pigs in blankets at four-thirty sharp." I bite my lip. "You in?"

He touches his chin. "Only if Earl burps the alphabet for me."

I laugh. "If you give him a Lucky Muck scratch-off ticket, he'll burp 'The Star-Spangled Banner.' " I take a big bite of my hot dog then stare at the flames. "I should warn you. My parents are rough around the edges."

Lonnie shrugs. "Have you met my father?"

"Okay, yes. Butch is special. But compared to my parents—" I shake my head. "For my fourth-grade open house, Earl walked into the classroom farting loudly, then asked Mrs. McKinlay to point him in the direction of the men's crapper."

Lonnie chokes a laugh. "That's funny."

"Not when it's your father doing it." I rub my forehead. "And Mom can be just as embarrassing. At my sixth-grade health fair, she lit up a cigarette at the Self-Care Bingo table."

He covers his mouth. "Ooh."

"Yep. And when Mr. Hurley told her smoking was prohibited, she said, 'Smoking relaxes me. How's that for self-care?' "

Lonnie laughs, and I lean toward him. "I know it sounds funny, but you don't understand." I clasp my hands in prayer. "When you're with them, whatever you do, don't pull anyone's finger. Or thumb. Oh, God, especially not the thumb."

He knits his brow. "Why would I pull anyone's thumb?"

I palm my forehead and whine, "Because they will ask you to."

"Ramona—"

I clutch my chest. "Oh, my God. You're going to hear me speak Snap Peas. When I'm there, it's like a switch that goes off in my left frontal lobe. The second I'm around them, I'm fluent again."

He chuckles. "You speak Snap Peas?"

"Oh, yeah. You'll be immersed. My family will chatter at you about meat raffles and donkey basketball and the fat, long-eared woodchucks underneath their shed who are multiplying like rabbits." I hold up a hand. "And, yes, they *are* multiplying like rabbits because, I've seen them, and *they are rabbits*. It's just…embarrassing."

He flashes a kind smile. "Ramona, *all* families are embarrassing. Listen, I'm looking forward to meeting them." He winks. "And hearing the belched version of 'The Star-Spangled Banner.' "

"Let's hope Earl *burps* it." I sigh. "If he stands up to belt it out, you'll want to clear the room."

Lonnie doubles over laughing, and I find myself laughing right along with him. Then he points to his empty plate. "Who needs prime rib when we have tofu dogs?"

"Not bad, right?"

He rocks forward and stands. "Going in for seconds."

As he walks toward the grill, my phone dings with an incoming message from Jules.

—Reminder! It's your last night at the campfire to stoke some wood. [three fire emojis]—

I bury a laugh. *—We're eating vegan hot dogs. On warm buns. [hot dog emoji]—*

—Warm buns are good. Now go get some real meat. [sausage emoji]—

I'm stifling a giggle when Lonnie returns with a full plate.

He watches me set my phone on the blanket, cocks his head, and I swear I see his jaw tighten before he asks, "Martin?"

I jerk back. "God, no. My friend, Jules." He sits beside me, and I turn to face him. "You saw Jules that day you walked by my trailer. She and her boys helped me move in."

"Sounds like a good friend." He bites into his hot dog.

"She's the best."

He arches an eyebrow. "If you don't mind me asking, what happened with Martin?"

I sigh. "We dated for two years. Jules and her husband, Chase, didn't like him from the beginning. And I get that. Martin can be difficult. He's arrogant, self-centered."

He grins. "So how could you resist?"

"We had some things in common. I used to live in a town house in downtown Jackalope near campus. Martin lived in a house nearby. We'd meet at restaurants and coffee shops and go to readings and events at the university." I move salad around my plate with my fork. "When I was a teenager, I dreamt of having that kind of life someday. My parents are hardworking, but their highest level of education is a GED. And there I was, Ramona Sadler, Ph.D., going to gallery openings and literary nights with Dr. Martin Smallwood, renowned psychologist." I shake my head. "It all feels silly now, but I think I was willing to put up with the reality of Martin to have the fantasy of what he symbolized. You know?"

Lonnie nods. "Yeah, I totally get that. Being so caught up in pursuing a particular life with someone that you don't realize that that someone is not a fit."

"Exactly. That, and when I met Martin, I was in a vulnerable place."

He knits his brow. "What was going on?"

"When my mom had the heart attack, I took the first flight out of Jackalope. She was out of surgery by the time I arrived, and I was just so relieved that she was going to be okay. When I saw her sitting up in that hospital bed eating pudding, I was just so grateful she was alive. I didn't know what to say or what to do to help her. All I wanted to do was sit beside her holding her hand, letting her know I was there for her, letting her know that I love her. But—"

"But?"

I let out a long exhale. "That's not how it works in my family. Mom had the TV blaring some soap opera. Earl sat around doing scratch-offs and complaining about the hospital cafeteria food. Ricky and Tina bickered with the nurses about when Mom should be discharged. I know this is selfish, but all I wanted was to have my mom to myself. But her hospital room was like a three-ring circus." I shake my head. "Then, when I told Mom and Earl I could stay in Snap Peas to help after she was discharged, they said that Ricky and Tina were all the help they needed."

He sucks air in through his teeth. "Ouch."

"Yeah, I doubt they meant to hurt my feelings, but that's how they are: blunt. Anyway, I realize now that I was hurt, really hurt, but at the time, I came home from the trip feeling angry, telling myself that I didn't want to be anything like them. The next night I met Martin. We were at a university gala. I was in an off-the-shoulder gown with stiletto heels, and Martin was in a three-piece suit with toilet paper stuck to his shoe." Lonnie laughs, and I go on, "He spotted me from across the room, brought me a glass of champagne, and we talked about literature and film, and, of course, Martin talked all about his feelings."

"Then what happened?"

"He asked if I wanted to see his *Flying Dutchman* in a Merlot bottle and we went to his place."

He snorts a laugh. "Ah, the old ship in the bottle line. Works every time."

I laugh. "Yeah. Dating arrogant guys was a pattern with me. In college, I dated a guy who was a lot like Martin. Chester Featherston. Captain of the Chess Team."

Lonnie smiles. "Captain Chess sounds like a winner."

I chuckle. "Our relationship was going strong until Captain Chess came to Snap Peas with me over Christmas break. He was supposed to stay for two weeks and stayed for two days. As soon as I returned to college for spring semester, he broke up with me. Said our backgrounds were incompatible."

Lonnie huffs. "Dickhead."

"Yeah, but I don't blame him. He came from an upper middle-class family in Connecticut. His mom was a banker, his dad an orthodontist. They lived in a wealthy subdivision. Then he's sleeping on the sofa in my parents' double-wide, listening to me speaking Snap Peas—"

Lonnie holds up his hand. "I blame the hell out of him. And I'll tell you something, Captain Dickhead missed out." He leans toward me, his eyes fiery in the glow from the campfire. "You're smart and funny and a badass truck driver in tight parking lots." I laugh, and Lonnie leans closer, so close that his shoulder brushes mine and my entire body warms, like a slice of golden-brown toast with melted butter. "Ramona, any man would be lucky—"

Lonnie's phone rings so loudly that our shoulders jerk. He holds my gaze for a few heartbeats, then looks down at his phone and sighs. I follow his gaze, my chest deflating at the sight of the name on the screen: *Shi-Yun*.

Chapter Sixteen

Lonnie stares down at his phone, arms crossed, waiting for the ringing to stop. Then he clears his throat and glances at me. "Speaking of exes."

I lean back on my hands, my jaw muscles tightening. *Am I...jealous?* "How long ago was the breakup?"

"About eight months ago. A few months after my mom passed."

Hmm. That long ago. Yet she's still calling. "So, you're still...friends?"

He stares at the night sky. "At first, since we were both surgeons at Cassidy Memorial and trying to be *mature* about things, we agreed to be friends." He turns to me. "That didn't work. Sent mixed signals, so I distanced myself." His shoulders slump. "But Shi-Yun is Ming's niece, and now Dad is dating Ming, so we're...cordial."

I swallow hard, thinking back to that time in the parking lot when Lonnie and Shi-Yun seemed to be in a very heated discussion until Shi-Yun was suddenly holding Lonnie's hand. I'm not sure what that was, but I wouldn't describe it as cordial. I bring a hand to my stomach that feels suddenly unsettled. *Well, shit. Yep, I'm jealous all right.* I stifle a sigh. *I really like Lonnie. During this trip, he's started to feel like a true friend. Not to mention, a friend with benefits that I'm dying tap into.* I bite my bottom lip. "So, Shi-Yun was almost Butch's daughter-in-law. Are they close?"

He stammers, "Not close, really. All I know is that it's all too close for comfort." His phone rings again. Shi-Yun. Lonnie flashes me an apologetic look as he lets out a long exhale. "You know, with Dad newly discharged from the hospital, I'd better take this." Picking up his phone, he stands. "Hello, Shi-Yun. It's not the best time for me to talk, but—"

I watch him walk off, then slowly get to my feet. I'd love to hear every word to get a better sense of their relationship, but he's out of earshot, pacing the gravel near my truck. I refill our mugs with tea then return to the blanket, and curl my legs under me, my body suddenly heavy with uncertainty. Too close for comfort. Just how close is Shi-Yun with Lonnie's family? Or with Lonnie, for that matter? In the parking lot, when Shi-Yun took his hand, he didn't look happy, but he didn't pull away either.

A few minutes later, Lonnie slumps down beside me.

I hand him his mug, studying the shadows the campfire's casting on his tight jaw. I ask, "Everything okay?"

He sips tea. "Shi-Yun's at Dad's house."

My pulse quickens. "Is Butch okay?"

Lonnie lifts his chin. "He's fine. I could hear him in the background yelling at the TV. His favorite baseball team is taking a beating."

I chuckle. "Glad he's doing okay."

"Shi-Yun said she was calling to update me on Dad's progress, but—" He stares off into the distance. "She was in the dining room, opened the buffet drawer, and found a stack of our wedding invitations. Then she started in on her guilt trip."

"Because you called off the wedding?"

He looks at me with tired eyes. "Because Mom helped design the invitations."

My shoulders drop. "Your mom helped with the wedding?"

He blinks slowly. "Mom and Shi-Yun planned every detail together. Right down to the pink peonies and bridesmaid's earrings."

My voice is small. "Sounds like they were close."

He grins. "They bonded over their common love interest."

I grin. "You."

He chuckles. "Shopping."

I smile then notice Lonnie's sudden pained expression and ask, "Hey, are you all right?"

"Just exhausted from the pressure. And the guilt." He scratches his face. "When Mom was near the end, she must have realized I was having second thoughts about the wedding. One day she started talking about how comforting it was for her knowing that Shi-Yun and I would be married, that I'd have a wife and wouldn't be alone." He swallows hard. "Then she looked me in the eye. I'll never forget the way she looked at me, her eyes pleading. She said, 'Promise me the wedding will go on without me.'"

I hear a sigh escape my lips, then ask softly, "What'd you say?"

He shakes his head the slightest bit and whispers, " 'I promise, Mom.' "

Instinctively, I reach over and place my hand on his.

He turns to face me, his eyes sad and warm and grateful. "Mom didn't understand the changes I'd seen in Shi-Yun." He frowns. "Shi-Yun acted like Mom's cancer was an inconvenience." His eyes search mine like he's trying to solve some impossible puzzle. "The day Mom went into hospice, we were told she only had a few weeks left. I was gutted, and Shi-Yun was upset with me because I wouldn't go to our wedding cake tasting party that night."

I bring a hand to my mouth and whisper, "Wow. Sorry."

He goes on, "A few days after that, she was furious that I'd canceled my tux fitting." He furrows his brow. "Here, I'd finally figured out what was truly important. I'd completely cleared my work schedule to devote time to my mom in her final weeks, and I was catching hell from my fiancée, the woman I was about to take vows with to love in times of sickness and health. That's when I realized that I was going through the hardest thing I'd ever faced in losing my mom, and instead of helping, Shi-Yun was making things harder."

I sigh. "I'm so sorry you didn't have more support during that time. That must have been so…" My voice trails off.

"It was rough, but I focused on being there for my mom and for Dad. And I went through the motions with Shi-Yun, swallowing back my unhappiness because Mom wanted the wedding so badly." He lifts his chin. "Then, a month after Mom passed, Shi-Yun called a realtor who showed us these extravagant places that looked like they came off the pages of My Trillion Dollar House is Better Than Yours." I chuckle, and he goes on, "We must have looked at twenty houses, and Shi-Yun couldn't understand why I wasn't willing to make an offer on any of them. Since we were both earning surgeon's salaries, we could afford them. But it all felt wrong." He shakes his head. "Then at the last house, this sprawling contemporary with a fountain and tennis court, Shi-Yun told the realtor that we were getting married in two months and I had a panic attack."

"Wow."

"Yeah, a full-on gasping for air, having to breathe into a paper bag, panic attack."

"That'll get your attention."

"It did. I knew I needed to change my life, that my priorities were all wrong. I broke off the engagement, quit surgery, bought twenty acres, built my barn, and put up a tiny house."

"Good for you." We clink mugs, and I sense that Lonnie's sadness has lifted, like it was helpful for him to tell the story out loud to someone who really wanted to hear it. I tilt my head. "I've seen your barn from a distance, but I didn't know you have a tiny house."

"I love it. It has a big loft, lots of windows." He shoots me a mischievous smile. "What? You thought I lived in the barn?"

"No, I figured I couldn't see your big surgeon's mansion through the trees."

He grins, and I notice that his jaw is relaxed again.

I arch an eyebrow. "So, any regrets about calling off the wedding and moving to Tiny Town?"

He chuckles. "No. It's been a relief." A thoughtful expression sweeps across his face. "Tonight, on the phone, Shi-Yun said the same old things. Told me that Mom would have wanted me to move on by now and go back to my old life, the way things were before she died."

I touch my chest. "Sorry that you've been pressured. Not just about the wedding, but about *moving on* from grief."

He nods. "People say things like that. They talk about moving on like it's some goal I'm supposed to achieve." His voice is soft. "Maybe I'm weird, but when it comes to grieving my mother's loss, I don't have a goal. The grief feels…so much bigger than me. So much bigger than all of us. I guess I just try to move *with* it instead of *past* it. You know?" His eyes are suddenly pleading, like he wants me to understand. Or maybe he wants to fully understand it himself.

I look up at the endless number of stars shining in the deep blue sky. "I've never heard grief talked about that way before. But it rings true."

We're quiet for a while. I savor the touch of the gentle breeze on my face and the sounds of leaves rustling on branches and pond frogs croaking their songs in the distance, and it feels like a perfect silence between two people who feel as natural together as their surroundings.

Lonnie's gaze sweeps across my face. "I've never told anyone that whole story. Thanks for listening. You took the sting out of Shi-Yun's phone call." He cocks an eyebrow. "So, what about you and Martin?"

"You want the whole break up story?"

"Spill it, Sadler."

I shrug. "Okay, long story short. Martin teaches at Sawyer Pickens University. He went to a committee meeting to supposedly get me rehired, but told the dean that, since I have a Ph.D. from a state school, I'm not in their league."

Lonnie jerks back. "God, what a prick."

"Yeah, there were plenty of other things, but that was my moment of clarity."

"So, no regrets?"

I widen my eyes. "About breaking up with Martin? God, no. The day Martin went to that meeting, I'd just moved out of my nice town house on Bluebonnet Lane and into my used trailer on Sawdust Loop. It was a low point, especially since I grew up in a trailer, and let's just say, kids can be mean." Lonnie searches my eyes, and I go on, "I was going through a tough time, and instead of being supportive, my boyfriend of two years made things tougher."

He shakes his head. "Sorry you went through that. How did your family feel about the breakup?"

I laugh. "Oh, yeah. Forgot. I haven't told them yet."

"Because?"

"Because I call my mom every other week and our conversations are brief, more about bowling and TV game shows than breakups and emotional well-being. When I called to tell her I was driving to Snap Peas, we talked for a few minutes about the trip." I touch a finger to my lips. "You know, it was funny. When I told Mom I was towing my trailer up here, she said, 'All by yourself?' You know, like she was…concerned about me."

"And that surprised you?"

"Yeah. By my mom's standards, that's downright gooey." He chuckles, and I go on, "Anyway, I told her you're helping me drive up, and she said, 'Okay, good. See you in a few days,' then hung up." I shrug. "I'll mention the Martin breakup when I'm there."

Lonnie cocks his head. "Mention? Didn't you say you dated for two years?"

"Yes, but they only met Martin once. He flew up with me last year. Stayed in a hotel. Came to my parents' place for dinner, then flew home the next morning. He didn't meet Ricky and Tina."

"Did your parents like him?"

I laugh. "Do my parents like anyone?" Lonnie smiles, and something in my stomach flutters. "They asked Martin if he wanted to go bowling."

"I'm guessing—"

"That Dr. Martin Smallwood would rather die than wear striped, rental shoes? Correct. So, we sat around in their living room trying to make conversation. Mom served Martin a bag of potato chips. Earl offered him a beer. Wasn't exactly a love fest."

A spark flies from the campfire, and when Lonnie reaches forward to brush it off the edge of the blanket, his warm shoulder leans against mine. Then he faces me, his green eyes looking dark as pine in the moonlight. "So, you and Martin are over?"

I lock my gaze on his. "So over." He leans even closer, as if he's trying to erase any distance between us, and I breathe in his torturous smell of honey, leather, and, I don't know, pheromones. "And you and Shi-Yun? Really over?"

His gaze darts from my eyes to my lips to my throat, and every nerve in my body lights up like that campfire spark. "Oh, yeah. Over."

He takes my hands in his. That simple gesture—the sensation of the warmth and strength of his hands cupping mine—makes me dizzy with pleasure. And I realize I've never felt excited like this with a man. All these years, I thought I was attracted to Martin and Chester and the handful of other men I had dated. I guess, technically, I was. I thought they were handsome, maybe even sexy. But here with Lonnie, there's no such thing as *technically*. Just the sight, the smell, the slightest touch from him stirs my body in ways I didn't know was possible.

Lonnie slowly stands, pulling me up with him, drawing me close, and I exhale a shaky breath in response to the heat radiating from his core. When he moves one hand firmly along my waist, curving it around to the small of my back, my legs go weak, unsteady, but I know I won't fall. Lonnie's holding me too securely to ever let that happen. He locks his gaze, gently brushes my jawline with his thumb, then his lips touch mine so gently and tenderly that it's like a whisper summoning me, *come closer...closer*. Instinctively, I wrap my arms around his neck, and he kisses me more deeply, passionately. I cup the nape of his neck, my kiss matching his passion, and he pulls my hips against his, making my back arch and my body moan for more of the heat from his mouth, the warmth of his tongue greedily exploring as our bodies draw closer and closer, yet nowhere near close enough because I want more of him. I need more of him. His touch fueling my longing is like every wonderful emotion on every turn of the Feeling Wheelhouse, my heart thumping and head spinning, then—

My phone rings.

Shit! My phone is ringing. I jerk back, bring a hand to my chest and shake my head as I glance down at the name flashing on the screen: *Ricky*. I furrow my brow. "It's my brother. He never calls. Like never."

Lonnie scoops up my phone and presses it into my palm.

My voice cracks as I stammer, "Ricky? Is everything okay?"

I feel every muscle in my body tense and hear my blood pounding in my head as I listen to Ricky's words. "Ramona, you're on your way, right? It's Mom."

Chapter Seventeen

Lonnie drives. I sit, knees curled to my chest, in the passenger seat staring out the window at my truck headlights beaming on highway asphalt, the weight of my heart growing heavier with each passing mile.

Ricky calls from his car as he's driving Tina and Earl to Mercy Upstate Hospital. Mom's being taken there by ambulance. She collapsed in the bathroom while brushing her teeth.

Later, Ricky calls again. Mom's hooked up to IVs, and a doctor's given them all "an earful of medical mumbo jumbo." Then Ricky says his phone battery is about to crap out, and the line goes dead. I stare at my phone for the next hour, willing the screen to light up in the darkness and to hear Mom's voice on the other end telling me she's okay.

But there's no light or reassuring words from Mom.

My cell reception goes to hell somewhere near Erie, Pennsylvania, and I doze off until Lonnie pulls into a service station, brings me two granola bars, unwraps one, and says in a voice so gentle that I think an angel has entered my dreams, "You'll need to keep up your energy. You know, to be there for your mom."

That's become my single focus: to be there for Mom. All that earlier passion stirred up between me and Lonnie, like a stoked campfire smoldering then igniting into red-hot flames—all from that one kiss—has been doused with a bucket of cold water of reality from one urgent phone call.

Now the sun rises as Lonnie pulls my truck and trailer into a spot at the far end of Patient Parking at Mercy Upstate. I rub the kink in my neck, squinting at the hospital building lit as bright as a beacon. Then Lonnie's at my door, offering his warm hand as I step from the truck. We stand facing one another, and I search his tired eyes, trying to find the words, summoning the strength to say, *About last night…right now, I can't.* I swallow hard. "Lonnie—"

Cupping my cheek with his hand, he gently kisses my forehead then steps back and takes my hands. His hands are still as warm and strong and sure as they were when he held me, mere hours ago, at our campsite. But there's no longer room to allow that sensation to take up space in my heart and soul that must now be held for my mom. Lonnie's voice is as warm as his hands. "At times like this, when you receive this kind of news about someone you love, the world stops. Everything else falls away. Right now, all of your emotional energy needs to go to your mom. Believe me, I understand."

Smiling sadly, I whisper, "Thank you."

Then he leads me across the expanse of parking lot blacktop, weaving us between rows of vehicles, his backpack swung on one shoulder. We hurry toward the big, red entrance sign, through the swoosh of opening doors to reception, up the elevators, then down the maze of long corridors to my mom's fifth-floor room.

The doors of Room Fifteen are closed when we arrive. I glance up at Lonnie and draw in a deep breath, trying to brace myself for the sight of Mom lying in a hospital bed connected to IVs and God only knows how many tubes and monitors.

Lonnie gently squeezes my hand, gives a quick knock on the doorframe, then pushes open the door.

Then I see it: the empty, stripped bed, nothing but a white mattress and bed rails. I double at the waist, slap my palm to my mouth, whispering, "No, no, no." I hear the thud of Lonnie's backpack against the tile floor then feel his arm around my shoulders. I straighten and turn to him, my gaze wildly searching his as I say, "She's gone." My voice cracks. "Oh, my God. My mom's…gone."

I exhale a rattled breath, my throat burning like a wildfire as I hold back tears, and collapse into Lonnie's embrace, my mind screaming, *No, no, please, God, no!*

Then I hear Ricky's voice from the doorway. "Ramona?" Our heads snap in his direction. Ricky looks at us like, *what the hell?* Then he says matter-of-factly, "Room change. We're in here."

Lonnie and I blink at one another then let out a huge collective sigh before rushing to the room next door where I see Mom, in her blue nightgown and robe, sitting in a chair with her purse on her lap.

Ricky shrugs at me. "False alarm. A bag of IV salt water and pint of orange juice and she's good as new."

I'm at her side in a nanosecond, bending to kiss her cool forehead. "Mom. You look—" I want to say, *so fucking adorable*. Because she is fucking adorable with her gray pixie all mussed up and bed-heady, looking up at me with her huge, round blue eyes. "You look good."

Then I look over at Ricky, in baggy jeans and flannel shirt pulled across his doughy belly, his dimpled face looking boyish as usual, and say, "Well, you might have told me she's doing better."

Ricky frowns. "I told you my phone was crapping out." He drags chairs over, gives Lonnie a quick handshake, and takes a seat.

I look at Mom. "So, you're okay?"

She blinks. "Took a tumble while brushing my teeth. Guess that's what I get for having superb oral hygiene."

I grin at her, shaking my head. "That'll teach ya." I wave to Lonnie, who's eyeing me and Mom with a warm grin. "This is Lonnie. He's—"

Mom flashes a smile as Lonnie walks over. "The neighbor who helped you drive here."

He takes her hand. "So nice to meet you, Mrs. Sadler."

"Please, call me Carol. Mrs. Sadler is my mother. And not a good-looking woman, may she rest in peace." She gestures toward the chairs. "Take a load off."

We sit. Then I look around. "Where are Earl and Tina?"

Ricky clasps his hands behind his head and leans back. "Earl started fighting with the vending machine when a packet of cookies he paid two dollars for wouldn't drop. Tina's plantar fasciitis flared up on her walk back from the hospital cafeteria. They went home to get some shut eye."

Mom looks at me then at Lonnie, sweeping her eyes from his head to his…holy shit, is she checking out his man package? "Glad you helped Ramona tow her trailer all this way."

Lonnie nods. "Happy to help." He grins my way. "Even though Ramona didn't need it. She's a much better truck driver than I am."

Mom grins. "Doesn't surprise me. She always was a tomboy."

I jerk my head. "Tomboy?" I hold a hand to my ear, pretending to make a phone call. "It's 1950 calling. It wants its vocabulary back."

Mom purses her lips. "You know what I mean. You were always climbing trees and rough housing with the boys."

Lonnie smiles. "That explains all the noogies she gave me on our way here."

I playfully nudge his elbow then glance over to see Mom grinning. Ricky leans forward. "Hey, Lonnie. What do you do for a living?"

"I'm the Patient Panda coordinator at a hospital." Ricky scrunches his face, and Lonnie adds, "Long, boring story."

Ricky grins. "I'm sure it's better than Ramona's story." He turns to me. "You got canned how long ago?"

I roll my eyes. "Five months ago. Thanks for the memories."

Ricky squints at me. "What are you doing now?"

Mom pipes up, "Ramona's a floater."

My jaw drops. "Mom, we don't call it that anymore. I'm a substitute teacher." I groan. "Floater. Jeez, sounds like something you'd find in the bathroom stall at a bus terminal."

Mom bursts out laughing which leads to a coughing fit that seems to turn her lungs inside out for a painful five minutes.

Lonnie's next to her in a flash, standing with his hand on her shoulder as she coughs, her hand pressed to her mouth and body lurching forward until her lungs finally begin to calm and she dabs her lips with a tissue.

Ricky cranes his neck toward me. "Happens every time she gets laughing."

I furrow my brow. "Do the doctors know?"

Mom says, "Oh, yeah. It's nothing new."

I flash a concerned look at Lonnie then there's a knock on the doorframe. "Mrs. Sadler, the EMT's are ready to transport you home." The nurse glances at us. "Your family can head to the lobby exit to join the ambulance now. We'll wheel you down in just a few minutes."

****

We step outdoors to see a Snap Peas Ambulance parked just outside the lobby. Two EMT's—one, a giant-sized middle-aged man with a long, gray ponytail and the other a younger athletic guy with a mop of beaver brown hair—stand near the side door shooting the breeze.

When they spot me, they lift their chins. Then the giant one strides over and pulls me into a quick hug. "Ramona. Good to see you. We're going to take good care of your mom."

I pat his shoulder and grin at Lonnie. "This is Big Jonny."

As Lonnie shakes his hand, Ricky says, "He's the boss. Owner of Big Jonny's Tires and Lube." He nods at the other EMT. "And that's Grizz."

Grizz waves and I wave back.

Then Ricky snorts a laugh. "Hey, Ramona, remember when Grizz mooned the tenth-grade pep rally?"

I cough. "How could I forget?" I look up at Lonnie. "So much hair. It was like staring into the ass of a grizzly."

Lonnie laughs. "Ah, hence, the nickname."

I nod. "You got it."

The lobby doors swoosh open, and the nurse wheels

out Mom.

Big Jonny smiles. "Ready to roll, Miss Carol?"

Mom gives a thumbs-up, and I swallow down a lump in my throat, thinking about her being transported here. Was she pale and scared? Did they carry her into the hospital on a stretcher?

Jonny looks at me and Ricky. "You two can ride in the back."

I knit my brow. "Oh, actually, my truck and trailer are parked here at the hospital." Then I look at Lonnie, feeling suddenly rattled that everything is happening so fast. "Uh, you're welcome to come over. I mean, if—"

Mom waves at me. "Hey, Ramona. Jonny brought a Beau Boopster music playlist for my ride home."

I give her a thumbs-up then grin at Lonnie. "Mom's a *huge* Boopster fan." I bite my lip. "Anyway, like I was saying, you can come over. Rumor has it that Tina brought over a big stash of Snap Peas Elementary cafeteria leftovers for breakfast."

He glances at his watch. "Thanks. It's tempting. But if I get to the airport soon, I can make the morning flight. Get back to the farm in time for evening feeding."

"Yeah. You have a long day of travel ahead." I force a smile even though I feel panicked. After three days on the road together, not to mention that kiss, I'm going to my parents' place and Lonnie's going back to Texas. "You're gonna miss Earl belching out the classics."

His eyes smile tenderly. "I look forward to the rain check." He winks. "I'll bring my tuba. We'll play a duo."

I glance over as Jonny wheels Mom to the ambulance. Grizz walks over. "Ramona, you should go with your mom. I'll drive your truck over."

"Thanks, but—"

Mom whistles my way. "He brought Boopster's *greatest hits.*"

Ricky turns to me. "Grizz is a good driver. Well, if you don't count the time he got our station wagon stuck in a cow pasture." He nods toward the ambulance. "I'm getting in the ambulance. I'll save you an uncomfortable spot on the floor."

I smirk. "Jeez, thanks, bro."

Lonnie smiles gently. "Go with your mom. You don't want to miss out on 'The Boopster Boogie.' "

I chuckle to hide my sadness. This is it. After eighteen-hundred miles on the road—enjoying campfires and tofu dogs, vegan bacon breakfasts, and that world-rocking, toe-curling, heart-thumping kiss—this is goodbye.

Grizz holds a hand out to me. "I'll need your keys."

Lonnie looks at Grizz then gestures toward the parking lot. "The truck and trailer are parked at the far north end of the lot." He reaches into his pocket and hands me my keys. Our fingers touch, and my world stops again.

I toss Grizz the keys, and he jogs off toward the parking lot as Ricky calls from the ambulance, "Ramona, Mom's ready to boogie."

For a moment, Lonnie and I search each other's eyes, speechless. Then he lifts his chin toward the line of taxis. "Guess I should get my ride." He takes my hand. "Hey, I meant what I said about all of your attention needing to go to your mom right now, but—" He bites his bottom lip. "Can I call you?"

"Yes, please."

Ricky calls out, "Ramona!"

I want to wrap my arms around Lonnie's neck, press

my head against his chest, and listen to his strong, beating heart and gentle voice tell me that everything will be okay. But my mom's waiting, and people are watching, and everything's happening so fast that I can barely catch my breath, so I raise my hand, wave, and turn to rush toward the ambulance.

Then I skid to a stop. "Lonnie!"

He turns back, his backpack hanging from his shoulder, his handsome face looking earnest.

I tell him, "Thank you for driving all night. You know, for getting me here safely."

He tilts his head and smiles. "Of course. Precious cargo."

Chapter Eighteen

I step inside my parents' place and wave at Earl and Tina, seated on the sofa with tray tables in front of them. Earl lifts his chin at me. "Look what the cat dragged in." He gestures to the plate of food on his tray. "I'd get up, but I might knock over my grape juice."

As Ricky and Jonny settle Mom into her overstuffed chair near the sofa, I head over to Earl and pat his shoulder. "I heard you got into a brawl with vending machine cookies."

He frowns. "Yep, and the damn cookies won."

Tina shifts on the sofa, flips her mane of blond hair, and points toward the kitchen. "Sausage and pancakes on the counter." She winks at Ricky. "Your favorite, babe. Patties, not links."

Ricky widens his big blue eyes, and I can't help but smile. He looks so much like Mom. He has her eyes, the cowbird brown hair she had before going gray, and, despite being a guy, he's got Mom's plump, pear-shaped figure. I'm the spitting image of Earl with his hazel eyes, wavy hair, athletic build, but thankfully, not the tufts of gray hair growing out of his ears and nose. Ricky glances at the wall clock then says to Jonny, "Plenty of time to chow down before the shop opens."

I set a tray table in front of Mom, then join the others in the kitchen microwaving breakfast plates. Tina calls over, "Last week's school theme was Mystery of the

Sea." I heat two plates heaped with sausage patties and mini-pancakes in the shapes of sea creatures, then slide a plate in front of Mom, and take a seat on one of the kitchen chairs Jonny dragged into the living room.

Earl clunks his fork down. "You know, Ramona, since last time you were here, I turned seventy-five." My parents are older than most of my friends' parents. Mom and Earl married in their twenties but didn't have Ricky until Mom was thirty-eight. She'd just turned forty when I was born. I asked them once why they waited so long to have kids. Earl said they didn't want to squander their peak bowling years chasing rug rats. Earl raises his eyebrows at me. "The big seven-five."

I stab a pancake with my fork. "I know, I sent you a Beer of the Year subscription, remember?"

Mom drizzles syrup on her plate. "Seventy-five. That's a lot of rings around the old tree."

Earl grins. "The other big news since last I saw you is—" He throws his hands out to his sides like, *ta da!* "I'm going to the University of Buffington."

I cough. "What?"

Earl chuckles. "That's right. Donated my body to science."

I nudge Ricky's elbow. "Has science *seen* his body?"

Mom looks at Earl. "You'll finally get that degree you always wanted."

Chewing on a pancake, it hits me. I'm back. Here in Snap Peas. Smack dab in the middle of my parents' world with Ricky, Tina, and Big Jonny. My stomach churns finding myself back here in this world that I know inside and out, yet feel lost in, a world that's familiar and foreign all at once. And I'm here for the whole summer.

Ricky holds up a pancake. "Got the starfish and shark."

Mom points to her plate. "Whale and octopus."

Jonny stabs a pancake then frowns. "Wait a minute. I got a Christmas tree and elf. How old is this?"

Tina shrugs. "You must have gotten one of the holiday freezer bags."

Jonny grimaces. "Yeah, and from the taste of things, it was Christmas, 1987."

I look over at Mom, who's grinning as she bites into a sausage patty, then chases it with a big gulp of juice. Maybe Ricky was right, and she is *good as new*. Maybe I've been worried for nothing and on a guilt trip for no reason. She had a heart attack, but that was two years ago, and now, here she is, eating whale pancakes and cracking jokes.

Jonny waves over at me. "Ramona, I forgot to mention that I put your mom's hospital paperwork on the table."

I glance over at an orange folder then look at Mom. "Are those your discharge papers?"

She purses her lips. "Probably just the same old hospital poppycock."

Ricky nods. "We get it every time. Bunch of stuff about how the goal for Mom is *comfort*."

I jerk my head. "Comfort?"

Mom arches an eyebrow at Ricky. "Everybody needs a goal."

He leans forward. "Yeah, but what kind of goal is *that*?" He holds up a hand. "Running five miles without tossing your cookies. That's a goal. Bowling a three-hundred. Goal. But *comfort*? No offense, Mom, but they set the bar pretty low for ya."

I open my mouth, but no words form. Comfort? As in comfort care? Like palliative care? I feel my pulse quicken. They must have read things wrong. They're always talking about how they can't make heads or tails out of the doctor's "medical mumbo jumbo." Too bad Lonnie's not here to flip through the folder then reassure me that everything's fine. I feel myself softly sigh. Too bad Lonnie's not here to…just be Lonnie.

The door opens, and Grizz steps inside. He heads for the kitchen, and Jonny calls over, "What took you so long?"

Grizz fills a plate. "Made a quick stop." He grins at me, jangles my truck keys, then sets them on the table next to the orange folder. "Goodenough's DIY Car Wash. It's got a great power washer."

I set my plate down and walk to the picture window, smiling at the sight of my shiny truck and trailer. "Thank you, Grizz."

He takes a seat, balancing his plate on his lap. "It was nothing."

Mom smiles, shaking her head at him. "Even in grade school, Grizz was the sweetest boy in Snap Peas."

I loud-whisper to Ricky, "With the hairiest ass in town."

Ricky coughs a laugh, and grape juice shoots out his nose.

Mom wags a finger at us. "You two. Don't make me ground you." She tilts her chin at Grizz. "Remember when you asked every girl in the fourth grade to marry you? Got right down on one knee."

Grizz chuckles. "It was fun until Ashley Gumper said 'yes' then demanded a ring."

Ricky straightens in his chair then eyes me. "Hey,

speaking of proposals. Why don't you tell Martin to put a ring on it? There are tax advantages, you know."

I shoot him a look like, *Are you insane?* "You never met the guy, yet you think I should marry him? Not that any of it matters because—"

I'm about to say, *because Martin and I are over*, when Ricky shrugs. "You've told me everything I need to know to approve the union."

I huff. "Like?"

"Like he's got his own teeth and makes a good paycheck."

I roll my eyes. "And don't forget about his opposable thumbs."

Ricky grins. "Tie the knot. You can go from trailer living to *Bigger Homes Digest.*"

I point out the window and chuckle. "Look at that power washed gem of an RV. What girl could ask for anything more?"

Earl cranes his neck to look out at my trailer. "Not for nothin', but even for us, your place is on the small side. Might want to take Ricky's advice."

Unbelievable. Even my own father, who spent one awkward evening with Martin, thinks I should marry the guy. I purse my lips. "Listen, about Martin—"

Ricky glances at me quizzically. "Yeah, about Martin. Why didn't he help you tow your trailer here?"

I snort a sarcastic laugh. "Martin? Connecting and reconnecting trailer sewer lines? Besides, Martin and I are—"

Mom sits straight. "Kaputski?"

I nod. "Kaputski."

She grins. "Well, it's about time. I mean, the ships and bottles and the Feeling Wheelhouse? Please." She wriggles her eyebrows at me. "Then there's that Lonnie fellow. Nice guy. And not too hard on the eyes." I bring a hand to my mouth, and she chuckles. "What do they call men who look like that? Man candy?"

Ricky bursts a laugh. "Mom!"

Earl snickers. "Man candy. Well, that does it, Carol. No more afternoon soap operas for you."

Laughing, Jonny gathers his plate and stands. "Time for me to get that rust bucket of an ambulance back to Snap Peas station." He walks over to Mom and places a hand on her shoulder. "Feel better, Carol." He side-eyes Earl. "And keep that old fart out of trouble."

I walk Jonny to the door. "Thanks for taking care of my mom." I grin. "I mean, what other volunteer EMT would play back-to-back Beau Boopster tunes for a patient?"

Jonny smiles. "Anytime." Then he nods toward the table. "Hey, Ramona. Your mom's hospital folder? You might want to take a look."

Chapter Nineteen

It's almost eight p.m. My trailer is dim, so I flick the wall switch for the light above the kitchen dinette. Ricky borrowed a spare generator from Big Jonny's, so I have electricity. I don't have water or sewer hookups, so I keep bottled water on the countertop and use my parents' bathroom and kitchen. And Ricky reminds me, "There's a hose out back with your name on it."

I sit at the table, tapping my fingers against the orange folder, my eyes fixed on *Carol Sadler* handwritten in bold, black marker. At my parents' place, I must have glanced at the damn thing a hundred times as I busied myself cooking and cleaning, trying to be helpful. Now it's just me and the stupid folder Jonny told me I might want to look at, his face flashing concern. I draw in a deep breath and pinch the cover, about to flip it open, when my phone rings. Looking at the screen, I feel my body immediately soften. "Hey, Lonnie. Back in Hill Country?"

His voice is warm. "Yep. And your mom? She's back home?"

"She's all comfy in her chair watching *Virgin Creek* season two, for the tenth time, and listening to Earl snore in his recliner."

He chuckles. "It was great meeting her. She's a real spitfire."

I smile, remembering her calling Lonnie *man candy*.

"Oh, you have no idea."

"It was nice meeting your brother, too. And he didn't ask me to pull his finger. Or thumb."

"Miracles happen."

I swear I hear a smile in Lonnie's voice as he asks, "How was your first day in Snap Peas?"

"Went grocery shopping, whipped up a cube steak dinner, and did two laundry loads of towels, Mom's nightgowns, and Earl's skid-marked underwear. Who knew old people produced so much dirty laundry?"

He snorts a laugh. "Uh, me. I'm at Dad's ranch now and just dumped a load of filthy socks, T-shirts, and baggy old-man shorts in the wash." I hear rustling and a muffled voice on the other end. "In fact, the old man in question would like to talk with you."

I smile, feeling a warming sensation in my chest. From the start, Butch has been my favorite patient ever, but now that Lonnie and I have become closer, I feel even more fond of Butch knowing that he raised a really good son. "Put him on."

Butch coughs into the phone. "Ramona, I'll just keep you a minute. Lonnie told me about your mother's hospital visit. How are you doing, Panda?"

"I'm okay. Glad I'm here." I stare down at the folder and run my finger along her name.

"I'm sure it means the world to her to have you there."

"Thanks, Butch. Hey, how's your knee?"

"Getting better every day. But don't tell Lonnie. He might start making me do my own laundry."

I chuckle. "Our secret."

"Listen, if there's anything you need, there's an old coot here in Texas you can count on."

My throat thickens. "That means a lot."

"Well, I don't usually say these things out loud, but you mean a lot."

I bring a hand to my heart.

He goes on, "You know, I wouldn't have survived that hospital stay without you…and the chocolate. If you need anything, just call."

"Aw, thank you."

"Just remember: I don't answer the phone during televised baseball games, or when the six o'clock news is on, but other than that—"

I shake my head.

"Now let me give you back to my pain-in-the-ass son."

I hear a door open, followed by footsteps, then Lonnie's voice. "Hope he behaved himself."

"He was downright sweet. You know, for Butch."

Lonnie chuckles. "So, what are you doing this evening?"

"Avoiding opening Mom's hospital folder." I sigh. "I'm nervous about reading the paperwork."

He sighs then speaks slowly. "What do you say, we switch to video call, and open the folder together?"

His words feel like a warm hug. "Okay."

There's a click then a ringtone. I prop my phone up, swipe answer, and blink slowly at the sight of Lonnie's compassionate expression. His voice is gentle. "Ready?"

I nod, then open the folder, realizing that my palms are sweaty. I remove the papers from the folder sleeve, my mind scrambling to process the first word that catches my eye: "hospice."

I've volunteered in a hospital long enough to know that doctors sign off on hospice care when a patient's life expectancy is six months or less. I rub my forehead, my chest squeezing, my heart melting into a puddle.

Lonnie's quiet on the other end, breathing steadily, giving me space to be sad or angry or anything I need to be as I scramble to grasp the implications of what I'm reading. Then he says in the kindest voice I've ever heard, "Can you tell me what your pain is about?"

I blink at his face on the screen, his eyes searching mine. "Hospice."

Drawing in a breath, Lonnie slowly nods.

Sighing, I tell him, "I guess I'm not really surprised. Ricky and Mom were saying that the doctor's goal for her is comfort. I thought maybe they'd misunderstood what the doctor said. But today, I noticed a shower chair in Mom's bathroom. She told me a nurse's aide delivered it last week then stayed to take her blood pressure and check her legs for swelling. I know extra services, like having a nurse's aide do home care, aren't handed out unless there's a need." I scratch my jaw. "But seeing it in writing—"

His eyes moisten. "I'm so sorry."

"Me, too." I cross my arms over my stomach, my throat burning from pushing back tears. "I've wasted so much time. So many opportunities." My voice cracks. "I taught at a university, for God's sake. I had academic breaks in the summer, spring, and winter. And I stayed in Jackalope when I could have flown here. All the holidays and birthdays and Mother's Days I've missed…with her." I throw up my hands. "She had a heart attack. I should have visited more. Gotten my ass on a plane. But I didn't." Heat rises in my chest. "I just flew up once a year, stayed for three days, like I was checking the visit off my fucking to-do list. Another pesky chore like cleaning the gutters. And now time is running out."

He tilts his head. "Ramona, it's okay to have regrets. We all have regrets."

I rub my forehead. "I should have been here."

"You're there now."

I sigh. "Yeah."

He looks thoughtful. "And you're there in a big way. You hauled your RV up for the summer. I'm sure your mom appreciates that beyond words."

"Yeah, she's not one to communicate that kind of thing, but I know she appreciates it." I search his eyes. "When you saw Mom in the hospital, did you know?"

He swallows. "Her cough concerned me. And I noticed the swelling in her ankles." He pinches his chin. "But she doesn't appear frail, and she was engaged in conversation." He cocks his head. "How is she at home?"

"She gets around slowly, but she has a good appetite. And even better sense of humor." I giggle. "She called you *man candy*."

He coughs. "Didn't think it was possible, but I like her even more now."

"She's a hoot. Earl was walking through the living room farting loudly, and Mom looked at me and said, 'It's his motor. I told him I'd prefer electric, but he went for gas.' "

Lonnie doubles over laughing. "Now I know where you get your sense of humor from."

My cheeks warm. Mom and I have always joked around. I guess it is a kind of connection, one I've taken for granted. "Luckily, I got Mom's humor instead of Earl's talent for turning flatulence into song." Lonnie chuckles, and I say, "She is funny. Despite being sick, she's still my mom."

Lonnie's voice is gentle, yet sure. "She'll always be your mom. *Nothing* will ever change that."

I close my eyes, my throat raw from swallowing back tears. "Promise?"

"Cross my heart."

Chapter Twenty

Days and weeks pass by in a blur of steadfast routine. I wake up around seven. Make Mom and Earl breakfast. Do dishes and laundry while they watch game shows. Buy groceries, serve them lunch, take a shower while Mom watches soap operas and Earl tinkers in the yard. Then Mom falls asleep in her chair, and I turn off the TV, place a thin blanket over her lap, and watch her sleep, thinking this whole hospice thing must be all wrong. Okay, she's lost a few pounds, and her hands and ankles are puffy. But I study her as she breathes steadily, her eyelids gently closed, and all I see is my mom, the woman I've known since the beginning of time.

It's Tuesday afternoon. Mom's napping. Earl's mowing the lawn. I'm in my trailer, lying on the bed, when my phone rings. I beam at the screen: Jules. Her voice is cautiously cheerful. "Hey. How's it going?"

I roll onto my side. "Made Mom's favorite dinner last night: smothered hamburgers. Ricky said I was heavy on the alphabet soup."

She snorts. "Ricky couldn't spell his own name with alphabet soup." I chuckle, and she asks, "Are you cooking again tonight?"

I sit up then lean against a pillow. "We're defrosting shit. Tina's stocked a gazillion plastic containers filled with school cafeteria leftovers in Mom's freezer. Come to find out, she's been doing that since Mom's heart attack. She told me she didn't want Mom to have to lift a finger if she didn't feel like cooking."

Jules coughs. "Really?"

"Yeah, shocking, right?" I stare down at my comforter. "And here all these years I thought Tina was freakishly self-absorbed."

"Well, in your defense, she does spend most of her time applying lip liner and adjusting the spacing of her basketball ass."

"True. But I have to say, my heart melted a bit when she showed me the meals, all perfectly stacked and labeled. There's enough popcorn chicken and ham mac and cheese to feed an army." I shrug. "I mean, it's not exactly heart healthy food, but Mom's idea of a vegetable is a glass of cheap red wine."

Jules laughs. "Sounds like frozen hamburger patties and rectangle pizza is Tina's love language."

"Yeah, between that and Ricky bringing me a twenty-four-pack of bottled water and Earl actually smiling at me and patting my head, I'm like, who are these people?"

"Emotional bonding with your Snap Peas kin. Nice."

"Don't get too excited. After the head pat, Earl gave me five dollars to go buy him scratch-offs." I sit cross-legged. "So how are things in Texas?"

She groans. "Summers are the worst. You know I love my boys, but twenty-four/seven? Every June I eat up half my vacation time to chauffeur two redheads to swimming lessons, science camp, and Lick Away Ice Creams. If I'm not doing that, I'm hand feeding them a side of beef every day. I swear, if I hear, 'Mom! What's there to eat?' one more time—"

I laugh. "I don't know how you do it. But they are sweet boys."

Jules sighs. "Dang, they are the sweetest. Yesterday, after helping Chase with the horses, they came into the kitchen and gave me a big hug and a bouquet of wildflowers *just because*." Jules clears her throat. "Speaking of hugs. Wish I could give you one while I ask this question: How's your mom?"

"Tired. She naps and goes to bed early. But she still has a pretty good appetite. And the nurse's aide said her walking is stable."

"Have you had a chance to get some alone time with her?"

I sigh. "Not really. I mean, there's always some distraction. If it's not Ricky, Tina, or Earl, it's the blaring TV."

"Sorry."

"Yeah, I was telling Lonnie that's the hardest part. It's tough for me and Mom to have a heart-to-heart talk while Earl is yelling out numbers during a game show or Tina and Ricky are talking about the latest scandal on the front pages of tabloids."

Jules sighs. "What did Lonnie say?"

"He sympathized. Asked how I'm coping."

"How are you coping?"

I swallow hard. "Well, when I got up the courage yesterday to tell Mom I love her and she didn't hear me over the roar of the game show audience, I grabbed *National Velvet* and climbed my favorite tree in their backyard."

"Back to tree climbing. Just like when you were a kid. Did it help?"

"It did until the wind picked up and I dropped my

book. Landed in a puddle."

"Oh, no, Ramona. I'm sorry."

I can't help but chuckle. "Yep, poor Velvet and The Pie took a nosedive into mud. But it's okay. Climbing trees does help. Just being up there, away from everything, feeling like a part of nature, it's my little leafy refuge." I run a hand through my hair. "But enough of my Snap Peas drama. I want some good ole Jackalope gossip."

Jules bursts a laugh. "Oh, I'll give you gossip. Tiffany Dicksteiner tried flirting with Chase again after church this past Sunday."

I gasp. "No."

"Yes. It's a thing with her. Tiffany puts the move on every married man in our congregation."

I huff. "Can't churches do something about stuff like that? What about a good, old-fashioned shunning?"

"That's what Chase does. He's like, talk to the hand. But I chose another route."

I lean forward. "Ooh, what'd you do?"

"In the parking lot, I followed Ms. Dicksteiner to her little car and said, 'I noticed you trying to flirt with my Chase again. I didn't say anything the first time, or the second. But looks like this third time's a charm.' "

"Good for you."

"I told her there's not a married man in this congregation who's interested in her big old hairy cooter."

I bark a laugh. "You did not!"

"Oh, I did. Called out Tiffany Dicksteiner's hairy cooter with church bells ringing in the background."

I double over laughing.

Jules goes on, "Then I said, 'My pastor tells me not

to exchange evil for evil, but if you hit on my husband again, I will go all Old Testament on your ass.' "

When I finally stop laughing, I say, "God, I miss this. I miss you."

"I miss you, too."

Then I surprise myself by blurting out, "And I miss my mom already."

I listen to Jules's long, heart-breaking sigh. Then she says, "I know you only have one mom. And I'm way too young and hip to be a mother figure for you. But I've always wanted a sister."

I jerk my head slightly. "You have a sister."

"You've met Joleen. I've always wanted a *good* sister. You in?"

I chuckle. "I'm in…Sis."

"Good, it's settled." Then she groans. "I just heard the refrigerator door open. I need to go rescue the leftover meatloaf before it's inhaled by twins. Okay, Ramona, you know the rule: call me anytime."

I'm still smiling from the phone call when I hear the rumbling of an engine coming from outside my RV. I step outdoors to see a mail truck pull into my parents' driveway. A man wearing a brown uniform and broad grin emerges from the truck carrying a large box. "Delivery for Carol Sadler."

"Thanks. I'll sign for it."

He sets the box down, then holds out the clipboard. "Tell Mrs. Sadler we hope she's back to calling Friday Bingo in no time."

I sign my name. "Will do."

He winks. "And tell her pain-in-the-butt husband to bring his best game to horseshoes this week. Another performance like last week and we're giving him the horse's ass trophy."

I chuckle. "Just like last year."

I wave as the truck pulls from the driveway, then squint down at the box and feel my jaw drop into a huge smile. To: Mrs. Carol Sadler and family. From: Lonnie Acres.

Chapter Twenty-one

I hold the phone close to my ear. "Your care package was a big hit." I feel a bit breathless just thinking about what Lonnie sent: the beautiful soft knit shawl and lilac-scented hand lotion for Mom, the Lucky Muck scratch-off tickets for Earl, a canvas gift bag embroidered, *Huge Hugs from Texas*, filled with chocolates, nuts, and cookies for everyone, and for me…I place a hand on my fluttering stomach…a book and a necklace. "Mom loves her shawl. She keeps saying, 'How did he know my favorite color is blue?' "

Lonnie's voice is gentle. "I was trying to match her eyes."

I hear a little *heh* escape my lips. "Wow. I mean, just, wow."

He chuckles. "Were any of the scratch-offs winners?"

"One was a lucky muck. Ten bucks."

"Nice."

I nod even though he can't see me. "*You're* nice. Thank you."

"My pleasure. Hey, video, please?"

Before I can say yes, I hear a click then the chime for video chat. I answer then hold my book in front of the camera. "When I opened the box and saw my brand-new, mud-free copy of *National Velvet*—" I turn the camera toward myself and smile. "So happy."

Lonnie smiles then squints at the screen. "Are you—?"

"Yep, up a tree with my horse book." I bring a hand to my throat, touching the simple gold chain and glass medallion with pressed bluebonnets. "And this necklace is beautiful."

"Thought you might be craving just a little bit of Texas Hill Country."

I study Lonnie's image on the screen. Since I last saw him in person weeks ago, his hair has gotten longer, and his face and neck are a deeper golden brown. It's evening, the sun just setting, and even in a small square of video I can see the green in his eyes. "So, what did your day look like?"

"Did farm chores, had fresh eggs for breakfast, went to the hospital and trained new volunteers, then went to the cafeteria and ate a tofuy salady thing."

I snort a laugh. "How's Butch doing?"

He frowns. "Unfortunately, he's feeling well enough to start getting on my case again. He was having lunch with a friend, who just happens to be the Chief of Surgery at Cassidy Memorial. Dad told me the department wants me back. Said it's a darn shame that I'm wasting my talent as a surgeon to raise farm animals."

"Ugh. Sorry Butch is being hard on you. When he told you the surgery department wants you back, were you tempted?"

"Not a bit."

I tease, "You could say goodbye to herding volunteer prairie dogs."

He smiles. "I want to go back to medicine, but not surgery. My mom was diagnosed with cancer a year and a half before she died, but I was working so much that I didn't spend nearly as much time with her as I should have. I'd plan to see her, then end up bowing out. She said she understood, and she probably did since she was married to a surgeon. But the bottom line is that surgery was all consuming. I don't want to live like that again, missing out on what's important."

I blink at the warm breeze on my face. "I get that."

"And what about you? Have you been up a tree all day?"

"Nope. The usual. Cleaning, grocery shopping, helping Mom get around. She uses a walker now. The nurse's aide wants her to use it for stability. We don't want her to fall." Lonnie nods, and I say, "I made dinner, did the dishes then hung around up here reading my book and waiting for Ricky and Tina to go home in the off chance I might finally get some quiet time with Mom." I turn my head toward the sound of a car door opening and closing then an engine revving. "In fact, I think they're leaving now."

"Be careful climbing down. We don't want you to fall either."

I press a finger to my lip, feeling touched by Lonnie's concern. "You're the first person who's ever said that to me, you know."

He knits his brow. "To be careful?"

"Yeah. As a kid, I jumped barbed-wire fences, rode on bicycle handlebars, dove off high banks into the river, walked on railroad tracks." I laugh. "It's amazing I'm in one piece."

"Sounds like your parents were not worriers."

"Mom and Earl would tell me and Ricky, 'Go outside and play,' and we'd walk three miles along

County Road 12 to buy candy at the gas station. Or we'd follow some trail in the woods for hours or ride our bikes down back roads to swim in the quarry. And it's not like we had cell phones. I think our parents just assumed we'd be fine. And, you know, we had bumps and bruises along the way. I broke my wrist once, and Ricky broke his collarbone. But we were fine."

His eyes flash a smile. "Way to be a country girl. But if it's all the same with you, I'll stay on the call until you're safely on the ground."

****

I pause outside Mom's front door and stare up at the moon in the dark blue sky. I love seeing a full moon, the kind me and Ricky gazed up at as kids, pointing to crater shadows, and repeating the silly myth that it was made of green cheese. There's something so hopeful about a big, bright full moon. But tonight's moon is a waning crescent, making me feel oddly sad. I suppose everything wanes eventually. I hear the TV blaring from the other side of the door and sigh. Mom looks up and grins when I step indoors, and I swivel my head. "Where's Earl?"

"Listening to the radio in the bedroom. Baseball game." I take a seat on the end of the sofa next to her chair, my heart warming at the thought that it's just me and my mom...and that blasted blaring TV.

I look at her sitting there in her nightgown with the shawl Lonnie sent wrapped around her shoulders and feel suddenly weepy, yet not a single tear falls. "Can I get you anything, Mom? Water? A snack?"

She gestures to the TV remote. "Can you turn this thing off?"

I gladly flick the remote. "I thought *Virgin Creek* was your favorite."

"I'm a big fan of Mal and Don, and that Jack Sheerington is a sight for sore eyes."

I chuckle.

"But Faith McCroy? Annoys the hell out of me."

I lean toward her. "Right?"

Mom grins then runs her hand along her shawl. "Did you ask Lonnie how he knew blue was my favorite color?"

"Yes. Said he was trying to match the color of your eyes."

She blinks. "Well, I'll be. That was some package he sent." Then a mischievous grin sweeps across her face. "Speaking of packages—"

I knit my brow, wondering where she's going with this.

She confirms my suspicions. "Lonnie looks like he fills out his jeans in exactly the right places."

My jaw drops. "Mom!"

She squints at me. "Like you haven't noticed. I mean, they don't grow men like that here in Snap Peas." I laugh, and she says, "And, by the way, I approve."

My face flushes. "But we're not…there's nothing to approve."

She cocks an eyebrow. "If you say so. But, in the hospital, I saw the way he looked at you."

I search her big, blue eyes, my chest tingling, like it's filled with champagne bubbles. Not just because of what she said about Lonnie, which definitely makes me giddy. But because, finally, it's just me and my mom having a heart-to-heart talk. I bite my lip. "Really?"

"Oh, yeah. He was all goo-goo eyed, like he was looking at something…precious."

I stifle a giggle remembering how, when I thanked

Lonnie for driving me safely to Snap Peas, he referred to me as precious cargo. That was so sweet, but sitting here with Mom, I'm awestruck by the one truly precious thing in life that there never seems to be enough of…time.

She pinches her chin. "When you opened that box and I saw that horse book, it brought back a lot of memories. You know, I always wanted to surprise you on your birthday with horseback riding lessons."

My head jerks back. "You did?"

"Oh, yes. I knew you'd love riding lessons since you ran down the road to feed carrots to the neighbor's horse and always had your nose in one of those horse books." She glances at the ceiling. "But somehow I never got around to giving you those lessons."

I raise my chin. "It's okay, Mom. Reading those books…it was like I was galloping through the fields. I remember the Christmas you gave me *Horse Crazy*. And by the time I was thirteen, you'd gotten me the complete series."

"You had quite the library. Always reading and writing and studying." She takes a sip of water and gazes out the picture window. "You know, you were always different from the rest of us."

My breath catches. There it is. She said it: the truth I've felt from the time I was a little girl. I never fit in. I was different. I knew it. They knew it.

She looks at me wistfully. "You've always been so smart."

I feel my jaw slacken.

She smiles. "I'd look at Earl and say, 'How did us two dumb-asses bring *this* into the world?' " I shake my head in protest, but Mom goes on, "Really. You're so smart, so…special."

I bring a finger to my lips, swallowing back the burning in my throat.

Mom shoots me an impish grin. "I mean, Ricky's great. But let's face it, he's not exactly the sharpest tool in the shed."

I snort a laugh. "He's special in his own way."

She nods then glances at my throat. "That's some necklace Lonnie sent you. Texas bluebonnets." She shakes her head. "Texas…so far away." A sudden pang of guilt washes over me for having moved so far away from Snap Peas. But then Mom adds, "You were so brave to move, to see the country."

A little gasp of surprise escapes my lips. "Brave?"

"Hell, yeah. We're all a bunch of homebodies. But not you. I remember when you went off to college. All the way to Minnesota and you were barely seventeen. Now that's brave."

"I didn't feel brave at the time. I felt homesick."

Mom raises her eyebrows. "Really? I thought you hardly looked back."

"I acted like I wasn't looking back. But that first year? I was so homesick. Remember all the letters I wrote?"

"Kept every one of them."

My throat thickens. "You did?"

"Of course. Reread them not all that long ago. You started every letter with Dear Mom, Earl, Ricky, and Big T-nana."

I laugh. "I forgot I called Tina that."

"That was one of your nicer nicknames for her." She grins. "And you ended every letter with Hugs and Kisses, Ramona." She purses her lips. "You were always such a mush."

"That's right. I'll own it. I'm a mush." I search her eyes that are shimmering like lake water, feeling like all I want to do is let myself fall into that blue abyss. But rather than falling, I take a deep breath and dive right in. "I love you, Mom. You know I love you, right?"

She reaches over and pats my hand. "I always thought I'd make it to Texas to visit you. I imagined how pretty Texas Hill Country must be."

I lean toward her. "It is. Where I live there are so many trees and flowers. Beautiful live oaks and hibiscus and crepe myrtle. And there's the San Gabriel River and tall grass and Texas sage."

A dreamy expression crosses her face. "Sounds so nice. I'm ready to pack my suitcase, get on a plane, and take off to Hill Country. It's been a while since I've been on a trip. I'm ready to go."

I chuckle. "It is nice. In my yard there are so many birds, Mommy." Mommy. It just comes out. After hiding in some undisclosed location for the past three decades, it slips out like a primal longing. "At my bird feeders, I see finches and hummingbirds and painted buntings, which are just gorgeous. And the flowers. You should see the fields of bluebonnets in the spring—"

"Wish I'd made the trip sooner."

I take her soft hand into both of mine. "Mom, you did. You didn't have to take an airplane or bus or a pickup truck to be in Texas Hill Country. You were always right there with me, watching the birds at the feeder, walking through the fields of bluebonnets, right there with me...in my heart."

"That's right." Her voice is soft and dreamy. "I remember now. It was so beautiful."

Chapter Twenty-two

The grief comes in waves—at times, it feels like the weight of an ocean crashing over me, and other times, it hits me like a rolling swell or courses through me like a steady current. No matter how it surges, grief is ever present.

At Rivermore Cemetery, I stand in the shade of an elm tree watching people tearfully mingle. On this sunny, seventy-five-degree, end-of-June day, Rivermore is in its glory. I take in the lush green lawn and breathe in hints of hydrangea and milkweed carried by the breeze, and feel my lips curl into a sad grin as I whisper, "You chose a nice place, Mommy."

The crew from Big Jonny's Tires and Lube are patting Earl's shoulder and nodding compassionately at Ricky and Tina. Jonny offers condolences. Grizz doles out tissues. Others lift their faces toward the sunshine, drawing attention to the beauty of the day despite the heavy clouds of sorrow in our hearts.

Lonnie offered to be here. I thanked him over and over, then turned down his offer. I didn't want him to travel this far when I felt like every ounce of my emotional energy needed to go to my family, and to just hanging on. He told me he understood that he'd be here with me in spirit and be there for me when I was back in Texas. He understood when I'm not even sure I understand it myself.

I gaze at the other funeral attendees, a sea of vaguely familiar faces, who echo reassuring sentiments to Earl. "We'll be checking in on you. If there's anything you need—"

If there's anything you need.

My mom gave me the one thing I truly needed. She blurted it out in the middle of a *Virgin Creek* episode during a scene when Don was tsk-tsking Faith for being a town busybody. Mom turned to me, her eyes suddenly flashing a look of desperation, and said, "Ramona, you know I love you, right? Always have. Always will."

That's what I needed, but there's so much more I want. I want my mom back. God, I want her back, all healthy and fiery and busting balls like usual. I want my regrets washed away and the hole in my heart mended. I want more time—time for just me and my mom.

I gaze out at Earl and Ricky, in their slacks, shirts, and ties and Tina, in her black yoga pants and cropped tee, and the town full of friends and coworkers consoling them, and I press a hand to my heart. They'll be okay here without me.

It's time for me to go home to the hibiscus and painted buntings and Texas bluebonnets that Mom finally saw in her dreams.

Mom's funeral service feels like a dream. A blur of being ushered to the burial site, listening to Reverend Tillerton give Mom a Jesusy send-off, pressing my trembling lips together as Mom's urn of ashes is nestled in the ground, and feeling lost, so utterly lost, when her ashes are blanketed with soil before I can get my head around the finality of it all.

Still, I do not cry. Despite the monumental ache in my chest and inferno burning in my throat. If I start crying now, I'll never stop. Never. Because my heart and soul are an ocean of tears that I somehow manage to push back as Beau Boopster serenades us through portable speakers, as I lay a bouquet of roses at Mom's gravesite, as people offer final condolences before making their way back to their vehicles, as Earl, Ricky, Tina, and I stand in the spot where, a month from now, a carved headstone will sit, engraved with *Carol Sadler, Beloved Wife and Mother*. I do not cry. Even though my heart is crushed to bits and filled with vast love all at once from the pain of my loss and the beauty and courage of my mom in her final days.

Tina holds Ricky's hand and shakes her head. "The music was a good choice. There wasn't a dry eye in the cemetery when Beau belted out 'Love You, Blue Eyes.'"

Ricky blows air through his cheeks. "I didn't think Big Jonny would make it through 'Best Mama Ever Lived.'"

I place a hand on Earl's shoulder and force a grin. "Thank God for 'Dangled My Woogie in the Boogie.'"

He nods. "Comic relief just in the nick of time."

We walk toward Ricky's beater sedan parked alongside the gravel loop of the cemetery. Then Earl turns to face me. "Drive safe. You know, it doesn't hurt to stop and stretch your legs more often than not."

I lift my chin at him. "Aw. You sound all worried about me."

He tries to hide a grin. "Maybe I'm worried about the other people on the road."

I search his tired eyes. "I'll drive safely. Promise. And I'll be back to visit in August, before the school year starts."

He looks at me quizzically for a moment, then his hazel eyes turn warm. "Back here in August? I like the sound of that."

Tina nods at me then takes Earl's arm. "We'd better get you home, Earl. You hardly touched your breakfast. There's mac and cheese and chocolate pudding with your name on it." She starts leading Earl toward the car then pauses, turns, and waves at me. "Safe travels, Ramona. Don't be a stranger."

I slowly blink. For so many years, I felt like a stranger here with my own family. But now, that's somehow all wiped clean.

Ricky faces me, then holds up a plastic baggy. "Got something for you."

I squint at him. The last time Ricky gave me a baggy, I was five years old. I'd found our goldfish bobbing belly up, and dead, in our fishbowl and got all upset when Earl was going to flush him down the toilet. Ricky scooped the goldfish out of the water, put it in a baggy and gave it to me. I secretly kept him in my room for days until Mom said, "What the hell is that smell?"

I study the baggy in Ricky's hand. It contains about a cup or so of ash. I shoot him a suspicious look. "That's not the same bag Bubbles was in. Is it?"

He snorts a laugh and hands me the bag. His voice cracks. "Mom always wanted to visit Texas Hill Country."

I stand frozen for a bit, searching his big blue Mom eyes that are now wet with tears. Then I stretch out my arms and wrap them around his shoulders. "Thank you."

Ricky nods then pats my back. "Aw, now. It was nothin'. Okay, drive safe."

I take a step back and grin. "Will do."

Ricky walks to his car, slides into the driver's seat, revs the engine, and they all wave through open windows, as they head for home.

I peer down at the baggy of ashes clutched in my hand. "Guess it's just you and me, Mom." It's been a month since I arrived in Snap Peas, yet it feels like a lifetime has passed. I gaze off in the distance where my truck and trailer are parked, feeling already exhausted by the thought of the long drive back to Nearly Heaven RV Park until I'm finally home.

I'm walking toward my truck when a car pulls into the cemetery moving slowly along the gravel path. I'm sure it's just another teary-eyed person bringing flowers to a gravesite. As I open my truck door and slide the baggy of ashes onto the console, I hear the car tires come to a halt. I listen to the opening of a door. Then something, or maybe someone, gently nudges me to turn around, and I cock my head at the sight of a man stepping away from the car that's now driving off.

He's tall and broad-shouldered, the type of man my mom would call "a looker." Or maybe even "man candy." His green backpack sways from his shoulder as he strides my way. I gasp in a breath so deep it's as if I've been underwater, on the dark floor of the ocean, trying to find my way to light and fresh air for an eternity, and have just now broken the surface.

Lonnie picks up his pace, breaking into a jog then into a full run. I try desperately to run to him, but my legs are weak, and my knees start to buckle, and I'm moving in slow motion like I'm melting into a puddle of sorrow and loss, surprise and relief. Then Lonnie's there, catching me as I stumble and fall into his arms, feeling washed ashore as I press my head against his warm chest, grounded in his strong, steady heartbeat.

And I cry. Hot tears pouring down my cheeks and rolling down my neck as Lonnie wraps his arms tighter around me, pulling me closer into his embrace, into his living breathing refuge. I double over in despair, choking sobs wracking my body. I'm literally and figuratively falling apart, shattering to pieces, gasping for breath as I cry and cry in Lonnie's arms—warm and sure and strong—as he holds onto me for dear life.

Chapter Twenty-three

One month later

It feels like a lifetime since I've been out for an evening. After arriving home from Snap Peas, I settled into a quiet, somber routine. Early morning jog. Chores around the trailer. Volunteer shift at the hospital. Grocery shopping. Dinner. A glass of wine. Dead tired by eight. Asleep by nine o'clock.

Tonight, Jules and Chase insisted I join them and their boys for Family Cowpoke Fun at The Mangy Mule. The parking lot is packed when I arrive, but I find a vacant spot between the donkey pasture and the decorative wooden outhouse with the sign: *What Happens in the Outhouse Stays in the Outhouse*. I open my truck door to the sound of Boots & Bangles playing "All My Exes and Ohs" then head toward the outdoor patio where men in jeans and cowboy hats two-step with women in ruffled skirts and leather cowgirl boots.

Jules and Chase wave from a table beneath a canopy strung with fairy lights. Chase is wearing a cowboy hat over his red wavy hair, and Jules has unleashed her honey highlights, letting her hair fall past her shoulders in soft waves. I grin at how natural Jules and Chase look together, as comfortable as fleece pajama pants on a lazy Saturday morning.

Jules stands as I approach, her arms opening wide. "Girlfriend, get over here now."

We hug, then Chase sets down his hat and stretches his arms in my direction. "Right here. Right now."

I smile. "Dang, y'all are demanding. You know I just saw you, like, three days ago." I get another big, warm hug and find myself wiping a tear, but unlike the other gazillion tears I've shed over the past month, this is a happy tear that tickles as it dances down my cheek.

Wyatt and Boone step away from their basket of hot wings and pitcher of soda. Boone pulls a chair out for me as Wyatt hands me a card. "Sorry it took so long to write. You can open it later if you want."

I sit, read the envelope—*For Ramona*—then study their soft, freckled faces. "Thank you. That's so sweet."

Boone's cheeks flush then he points across the lawn. "Dad, there's a horseshoe pit that's free."

Chase puts his hat on and looks at Jules. "You won't be too lonely without us guys around, will you?"

Jules grins. "Please, give me some lonely."

Chase tips his hat. "Game on, fellas." Then they barrel off.

Boots & Bangles starts playing, "Save Your Horse, Ride That Cowboy," and I laugh over the song's title and also because I feel…happy. I know it's fleeting. Grief is still a close friend. But tonight, here with Jules, her family, and the best hot wings in Jackalope, I am certifiably happy.

Jules slides the basket of wings, plate of loaded nachos, and a mug of beer my way. Then she takes a seat, and a broad smile sweeps across her face as she watches Chase and the boys race across the lawn.

I wave the envelope. "I'm opening this now." Ripping the flap, I pull out the card that reads, *Sorry for your loss*. Inside there's a photo of stars in a clear, night sky. My throat thickens as I read their words:

Dear Ramona,

We're sorry about your mom. We took this photo the night our mom told us the sad news. There were so many stars that night. They were all so bright.

I bring my hand to my mouth as tears sting my eyes.

Then we remembered something we read when we were in our Eskimo phase.

Chuckling, I look at Jules. "Eskimo phase?"

She grins. "Fourth grade. Somewhere between their land irrigation and Civil War phases."

I keep reading.

There's an Eskimo proverb: Perhaps they are not stars in the sky, but rather openings where our loved ones shine down to let us know they are happy.

Take care and good luck,

Wyatt and Boone

I shake my head at Jules. *Take care and good luck.* I laugh again, only this time tears are running down my face.

Jules pats my hand. "You must have read the 'good luck' part."

I wipe my cheeks with a napkin. "God, they're good kids."

Jules tears up. "They are. And they'd be perfect if it weren't for their vegetable phobia." She holds up a nacho. "Wouldn't even eat these because they have tomatoes on them." She looks out across the lawn toward the horseshoe pit. "I'm glad to see them having fun. They've been having a tough summer."

"Oh, no. You never told me that."

She purses her lips. "I know. Seemed insensitive to bring it up considering what you've gone through."

I sigh. "Give it up. What's happening to my boys?"

"They've been dealing with a bully in science camp. Hawk Astor. Captain of the football team, of course."

"Hawk? Ugh. Hate him already."

She sucks in her cheeks. "The problem is that we're just inside Lime Rock School District. It's a great school. Advanced classes and summer day camps. But we live on a farm, and most of the other kids live in ritzy housing developments where the parents hire people to do everything: mow their lawn, clean their house, hang their Christmas lights." She narrows her eyes. "They even hire people to pick up the dog shit in their yards."

I jerk back. "What?"

Jules throws up her hands. "Pup Poo Patrol. The name's spelled out on the side of their truck. You can hire them for five bucks a poo."

"For five bucks they should bronze it."

Jules slaps the table. "They hire people to pick up their damn dog poo." She shakes her head. "Anyway, so this Hawk Astor—"

"You mean Birdass Astor."

"That's him. He's a big loudmouth. Talks crap about my boys' clothes, their haircuts, what I pack them for lunch."

I huff. "He's jealous. You pack the best lunches."

"You got that right. The other day I made them meatloaf sandwiches." She slumps back in her chair. "Birdass started posting stuff on social media. He calls them Cow and Dung."

I squeeze my hands into fists. "Let me at him. Feathers are gonna fly."

Jules chuckles. "If I don't get to him first." She nods toward the horseshoe pit. "Chase is staying calm so the boys will keep talking to him about it. We've talked to their teachers, and Chase feels confident that they're handling the situation at science camp. But I'm Mama Bear." She bites into a nacho. "I cannot hide the fact that I want to eat this kid's liver."

I take a swig of beer. "Hawk liver for lunch. You can put it in a sandwich." I blink at her and sigh. "Sorry y'all are dealing with this."

She rolls her shoulders, then dips a hot wing in Wasabi ranch. "Yeah, it sucks. But I'm feeling better already after blowing off some steam. Chase is so measured about it all. I just needed to spill my guts to my best friend on the planet. Thank you."

"Anytime."

She studies me and grins. "By the way, you're looking cute. Love the sundress."

"Prisha—you know, my neighbor who owns that ginormous motor home on lot twelve—bought it for her daughter. Prisha said the dress was a bad color on her. Actually, her exact words were, 'My daughter looks like a sick tuna in this shade of peach.' " Jules chuckles, and I point to my ear. "She also gave me these bauble earrings."

"That's nice."

"Yep, they were in a gift bag along with a scented candle called The Heiress's Vagina."

Jules slaps the table again. "Talk about sick tuna."

We laugh and dig into wings and nachos. Then she wriggles her fingers at me. "Okay, time for a Lonnie update. Pleeease tell me he's stopped being a gentleman."

Over the past month, Lonnie's been the best guy friend a girl could ever have. On the road trip back home from Snap Peas, he gave me space to be sad, served me soup and hot tea, real burgers and cold beer. He was a steadfast comforting presence at a time when I was raw with grief. Since our return to Jackalope, he takes me out for coffee or lunch and invites me to his front porch for glasses of lemonade. He tapes cards to my trailer door reminding me to call anytime. He stops by with fresh eggs and wildflowers. I sip my beer. "He's been the perfect gentleman."

Jules frowns. "Ugh. Enough already."

I bite my lip. "But I think he's cracking."

Jules's jaw drops into a big smile. "Tell me now."

I laugh. "Like I said before…you're so demanding."

"I'm the mother of twin boys. I speak in directives."

I sit straight. "Okay, I'll start with Butch and Ming."

Jules throws her head back. "What? No. I want to hear about Lonnie."

I shake my head. "It's related. So, Butch and Ming stopped over and—"

"Stopped over? At your trailer?"

"Yeah, it felt a little strange. They kept looking around saying how *cozy* my trailer is. I mean, they said nice things. Butch liked all the trees in my backyard and the picnic table, and Ming liked my cheerful kitchen towels. But I got that same feeling I'd get as a kid when some lady who lived in a big house on the other side of Snap Peas would tell my mom that she just loved the color of our front porch, and the petunias planted around our mailbox."

Jules knits her brow. "Yeah, I can see that. Why'd they stop by?"

"Actually, it was really sweet. Butch gave me a baseball cap embroidered Ranch Z." Jules cocks her head, and I explain, "Z for Zimmerman, Butch's last name." I throw up my hands. "Shoot, I brought it here to show you, then left it in my truck. Anyway, Lonnie has one just like it, only his is blue and mine is pink." I smile. "Butch said now I'm officially part of the Ranch Z team, which makes me think—"

Jules claps her hands. "That Lonnie told Butch—"

"About our kiss at Squirrels n Nuts." I rub my hands together in front of my chest. "And it gets better."

She leans forward. "You are killing me. Spit it out."

"Lonnie stopped by a few hours ago, wearing a nice button-down shirt, his hair damp from the shower. He looked kind of nervous. You know, in a boy asking a girl out on a date kind of way."

Jules throws a hand in the air. "Yes!"

"That's what I said." I jiggle my leg. "When he asked me out to dinner tomorrow night at Lou's Longhorn."

Jules smiles. "I'm so happy. You deserve to be with a great guy." She empties her beer mug. "Aren't you so glad you finally dumped Smallwood?"

"Oh my God. Martin out of my life. So glad." I shake my head. "Remember how, when I first broke up with him, he kept calling and texting me?"

"Yeah, especially after he realized you were driving to Snap Peas with Lonnie. Totally freaked him out."

"Exactly. So, I just blocked him. I blocked his phone. I blocked his emails. I just blocked him out of my life." I lean forward. "And I haven't missed him one bit. If I knew breaking up with Martin would be this easy, I'd have done it a year ago."

"Sometimes we just need some space to get perspective." She grins. "So, tomorrow night. Finally, a date with Dr. Hot Potato."

I shoot her a sheepish smile. "That's all I've been thinking about. You know, I was so sad for so long in Snap Peas. Then Mom died, and I was even sadder. It was like my body just shut down." I bite my lip. "But these past few days it's like my hormones have gone from zero to infinity. Yesterday, I walked past the hospital cafeteria and saw Lonnie eating a salad. My panties were destroyed."

Jules laughs. "How are you going to make it through three courses at Lou's Longhorn tomorrow night?"

"Already thought that through. Bought a box of panty shields."

"If your panties were destroyed over salad, imagine watching Lonnie eat steak. You might need a box of adult diapers." I laugh then she goes all mama bear on me, wagging a finger. "Condoms. Remember to slip a condom in your bra cup. In the heat of passion, you don't want to have to scramble across the room for your handbag." She winks. "Safety first."

I smile. "Good tip."

"Chase and I were college freshmen when we met. I had condoms in my bra, the pockets of my jeans, underneath my bunk pillow. I even used them as bookmarks. You never know when you're gonna get all horny in the library." She smiles. "Now what are you going to wear for the date?"

"I'm thinking my floral flounce skirt?" I eye her for approval. "I'm tempted to wear my new Ranch Z cap, but I don't want hat hair."

Jules pinches her chin. "Has Lonnie seen your Ranch Z cap yet?"

"Nope. Butch said it's hot off the press."

She tilts her head. "Hmm. I'm sure he'd love to see it."

"Yeah, I'm kind of excited about showing it to him tomorrow. I mean, it really was sweet of Butch, and it's cute that mine is pink and Lonnie's is blue."

Jules chews a fingernail. "Ramona, go show it to him." Her eyes shine. "You say that cap is in your truck?"

I nod.

"Drive your truck over to Lonnie's and show him that cap *now*."

Chapter Twenty-four

I turn onto Salt Lick Trail and pass the entrance of
Nearly Heaven headed toward Lonnie's driveway. My
spine tingles. I glance over at my Ranch Z cap on the
passenger seat, feeling my palms moisten against the
steering wheel. I'm practically quaking with hormonal
adrenaline, and for all I know, Lonnie's not even home.

I pull into his long driveway, then lick my lip at the
sight of his pickup parked in the shade. Taking a deep
breath, I park, then step from my truck. I've been here
plenty of times, helping Lonnie feed his sheep and
collect eggs from his flock of chickens. We've sat on his
front porch drinking lemonade and shooting the breeze.
It's a beautiful property with lots of shade trees and a
spacious, covered outdoor dining area with a stone firepit
and grill. I haven't been inside his house because Mr.
Gentleman Complex has been keeping me in the friend
zone. But it looks big for a tiny house and has
contemporary cedar siding and a huge wooden deck that
leads to the front door.

I'm about to grab my cap and head for the house,
when I hear "Ramona?"

I turn toward the sound of Lonnie's voice. There he
is. God help me.

On the drive over, I gave my hormones a good
talking to, reminding them that tonight is not date night.
I'm simply stopping by to show Lonnie the cute cap his

father gave me. And now I see him standing in a spray of soft sunlight in front of his big red barn wearing jeans without a shirt, his muscular shoulders glistening, and his body looking so man-gorgeous that I swear I smell his salty goodness from here. I wipe the corner of my mouth with the back of my hand.

He walks toward me, his abs rolling like hard waves to the muscular V where his jeans hang on his hips. So not fair.

As he nears, then turns toward me, I open my mouth and manage, "Hi."

His full lips turn into a grin. "You look—" His eyes take in the length of my body. "Uh, nice dress."

He faces me, then takes a step forward, his body mere inches from mine, and I'm flooded with warmth from the heat from his core. "Nice—" I run my eyes from his neck to his chest to his beltline then to the perfect bulge in his jeans and swallow hard. "Uh, skin."

We pause for a moment, his eyes asking permission.

My eyes screaming, "Permission granted!" I inch forward, and my lips part, and a shaky breath escapes, as he brushes his thumb against my jaw, slides his hand along my waist then presses it against my lower back. He kisses me tenderly, and I close my eyes, savoring the soft saltiness of his moist lips. I want to linger there, in his gentle kiss, for a long time. But my hormones are not listening. I need more. I tangle one hand in his hair and rake the other down his bare back, pressing my body against him until he kisses me hungrily, greedily. When I hear a soft growl rise in his throat, I become undone in a way that I never imagined possible. All from a kiss. From his lips on mine, from his warm tongue exploring my mouth in a primal rhythm that draws us closer together, deeper into one another. How does he do this to me? Our sexual tension sounds in my ear like a pounding drum beating the reminder that time is wasting, time is running out. I can't waste one more minute. I need him now.

I grasp his wrist, tugging him toward the porch. He rumbles a laugh as we take the steps in leaps and bounds. Pushing open the door, Lonnie sweeps me into his living room, and I spin my back against the cool wall and pull his hot body against mine. It's all so deliciously too much: the feel of his bare chest as I skate my hands over him, the salty, musky smell of his skin as I press my open mouth to him, the sensation of his hardness against my belly driving me crazy. It's a sensory explosion, and when he picks me up, cradling my ass in his strong arms, I hear myself cry out, "Oh, God. Lonnie." The skirt of my sundress is bunched at my waist, and I hear Lonnie's throaty groan when I wrap my legs tight around him. Grabbing his shoulders, I rock into him, needing to feel impossibly closer, surprising myself when I cry out again, "God, Lonnie, please." I'm never verbal during sex, like never. With other men, I've hardly made a sound, let alone formed words. But with Lonnie? With Lonnie, when his warm mouth is against my throat, and he cups my ass with both hands and pushes the hard length of himself against me, I cry out yet again. "Lonnie, more. Oh, God, please, more."

With each palpable beat of Lonnie's pounding chest, I need him closer. I need him inside me. I reach between his legs, run my finger along his fly, and pull down the zipper, feeling his entire body shudder from my touch. Sliding the condom from the cup of my bra, I pull my wrecked panties to the side. I want to be ravished right here against this wall, right now, with every hot, hard inch of him.

But Lonnie has another idea. With his arms tight around me, he carries me to the sofa and cruelly takes his time with me. Pulling the straps of my sundress off my shoulders, cupping my breasts in his hands, teasing my nipples with his tongue before devouring them in his mouth. I'm transported then, into full-blown delirium. And when he moves his mouth lower, grazing his tongue from my cleavage to my sternum, to my belly, then lower still, I let go of all inhibitions. I completely indulge my lust and fully surrender myself to Lonnie's touch, my mind and body unrestrained. And when he finally enters me, slowly, deeply, my hips move on impulse, writhing beneath him with abandon. My voice calls out, pleading, begging, demanding with a reckless kind of freedom. I'm lost in his touch, his taste, his smell, his voice, the steadfast rhythm of his body moving inside of mine until I'm flooded in a euphoria so big and bright and otherworldly that it seems to have no beginning or end.

When we're sated, our bodies melt together as we lay on sofa cushions. Slowly awakening from my daze of desire, I blink open my eyes and stare up at the wooden beams on the cathedral ceiling, my mind spinning back to the heat of our passion.

I remember my body growing feverish as his hands and mouth explored every curve of me. My breath quickening and mouthwatering as I touched and tasted every contour of him. I remember his pulse racing, muscles tightening, body thrusting, and his moans and groans of passion and pleasure. I remember my hips rocking, pleasure centers throbbing, and my heated groans, delirious moans as he satisfied me completely.

Again. And again. I bite a fingernail. And I remember that I talked. A lot.

Lonnie rolls on his side and drapes his arm across my belly. And it all comes rushing back. I cringe. Wow. I was verbal. I rub my forehead. And I think I had some kind of food/cooking theme going on. I bite my lip. Damn those hot wings and nachos at The Mangy Mule. I feel my neck flush. I think I remember saying, "Eggplant." Oh, God. And something about his special sauce in my messy taco. Panic shoots through me. I've never even told a man I was coming before. But tonight, with Lonnie, a man with a self-professed gentleman complex, I turned into a sex crazed, insatiable Jackalope.

I pat Lonnie's arm and bolt upright. "This, ugh, was…great." Swinging my legs off the sofa, I stand and frantically collect my bra and crumpled sundress.

Lonnie sits up. "Ramona?"

Stepping into my dress, I shoot him an awkward smile. "Really, it was just so…great."

His brow furrows. "Yes, it was." He reaches for his jeans. "Listen. What do you say, I whip up a few omelets? We can hang out here, maybe watch a movie together—"

I clutch my bra and panties to my chest then slip my feet into my sandals. "Thank you. That's so sweet, but—"

Pulling on his jeans, Lonnie stammers, "Ramona, are you okay?"

I sound way too enthusiastic. "Yes! You were great, like, beyond great." I swing open the door. "Just…gotta run."

Chapter Twenty-five

As soon as I got home, I texted Jules. *—Went to Lonnie's house. He had no shirt. Left cap in truck. Sundress off. Panties obliterated.—*

—OMG! That's great!—

My face warms. *—That's what I said, like way too many times.—*

—Wait. You're texting? Is he in the shower?—

—I'm home.—

—Home?????—

Jules called. I rambled. And now, twenty minutes later, Jules steps through the glass doors of Road Runner Café and I wave her over to my booth.

Sliding in across from me, she gives a warmhearted grin. "Don't get me wrong, Girlfriend. I'm happy to see you for the second time in one evening, but—" She puts her hand on mine. "Why are you at a diner with *me* when you could be eating omelets in bed with *him*?"

I chew my knuckle. "Because that wasn't *me* at his place." I lean forward and loud-whisper, "I'm quiet in bed. Or at least I *was* quiet. And when I came down to Earth from Planet Sex Stupor and realized just how not quiet I was with Lonnie, I panicked."

A waitress places tall ice waters in front of us then smiles. I slide Jules the laminated menu with dancing road runners. "Ladies? What can I get for ya?" She eyes us. "Insider tip: lean toward the Ranch Hand's Rump

Roast and run like hell from the Cheesy Chicken Steak."

"Rump roast it is." I glance at Jules who nods. "Make that two."

Jules takes a drink of water then squints at me. "From what you said on the phone—" She gives a quick look around to see if anyone's within earshot. "It sounds like you were just a horny woman being body positive."

I shake my head. "My body was not the problem. It was my mouth." I drag a hand over my face. "Oh my God. The things I said. Loudly. So loudly." I widen my eyes. "Before tonight, the dirtiest thing I ever said to a man in bed was when I referred to Martin's penis as Dr. P. And I was wearing flannel pajamas at the time."

She shrugs. "Progress. It was you finally letting go a little."

The waitress returns and slides steaming plates onto the table. She winks. "Careful, ladies. This rump is hot."

Jules snickers, and I rub my forehead.

Before heading off, the waitress adds, "Just give a holler if there's anything else I can getcha."

Spooning mashed potatoes into my mouth, I stare down at my plate. "Surprised I didn't say 'rump roast' in the throes of passion. It was so weird. I had this food thing going on. I blame it on the hot wings and nachos at The Mangy Mule."

"Maybe after two years of snack bites with Martin, you were just fucking hungry. Sounds like Lonnie was just the man to finally offer you a proper man-meal and fill you up."

I carve off a piece of meat. "I told him to shove his flaming sausage into my Hottie Pot."

Jules laughs so hard, she sprays mashed potatoes into her napkin. "Harmless. There's nothing wrong with a little dirty talk."

I can't help but chuckle. "But did I have to talk dirty vegetable? I'll never be able to look at an eggplant or cucumber again without being triggered."

She wags a finger. "No need to be embarrassed. You have a new skill. You speak Cooter. Fluently, I might add."

I laugh, then my shoulders slump. "It's just that, I was finally starting to feel like myself again. You know, after my mom passed away."

Jules's gaze turns sad. "I know, Sweetie."

"Then tonight, after all these years of being so…vanilla in the bedroom—"

She jerks her head. "Well, I'm not sure I'd say you're vanilla. I mean, you could open a museum with your collection of vibrators."

I shrug. "I'm not inhibited with *myself*. But with *men*, I never really found my groove."

"Maybe before Lonnie, you dated men who didn't have a groove."

I bite my lip, heat rising in my chest. "Lonnie has so much groove. So. Much. Groove."

Jules grins. "That's how it's supposed to be."

I nod. "You know, even before Lonnie and I had sex, it felt like we were already intimate. We could talk about anything together—our weird families, past relationships, our jobs, our struggles, the things that make us happy—and it was so comfortable. So…safe." I throw up a hand. "I know I shouldn't bring up the M word, but you'd think I could've talked with Martin, the *psychologist*, about those things. But whenever I tried, instead of just listening, there'd be all this pressure to categorize or label or process every feeling." I take a sip of water. "It's different with Lonnie. We just talk and listen and share. We feel our feelings. And it's nice."

She smiles warmly. "Have you told Lonnie all this?"

I cough. "No. Didn't have time. Tonight, I was too busy telling him to pound my juicy kumquat."

She doubles over laughing. "You do know that for Christmas, I'm giving you pajama pants that read, *Pound My Juicy Kumquat*."

I laugh, then search her eyes. "I mean, who am I?"

She sits straight. "Who are you? You're Ramona, an amazing woman on a journey of sexual self-discovery."

I jut out my bottom lip. "Okay. I like that."

She flashes a mischievous grin. "And you're a woman one step away from buying booty plugs."

I burst out laughing, feeling a surge of gratitude for my best friend who always makes difficult times feel easier.

"Ramona, give yourself a break. This is a good development. You're learning to let go instead of bottling things up."

"Yeah, I guess you're right. I do have a long history of keeping things bottled up inside."

She nods. "Like tears. I'm glad Lonnie burst that dam."

"Yep, ever since he showed up at the cemetery, I've been crying my eyes out."

"It's a good thing. You feel safe with him."

"Yeah, I do. But now the question is: After tonight, does Lonnie feel safe with me?"

She grins. "Might want to hide the booty plugs for a while." Jules wriggles her eyebrows. "No worries. I'm sure Lonnie loved it."

"He did seem to, you know, enjoy things." I sigh.

"Then afterward, I couldn't get out of there fast enough."
I rub my temple. "Ugh. I've messed things up with him
already."

She gives me her, *oh, please*, look. "Ramona,
Lonnie's a man who had incredible sex with an
incredible woman. *And* wanted her to stay and eat
omelets at his place. Believe me, he'll offer again."

Chapter Twenty-six

I wake up early the next morning, sit on my patio sipping hot coffee, and take in the stillness of Nearly Heaven RV Park. In an hour, neighbors will stir, emerging from their motor homes and gooseneck trailers to water their potted plants and walk their dogs before heading off to work or out for a pancake breakfast at The Yello Armadillo. But right now, it's deeply peaceful as the sun gently rises, creating a cotton candy sky filled with wispy blues and pinks. I close my eyes listening to the rustling of cedar leaves in the breeze, the sound of juncos and cardinals bursting into song, and, from a distance, the crooning call of Lonnie's rooster, Mr. Roo.

I shake my head at the realization that life goes on. I lost my job, my home, and most sadly, my mom, but I wake up to birds singing and Mr. Roo crowing at the rising sun. A fat tear rolls down my cheek, and I don't bother to wipe it away. There will be a tear after this one and more after that. Far too many to try to clean up after. Grief will not be tidied.

My heart sinks at the thought that I may have lost Lonnie, too. Or, at the very least, made a mess of things. He called last night, but my phone was on silent. By the time I saw his missed call, it was nearly midnight, and I didn't want to wake him. Besides, what would I say? I showed up at his place unannounced with a condom in my bra, channeled my inner porn star, then ran out of his house with zero explanation. I rub my forehead. Jules told me I deserved to be with a great guy. But she was wrong. Maybe someday I'll deserve that, but right now, I'm a mess. And Lonnie's a gentleman. He probably called to suggest we go back to the friend zone.

I drink the last of my coffee and set the mug beneath my chair, listening to a squirrel chatter from a nearby tree branch. The sun has fully risen, and Mr. Roo is cock-a-doo-a-doodling like crazy. Then I hear shoes crunching on gravel.

I turn my head, blink, and draw in a slow breath at the sight of Lonnie walking toward me. He's carrying wildflowers in one hand and a basket in the other. I stand then take a step toward him as he hands me the bouquet of beebalm and pink ladies.

He tilts his head and gives me a quizzical look. "Is this okay? You know, me showing up here." He lifts the basket. "With wicker."

I smile, tears suddenly stinging my eyes. "Very okay." Pulling the bouquet to my chest, I search his eyes. "I mean, how could it not be okay? You brought flowers and a man basket."

He chuckles, then turns the chairs so they're facing each other, takes a seat, and sets the basket on patio brick.

I sit across from him, our bare knees touching, and gingerly set down the bouquet.

Pointing to the basket, he says, "Fresh eggs from the flock." He bites his lip. "My table's set. I have sliced homemade bread for the toaster and orange juice in the fridge." He reaches over and clasps my hands. "Thought I'd offer again. Can I feed you omelets?"

I choke out a sigh of relief. "Yes, please. And

homemade bread." I feel a tear trickle down my cheek. "And vegan bacon if you have it."

Lonnie smiles then brushes my damp face with his fingers. "But I think first, we should talk? When you left so quickly last night, I was worried… Did I do something to upset you?"

I slump back in my chair. "No, it wasn't you. It was me. Actually, I don't know who that was last night. You must think—"

He knits his brow. "I must think what?"

I palm my forehead. "That I'm a cross between a port sailor and Diana Does Denver."

He buries a chuckle. "Ramona—"

I hold up a hand. "I don't have any issues whatsoever with people saying things like that. It's just that *I* don't say things like that. At least I never did before and—"

"What you said was fine. More than fine because I was with *you*." His lips curl into an impish grin. "I mean, when you said you wanted me to stir your Hottie Pot with my big wooden spoon, I thought, well that's…creative, but—"

I burst out laughing, covering my face with both hands. "Oh, God."

Lonnie gazes into my eyes. "The thing is, I'm crazy about your creativity." He cups my face and gently kisses my lips. "And even crazier about your Hottie Pot."

I run my thumb along the stubble on his cheek. "I'm a huge fan of your big wooden spoon."

Lonnie stands and pulls me up to him. "Then what do you say we spoon up some omelets?" Before I can answer, he wraps his arms around me. "But first this." He pulls me into a hug so warm and strong and close that, as I bury my head against his chest, I feel each beat of his heart. He kisses the top of my head. "Now, *this* is nearly heaven."

Chapter Twenty-seven

"Wow. It really is big." I sit at Lonnie's kitchen table, taking in his open concept dining/living area with beamed cathedral ceilings. "For a tiny house, this is super roomy."

He nods. "At nine-hundred-sixty-five square feet, it just squeaks into the category."

I nibble on buttered toast. "By the way, the flowers, the man basket, your table set with a centerpiece and candles—" I grin at him. "Pure romantic mastery."

He chuckles. "Glad you like it."

Last night, blinded by my hormonal daze, I hardly noticed his house. This morning, I've had a chance to take in his modern, sunlit home with custom windows, large loft, gorgeous hardwood floors, and marbled quartz kitchen island. His furniture is amazing: upholstered accent chairs, contemporary end tables, and the luxury leather sofa that Lonnie and I put a dent in last night. I take a bite of omelet, suddenly feeling the muscles in my neck tighten. Did Lonnie pick out this furniture? Or was it Lonnie and Shi-Yun? How many times did Lonnie and Shi-Yun dent the sofa?

I set my fork on the plate. "Your house is beautiful."

He grins. "Thanks. And I like your trailer."

I huff. "You don't have to say that."

He furrows his brow. "I'm saying it because I mean it. It has an efficient layout, comfortable table bed, and you've got the best oversized lot in Hill Country."

I shrug. "I did luck out with the lot."

"And it's cute. Like you."

I smile. "Thanks, but let's face it. I'm living in that trailer because I got fired from Sawyer Pickens and couldn't afford my town house anymore."

Lonnie takes a drink of orange juice. "Do you miss teaching at the university?"

I'm about to say, *of course*, when I pause and gaze at the ceiling. "I mean, I'd give anything to have my job back. I'd much rather be called Professor Sadler by college students in a lecture hall than Miss Mona by fourth graders in the middle school gymnasium. But do I miss it? You know, I really don't." I squint at Lonnie. "I was so excited when I was hired. I loved student teaching when I was in graduate school in Idaho. The students there worked hard, and they appreciated me spending time after class explaining an assignment or how to structure their research paper. I felt like I was making a difference. But at Sawyer Pickens, the students act entitled. I gave Madison Turnfellow a C- on his Against Moral Rationalism paper because he, uh, *earned* a C-. His father showed up in my office threatening to have me fired if I didn't change his grade immediately."

Lonnie groans. "But you still want your job back?"

"I want my life back. Being a professor. Living in a nice place downtown. I started applying for university positions, but then I went to Snap Peas and…" My voice trails off.

He sighs. "It's okay to take some time. Losing someone you love can turn everything on its head. At least it did for me. My mom died a year ago, and I'm still trying to figure out what I really want to do with my life."

His eyes flash a smile. "I mean, besides being the Patient Panda scheduler, of course. Livin' the dream."

I chuckle. "I'll be livin' the dream later today. I'm headed to Ward Four to check in on Mrs. Sonali. The poor thing fell and broke her hip two weeks after her husband broke *his* hip."

His eyes go soft. "You mentioned that in Idaho you felt like you made a difference with your students. I hope you know that you make a big difference with your patients on Ward Four. Dad tells me all the time how helpful you were to him." He wags a finger at me. "In fact, last week he mentioned that when he was in the hospital, you put his compression hose on."

I hold up my hands. "Okay, I know it was out of my scope of practice, but Butch was getting all antsy waiting for the nurse, and I was out of chocolate to shut him up."

He laughs. "I don't know which is worse, dealing with my father, or dealing with compression hose. Those things are a royal pain to put on."

"I use a little trick I saw on a medical training video. You wrap a plastic bag around the leg, put the compression hose on over it and pull the bag through. Worked like a charm." I smile. "Hey, speaking of Butch. He gave me a pink Ranch Z cap. It was the reason I came over last night. I wanted to show it to you."

His eyes shine mischievously. "Funny, you showed me all sorts of things last night...but I don't remember seeing that cap."

"Somehow never got around to it." I study Lonnie sitting across from me at this beautifully set table. He looks relaxed, like he's in his element, having just served me an incredible breakfast complete with homemade bread and preserves. I feel my chest expand with gratitude. "Hey, I know we'd planned to go to Lou's Longhorn tonight, but you just cooked me omelets. How about if you come to my place for dinner tonight? I make a pretty good pappardelle with wild boar ragù."

He sets his napkin on the table then comes around and stands behind me. I lift my head to look at him, and he glides his fingertips along my throat, making my spine go all tingly again. "Wild boar? I'm in." He pulls my chair away from the table then steps in front of me and bends to kiss me so tenderly that, for a second or a minute or maybe even a light year, time stands still. Then he kneels, runs his hand along my bare thigh, and in an instant, an ache of longing throbs between my legs. *There goes another pair of panties.* He arches an eyebrow. "What time did you say you need to be on Ward Four?"

Placing both of his hands firmly against the insides of my thighs, he pushes them apart then skates his thumb beneath the inseam of my shorts. I shudder at the sensation of his hands on my skin, strong and sure, slightly and perfectly calloused, as he caresses me higher, then higher. Swallowing hard, I manage to murmur, "Not for a few hours."

He drags the fingers of one hand over my lips, and I take them in my mouth, swirling my tongue then sucking, as he unbuttons my waistband with his other hand. "Good. Because I have plans for you, Professor Sadler." He slowly unzips my shorts. "And it begins with an oral examination."

Chapter Twenty-eight

The nurse's station on Ward Four is buzzing. James leans back in his seat and shakes his head at Meg. "Uh-uh. I've been on poopy duty all morning. When Room Sixteen lights up again, it's your turn."

Meg purses her lips. "Listen, mister. I have a toddler and five-month-old at home. I'm *never* off poopy duty."

James glances over at Luciana who's staring intently at her computer. "Maybe Lulu will—"

Luciana jerks her head. "Oh, no you don't." She lowers her voice. "This morning, I gave three bed baths. I don't have it in me to wipe one more hairy ass before noon."

James looks over at me. "Ramona, you settle this. But before you answer, you might want to remember all those times I paid for your Texas Hurricanes at Suds and Spurs." He winks at the other nurses. "Talk about a hollow leg." The call light for Room Sixteen blinks. James picks up the phone receiver. "Yes, Mr. Nardovino. How can I help you?"

Mr. Nardovino, hard of hearing, barks his answer, "Should have stayed clear of the Tex Mex Breakfast Tostada this morning. Guess my bowels didn't like the spice. Got a big mess in here for ya."

James pinches his forehead then stares down Meg. "Let's make a deal. You take this, and I'll bathe the new patient in Room Five."

Meg widens her eyes and whispers loudly, "The one who smells like sauerkraut, menthol cream, and wilted rose petals?"

James nods. "That's the one."

Meg stands and pulls on a mask. "Okay, Mr. Nardovino. I'm coming in."

Luciana flashes me a smile, and my heart melts as I remember the sweet emails she sent when I was in Snap Peas telling me that all the nurses on Ward Four were thinking about me. She smooths a hand over her shiny black hair twisted into a fat braid, then squints her huge brown eyes my way. "You look great."

James stands, eyeing me up and down. "More than great." His jaw drops into a smile. "Wait. I know that glow."

My face grows hot. "What?"

He leans toward me and says in a sing-songy voice, "You and Lonnie did the nasty." I shush him, trying not to giggle, but he goes on, "You finally unleashed that dog and buried that bone."

I burst a laugh. "Did not."

"Did so. And I want every sordid detail. Me and Miguel have been together ten years. We haven't tried a new position since *Gone with the Wind* was playing in theatres."

A shiver runs through my body just thinking about this morning. What Lonnie did to me with his mouth as I sat on his kitchen chair. Then what we did to each other on his king-size bed in the loft. And I did not talk about food once. No mention of eggplant or juicy kumquats. The only words that escaped my lips were, "Yes! Oh, God, yes!"

James wriggles his eyebrows. "You look happy. Do

I get a full account of date night at Suds and Spurs later?"

"Sorry. Rain check? Lonnie's coming to my place tonight for dinner."

"Ooh, what are we serving?"

"Wild boar."

He throws up his hands. "Of course you are. While I sit home with Miguel eating pretzels and putting together our thousand-piece jigsaw puzzle of the Grand Tetons, you'll be eating wild boar with Lonnie, a wild boar."

I smile. "Jeez, when you put it that way, it sounds so unfair."

The call light for Room Five blinks, and James flips his braids behind his back. "We have a new patient. Sixty-two-year-old woman admitted yesterday after getting run over by a bread truck."

I wince. "Seriously? That really happens?"

James nods. "Yep. She was walking to her car in the grocer's parking lot, and Dough Boy Bunworks rammed it in reverse without checking his mirrors. Broken hip. Surgery went well."

"Yikes.

He sighs. "Yesterday she pushed her call button three times in twenty minutes."

"For—?"

James holds up a finger for each call. "One: Butterscotch pudding. Two: Crackers. Three: Pillow fluff."

I roll my eyes. "Ugh."

"Right? Annoying. But I think she's lonely. She lives out of town. Houston, I think." A call light flashes for another patient, and James shakes his head. "When it rains, it hails."

"No worries. I'll take Room Five. I can handle pudding and pillow fluffs."

James says in a low voice, "Warning: The doctor ordered her pain meds on tap. She's loopy as a goose."

I chuckle. "On my way."

He flutters his fingers in a wave. "Thanks. Give Malvina my best."

Chapter Twenty-nine

Malvina. From Houston. Who smells like sauerkraut. I pause outside her room, suck in a deep breath, then give a courtesy knock on the doorframe. "Mrs. Smallwood?" I step inside. "You rang?"

Malvina sits straight in her bed and blinks at me. "Aren't you—?"

I give a cheerful wave. "Ramona. I know. Awkward, right?" It is awkward. I mean, what are the chances of Martin's mother getting rear-ended by Dough Boy Bunworks and sent here to Cassidy Memorial? The last time I saw Malvina—and Martin, for that matter—was over two months ago on the day I stormed into Martin's house to grab my stuff and break up with him. That day Malvina looked stylish in her linen tunic with coiffed hair and makeup. Today, in her pale blue hospital gown with bedhead and no makeup, she looks sad. I smile warmly. "I'm sorry to hear about your accident, Mrs. Smallwood. Is there anything I can help you with? I could score you some extra crackers and pudding."

She holds up her med pump and pushes the button. "Who needs pudding when you can have Happy Milk?" She lifts her chin, and her eyes shine. "Please, call me Malvina." She gestures to the chair beside her bed, and I take a seat. "You know, Ramona, the last time I saw you, you were grabbing dirty underwear out of Martin's hamper."

I wince. "Yeah, like I said, awkward."

She smiles, looking loopy on Happy Milk. "What was that thing you called him?"

I bite my lip. "Asswipe?"

She shakes her head. "No. As you were storming out the door."

I bring a hand to my chin. "Gasbag?"

"Hmm. I don't think so."

I hold up a finger. "Oh, yeah. Pencil-dick!"

She bursts a laugh. "Bingo." Grinning, she rolls her head from side to side. "I'm afraid Martin's a lot like his father."

I bury a chuckle. "I never met Mr. Smallwood."

She pushes her med pump again. "You didn't miss much. I divorced the ding-a-ling in 2010. He was a good-looking man, I'll give him that. But he was arrogant, self-centered, always flaunting his Ivy League degree." She squints at me. "And talk about pencil-dick!"

I cough. "Malvina, are you sure there's nothing I can get you—?"

She holds up a finger. "Not to mention a one-trick pony in bed."

Wow, Martin and his father really do have a lot in common.

She shoots me a mischievous smile. "Luckily, I had the bunny."

I knit my brow. "The bunny?"

She chuckles. "Premium vibrating rabbit."

"Oh, the V-Rabbit." I giggle. "It's a good little bunny."

"Sure is. Wouldn't have survived my marriage without that buck-toothed rodent." I bring a hand to my mouth as she continues, "That, and my candle that smells like a meatpacker's junk."

I laugh. "How do you know that's what that smells like?"

"Because that's its name: The Meatpacker's Junk."

"Sounds like an interesting candle."

She nods. "I'll get you one for Christmas. It smells like man-sweat and wiener schnitzel."

I laugh harder. "Who needs the smell of Christmas cookies and hot cocoa when you can light up a whiff of wiener schnitzel?"

She beams. "To make the holiday extra special, I'll throw in the V-bunny, too."

I study loopy Malvina and smile. Too bad Martin didn't get her sense of humor or her less-than-uptight attitude toward sexuality. I lean toward her. "Actually, thank you, but I don't need the V-Rabbit anymore."

Malvina raises an eyebrow. "You've met a two-trick pony?"

I wink. "More like a ten-trick fucking unicorn." I cover my mouth. "Sorry—"

Malvina howls a laugh. "Good for you. And good for that unicorn."

I bite my lip. "He's a very good unicorn."

We laugh together for a moment, then she looks at me with warm eyes and says, "I'm happy for you. I love my Martin, but quite frankly, he doesn't deserve you." I feel my jaw drop, and she goes on, "You know, my parents emigrated from Hungary when I was four years old, and I grew up in a housing project in Boston."

I jerk back. "Really? Martin never told me that."

"Oh, yes. My family just scraped by, but they taught me about hard work and the importance of education. I was valedictorian in high school, then earned straight

A's in college and graduate school." She locks her gaze on mine. "I'm guessing you and I might have a thing or two in common?"

I nod. "Yep, switch out the housing project for a trailer park, and we're practically the same person."

She nods. "I eventually married Martin's father who came from a very wealthy family." She flicks her wrist. "I married him for love, not money. At the time, I really was in love with him. I was a literature major in college, and he and I shared a passion for books and film. We'd sit in coffee shops and talk for hours." She stares off at the ceiling then squeezes her med pump. "Eventually, I had Martin and a teaching career. I thought I should be happy. I had a full life with a successful man who said he loved me, but in my heart, I knew he didn't see me as equal, with us being from such different backgrounds and all. And I never felt…good enough."

I sigh. "I can relate to that."

"That day when you came to Martin's house, and I heard what he'd said to the university committee—that you're not in their league—my heart broke for you." She looks intensely into my eyes. "You are good enough on your own, Ramona. Never spend time with a man who doesn't value you."

I swallow, slowly nodding.

Then she says, "Those are all the words of wisdom I have for today." She wriggles her eyebrows my way. "That, and light the meatpacker's candle. You won't regret it."

****

I'm walking toward the nurse's station to sign out, still smiling over my encounter with Malvina on Happy Milk, when I hear Martin's voice. "Ramona!" Then he's

211

there beside me, holding a bouquet of Get Well Soon balloons. "I've been trying to talk to you. I've texted, called, emailed."

I roll my eyes. "Guess you should have figured out that I blocked your texts, your calls, and your emails." I draw in a deep breath. "I'm sorry about your mom's accident."

He holds up the bouquet. "I'm on my way to see her now. And I'm sorry about your mom's—"

I feel myself stumble back a bit, my heart all at once heavy with sorrow. "Death," I say.

He looks suddenly uncomfortable. "Yes, I was sorry to hear about that." He sighs, his eyes pleading. "Truth be told, I'm sorry for everything. For missing your birthday. For not fighting for you at the dean's meeting."

I study Martin in slacks and a long-sleeved shirt buttoned all the way up, even though it's summer in Texas. I squint at his perfectly coiffed hair and manicured, uncalloused hands holding that stupid balloon bouquet and swallow back the vile taste in my mouth. He didn't *miss* my birthday party. He no-showed. He didn't *not fight* for me. He hammered the nail into my career coffin. I wave him off. "You know, Martin. That's all behind us. I've moved on."

He cups my wrist. "I haven't moved on. I miss you."

I snap my arm away. "Not doing this. We're over."

Martin throws up his hand. "Even after I explained everything in those cards I sent you?"

I shoot him a blank look. "What cards?"

He jerks back. "Don't you ever check your mail?"

"Of course. Yesterday I got my water bill, two fliers from Ranchos Pizza, and a letter from Ricky and Earl. God, Earl's spelling is atrocious."

Martin shakes his head. "Your *hospital* mail. I sent them here."

"I have a mailbox here?" I shrug. "Huh. Who knew?"

He sighs. "I did."

I narrow my eyes. "Why didn't you send them to the RV park?"

He pffts. "The hospital mailroom is, you know, safer."

"Yeah. That's right. As we speak, Prisha and Ugly Jim are picking mailbox locks and stealing fliers from Panhandle Realtors."

He nods. "Which is why I sent everything to your hospital mailbox."

I shoot him an exasperated look. "Listen, Martin, I'm out of here. I've got to get ready for my hot date with a sheep farmer who lives in a tiny house."

He looks at me like I've lost my marbles. "But I'm a renowned psychologist who lives in a three-story colonial with a library."

I snort a laugh and head down the hall, hearing Martin call out, "Ramona, check your mail! I explained everything.

Chapter Thirty

I *was* excited—like naked happy dancing in my kitchen excited—about my hot date tonight with Lonnie. But *now* I'm panicked—like sweaty upper lip, palpitating heart, practically hyperventilating kind of panicked.

It's five forty-five p.m. Lonnie's coming over at seven for my signature fancy date night dinner: pappardelle with wild boar ragù and roasted butternut squash. It's my Uh-uh-Ramona-did-not-grow-up-in-a-trailer-park dinner that I learned in culinary class and have made successfully many, many times.

Before tonight, that is. Because tonight, there's no way in hell I can pull this off.

I thought I had it all figured out. I knew that cooking an elaborate meal in my tiny kitchen would be a challenge. So, I set up a folding table on my patio to use as extra space for gutting and chopping the butternut squash, and dicing the onion, carrots, and celery that go into the ragù. I cleaned the outdoor grill to use as an extra heat source to sauté the vegetables for the stock and boil water for the pappardelle. And, for our romantic dinner, I prettied up the picnic table with a linen cloth and ceramic plates, white candle sticks and a juniper centerpiece.

Then it started raining. The kind of good, ole Texas downpour that comes in torrents.

I tried to make do with my square foot of counter space, two working stovetop burners, and my crap oven that won't heat higher than 325°F. Somehow, I thought I still might have a shot at making it all work.

Until I realized that the wild boar had gone bad.

I had two pounds of marinated boar meat in my freezer, along with a jumbo bag of tater tots. About a week ago, the electric in my trailer went wonky, turning off for a while, then back on. I didn't think much of it. I called Ugly Jim who came by the next day to fix the electrical connection, but my brain never made the logical connection that the food in my freezer repeatedly thawed and refroze. Now I have a bag of fuzzy taters and a wild boar that smells as gamey as Malvina's meatpacker's candle.

I slump onto my dinette bench, shaking my head and smoothing the apron my mom gave me—the one that says, *This Bitch Can Cook*—feeling like a total failure. Lonnie's going to show up tonight to a heap of uncooked squash and boar gone bad. The worst part is, I should have known something like this would happen.

Ever since my mom died, I've had brain fog. I forget to put gas in my truck until the red warning light comes on. I misplace my sunglasses and sunblock and forget where I put my phone. The other day, the library called to tell me my books were two weeks overdue, and I couldn't even remember going to the library. Instead of trying to impress Lonnie with my fancy date night dinner, I should have just taken him up on his Lou's Longhorn offer.

I startle at a knock on the door and open it to see Lonnie in jeans and white button-down shirt with sleeves rolled to his elbows. Smoothing a hand through his slightly damp waves, he holds out a bottle of wine. "Thought I'd run over between downpours to see if you need any help cooking."

I look around my kitchen, at the cutting board piled with vegetable shards, the sink filled with dirty dishes, the plate of cubed squash on the countertop, and burst into tears. "Dinner's a shit show!"

In a flash, Lonnie sets the wine bottle aside and wraps his strong arms around me in his perfect man-tender way. I bury my face in his chest. "My oven won't heat up enough to cook the squash."

He strokes my hair. "Who needs squash? It's so overrated."

I wrap my arms snug around his waist. "One of my stovetop burners isn't working. I planned to use the outdoor grill, but—"

He kisses the top of my head. "The weather's not cooperating."

"No, it's not." I look up at him, my chin trembling. "And my wild boar smells like The Meatpacker's Junk."

His head jerks back the slightest bit. "You kind of lost me on that one, but…it's okay." He cradles my face in his hands and looks intensely into my eyes. "It'll all be okay."

I wipe my wet cheek. "It feels like all I do these days is cry."

He leads me to the dinette bench, takes a seat, then pulls me onto his lap. "I know. And that's okay, too. You lost your mom. It's good to cry."

I sniffle. "Last week, at Buckeroo Grocers I bounced a check. It's not that I didn't have the money. I just forgot to transfer money from savings to checking." I shake my head. "I've had a checking account since I was sixteen years old. There were times I had to squeak through the weekend with five dollars to my name, but I *never* bounced a check." I look up at him. "Sometimes it feels like I'll never be myself again. You know?"

He gently rubs my shoulder. "I know. Months after my mom died, I had to reschedule my dental cleaning appointment three times. I'd see the appointment on my calendar, set a timer, then somehow it just escaped my brain." He sighs. "Let's just say Dr. McCavity was not happy with me."

I jerk my head. "Is that really his name?"

"Yep. And he's married to Dr. Cockburn, the urologist."

We both laugh hard, then I remember something my mom told me. "When I was in Snap Peas, Mom said she went to school with a girl named Cherry Bottoms. Then she added, 'You guessed it. She became a stripper.' "

He chuckles then touches my face. "I know you miss your mom."

I slowly blink my eyes. "I really do. This sounds kind of bad, but since my mom and I lived so far apart and we weren't exactly warm and fuzzy, I guess I didn't think I'd miss her as much as I do." Lonnie tightens his arms around me, and I lean my face into his neck. "But I think about her all the time. I hear her voice, see her face—"

"She's alive in your memory."

"Yes, and as painful as those memories feel sometimes, it keeps her close to me." I look up at him, a sense of desperation washing over me. "In some ways, I don't want that to end, you know?"

Lonnie's voice is gentle. "Yes. I remember lying in bed one night and realizing I hadn't thought about my mom all day. It felt bittersweet."

"You missed her all over again."

"Yes, until I realized that even though she wasn't constantly in my thoughts anymore, she was still in my heart." He kisses my forehead. "Ramona, having your mom in your heart? That will never end."

We're quiet for a while. Then I slowly stand up and smooth the front of my apron. "Today I do not deserve to wear this."

"Ramona, I'm sure you're a great cook."

"Pappardelle with wild boar ragù? It's all I've got. It's the one meal I know how to make besides smothered hamburgers and pigs in blankets." Grabbing the bottle of wine, I fish through my kitchen drawer for a corkscrew.

He grins. "Not true. You make a mean tofu hot dog."

I set two glasses on the table, pour, then sit across from him. "I had this meal down perfectly in my real kitchen."

Lonnie sips wine. "Ramona, it's not all you've got. Not even close. You've got beauty, intelligence, a wicked sense of humor—" He nods toward the door. "And Prairie Pizza two miles down the road."

I can't help but chuckle, then sigh dreamily. "You should have seen my town house kitchen. Big island with teal blue stools. Roomy cabinets, yards of counter space, and a nice big oven with a six-burner stovetop."

"Sounds nice. You know, you can use my kitchen anytime, right?"

"Thanks, but I wanted to host a meal for you the way you hosted breakfast for me. World-class omelets, homemade bread. I mean, please, you even make your own strawberry preserves."

"Big deal, so I can whip up a few eggs. I also love

eating pizza." He grins. "As long as I'm eating pizza with you."

"Good thing since I have a kitchen made for weekend camping trips and a big plastic container of wild boar gone bad on my counter. Looks like we're having pizza tonight."

He clinks his glass to mine. "So, tell me about your day."

I raise my eyebrows, remembering our passionate morning at Lonnie's place. "Well, it started out with a bang."

"Yes, it did."

"I volunteered, got a letter from Earl. Did I tell you Earl and I have become pen pals?"

He smiles. "That's a new development."

I shake my head. "Yep. Earl writes about his bowling scores and fishing trips with Ricky. I tell him all the RV park gossip then stick a few scratch-offs in the envelope." I sip my wine. "When it comes to Earl, I've decided that scratch-offs are my love language."

"Nice."

"Yeah. He said he's looking forward to my visit in a couple of weeks."

"Are you still planning on flying up?" Lonnie reaches over and places his hand on mine. "Because if you need a driving partner, I'm your man."

My heart squeezes. "That's nice, but with substitute teaching starting back up the end of August, it's faster to fly. I figure I'll stay for a week. Earl said he replaced their old, saggy couch with a sleeper sofa, so I'll be more comfortable."

Lonnie grins. "Sounds like you and Earl are getting closer."

"We are. One scratch-off at a time." I pour more wine into Lonnie's glass then tilt my head his way. "So, I was thinking that when I order from Prairie Pizza, I could get an extra-large." I run my finger along his knuckles. "You like cold pizza for breakfast, right?"

He leans forward and brushes his fingertips along my neck then down to my cleavage. "Even more than fresh eggs from Big Bertha." He stands, pulling me to him, and I run my palm up his hard chest, then stroke the back of his neck. He cups my face and kisses me deeply, like he's searching and discovering all at once.

As I search his hot mouth with my tongue, my hands kneading the muscles in his back, I realize that all the panicked tension I felt earlier has completely blown away like the Texas downpour that passed through.

He pulls back slightly and playfully nibbles my lip. "But I have a question about the pizza: Do you prefer pepperoni—" He nips my top lip. "Or flaming sausage?"

I kiss him greedily then, my legs instinctively parting and my body throbbing from mere mention of what he's offering. "There's nothing like your flaming sausage."

Lifting my ass up onto the table, he spreads my thighs and steps between them, and I moan at the feel of his bulge against the V between my legs. Right then, I'm transported to a place so deliciously enticing that my entire body melts into a puddle of yearning. He moves his hips harder against me, his hands firmly cupping my breasts, and my back arches in response to his touch, then—

There's a knock at the door followed by a woman's voice, "Ramona, honey! Yoohoo!"

Chapter Thirty-one

My trailer's too small to pretend I'm not home. Lonnie and I scramble to compose ourselves, then I open the door to see Prisha's beaming face. "My cousin, Urdu, brought over enough chicken tikka masala to feed an army. And it just happens to be Ugly Jim's fortieth birthday." She touches my arm, cranes her neck, and grins over at Lonnie. "The storm has passed. It's Saturday night. Time to party."

I smile. "Now?"

"No time like the present."

"Speaking of which, should we bring something for Ugly Jim?"

Prisha shakes her head. "His sister gave him a brand-new video game player, and Bacon Joe got him Big Truck Racers. Ugly Jim says that's everything a forty-year-old guy could ever want." She eyes Lonnie then winks at me. "It'll be fun. Bring your handsome farmer." Then she wrinkles her nose. "What's that smell?"

I turn up my palms. "Oh, wild boar."

Prisha shrugs. "Huh, smells like a candle I used to own. Anyway, come over as soon as you can." She starts to leave then faces me. "By the way, Ramona, I love your apron."

News spreads fast in Nearly Heaven. By the time Lonnie and I clean up my kitchen and head over to

Prisha's place with patio chairs and a six-pack of wine coolers, the party's in full swing. We set our chairs on the lawn and look around. Prisha's spacious patio is strung with fairy lights. Neighbors have set up tables and chairs in her yard and on their patios as well. People chat, laugh, and swig beer as they stand in line near Prisha's picnic table filled with buffet warmers heaped with Indian food.

We walk over to Prisha, who's wearing black slacks, a blue tunic, and an apron that reads, *I'll Feed All You Fuckers*. I laugh. "I like your apron, too." I gaze over at the food, breathing in the sweet, spicy aroma of curry and naan. "This is amazing."

Prisha's deep brown eyes shine. "Urdu's a caterer. His gig tonight at an outdoor food festival was canceled because of the storm." A woman and a girl, both with jet black hair, walk over, and Prisha waves enthusiastically. "Ramona and Lonnie, this is my daughter, Bushra, and my granddaughter, Myra."

Bushra holds her hands over Myra's eyes. "Let's pretend we don't see your grandmother's apron."

We all laugh then Prisha shrugs. "You've known me long enough to know, I gotta be me." Then she rubs Myra's arm. "I can't believe this young lady is going to start seventh grade this year."

I nod. "My best friend's sons are going into seventh grade. Lime Rock School District."

Myra smooths her long braid. "That's where I go."

I smile. "Do you happen to know redheaded twins named Wyatt and Boone?"

Bushra pipes up, "They're in science camp with Myra. Nice boys."

Prisha smiles. "Small world." Then she pats Myra's

shoulder and waves toward the food. "Please, everyone, go fill a plate. The saag paneer is to die for."

It's a beautiful evening. The passing storm left the air fresh and clean, and the blue sky is tinted with puffy pink clouds as the sun thinks about setting. The fairy lights, strung on patios and RV's, blink on like fireflies.

I lounge on a lawn chair, nursing a beer, my belly full of chicken tikka masala and samosas, as I watch Lonnie mingle. He chats and laughs with Ugly Jim, Bacon Joe, and Frank, the retired gentleman with the three-legged schnauzer. He glances over, and I try to hide my silly grin. The only thing more full than my belly right now is my heart.

I am falling for Lonnie, this man who helped me drive eighteen-hundred miles to Snap Peas and has been supportive beyond words ever since. This strong and tender and funny man who makes me feel safe enough to be myself. Safe enough to cry. Safe enough to lose myself in the throes of passion and come completely undone.

Lonnie walks toward me, pulls up a chair, and sits facing me. The mere sensation of my knees touching his makes my stomach flutter and pulse quicken and my mind doodle hearts and Cupid's arrows across the summer sky.

He kisses the back of my hand, turns it over, and presses his mouth against the inside of my wrist, his tongue against my racing pulse. He searches my eyes. "So, Dad called today."

Butch. I smile. "How's my favorite stubborn old man?"

"You can ask him yourself Monday evening." Lonnie bites his lip. "He and Ming are having a little family get-together. He apologized for having it on a Monday. Said the weekend's been busy. I'd love it if you joined me, and I know Dad would love to have you there. You in?"

I search his eyes, my heart dancing. Lonnie and Butch are inviting me to their family gathering. "Can I wear my Ranch Z cap?"

"It's required attire." He winks. "After dessert, you'll need it for the Ranch Z hat dance."

Country music plays from portable speakers. Bacon Joe calls out, "Feel free to make requests. Otherwise, Ugly Jim will have me playing honky-tonk all night."

Lonnie stands and kisses my forehead. "I'll be right back." He walks over, says a few words to Joe, then returns to me.

I tilt my head. "What time should we be at Butch's house on Monday?"

"It starts at seven, which might be a little tricky for me. Remember the job interview I told you about?" I nod, and he goes on, "My interview doesn't start until five-thirty, after the clinic has seen its last patient, so seven o'clock might be cutting it close."

I chuckle. "And Butch is a big fan of punctuality."

Lonnie nods. "I should be out of the clinic on time, but if I'm not, would you mind driving over at seven to keep Dad and Ming company, and I'll meet you there? Dad's already unhappy that I'm interviewing for a family doctor position at the clinic, then if we're late—"

"Sure. I'll save you a big wedge of brie from the charcuterie board." I search his eyes. "Are you looking forward to the interview?"

He knits his brow. "I'm looking forward to hearing more about the job. It fits in terms of work/life balance.

I'd work Monday through Friday, be home by around six, and rotate on-call about four days a month. That all sounds good."

"But?"

"But I keep thinking there's something out there for me that I'm—" He shakes his head. "I don't know, meant to do. I just need to figure it out."

I place my hand on his knee. "You will. You figured out that you needed to leave surgery, and you'll figure out what you're meant to do next." He gives a warm smile, and I skim my finger along his arm. "And in the meantime, mister, you can always do me."

He leans forward and kisses me. "Oh, that's definitely one of the things I'm meant to do." A new song begins, and he takes my hand. "It's the song I requested. Care to dance?"

Smiling, I stand. "It's a Beau Boopster tune. I'd know that voice anywhere."

Beneath a starry night sky, Lonnie and I press our bodies together, his hand firm against my lower back, my arms draped on his shoulders as we sway to the beat of a sweet, slow tune. He twirls me around then pulls me close again, nuzzles my cheek, and says, "I'm more of a Rhythm and Blues kind of guy, but this song, well, it just rings true."

I tilt my chin up. "I thought I'd heard all the Boopster songs by now, but I'm not sure I've ever heard this one."

"It's his new release."

"What's it called?"

Lonnie grins. "Just listen. The chorus is coming up." He twirls me again, then dips me. When he kisses my throat, a moan of utter delight escapes my lips. Scooping me up, he pulls me tight against him and looks into my eyes as Beau's voice sings the chorus. "After these past few days, this song says it all." Lonnie smiles. I'm 'The Dang Luckiest Man in Texas.' "

Chapter Thirty-two

It's Monday evening. I showered, loofahed, shaved my legs, then slipped into my skinny jeans, peach camisole, and strappy sandals. I'm sitting on my bed trying to figure out what jewelry to wear, when Lonnie calls. "Looks like my interview's running late. The clinic's busy, so the docs can't meet with me yet. That's Mondays for ya."

I bite my lip. Just the sound of Lonnie's voice takes me back to the weekend and fills me with longing. That dance on Prisha's lawn. That night in my trailer with Lonnie in my bed beside me. Waking up to him the next morning, to the touch of his warm arm across my bare belly, to the sight of his stubbled square jaw and tousled wavy hair, to the tenderness in his voice when he wished me a good morning. Then the morning only got better. I say into the phone, "No worries. I'll be at Butch's place at seven and tell him you'll be there soon."

"Thanks. When I talked to Dad yesterday, he gave me a hard time again about my interview here at the free clinic. Then he reminded me that the get-together starts at nineteen-hundred-hours sharp. You know he still lives on Army time. At least if you're there—"

"No worries. I'll knock on his door right on time then mesmerize him and Ming with Patient Panda stories. He won't even know you're missing." Lonnie laughs, and I chew my fingernail. "It's strange. I'm actually nervous about going to Butch's ranch."

I hear Lonnie take in a sharp breath. "Oh, then let's go together. I'll pick you up. If we're late, we're late."

"No. I'm not nervous about hanging out with Butch on my own. I mean, please, I put compression hose on the guy. It's more about feeling like a fish out of water at his ranch. I'm picturing this huge, ritzy property."

"Oh. It's not so much ritzy as…Big Tex."

I knit my brow. "Big Tex?"

"Yeah, twenty-foot beamed ceilings, stone fireplaces, lots of huge leather furniture."

I cringe. "Just the kind of place where I'll spill red wine on the five-thousand-dollar cowhide rug."

"Not a problem. The cow will not care."

I chuckle. "It's just…you know, Butch and Ming stopped by my place to give me the Ranch Z cap. They've seen my trailer, and tonight I'll be at Butch's Big Tex estate trying not to drop crumbs on the leather sofa."

"Ramona, please, if you spill wine and drop crumbs, it does not matter." I hear a voice in the background. "Oh, they're ready for me now. I have to go. Listen, there is no reason to worry. Just be yourself."

At six fifty-five p.m., I turn my truck onto Barnstorm Road and run a finger over the Texas bluebonnet necklace Lonnie sent me when I was in Snap Peas. *Just be yourself.* I let out a long exhale. *And drink white wine, not red.*

I slow down as my GPS tells me that my destination is on the left. I peer at the sprawling stone property, its circular drive filled with parked luxury vehicles, and mumble, "All these vehicles. This can't be—" I check the house number against the address in my phone and rub my chin. "I guess this is it."

I pull behind a black SUV parked along the road, and turn off the ignition, feeling that familiar tinge of nausea I felt as a kid when Mom dropped me off, in her beater station wagon with the loud muffler, at a birthday party on the nice side of town.

Donning my Ranch Z cap, I step from my truck, take in the expansive estate, and sigh. *Okay, get a grip, Ramona. It's just a house. Now go knock on that huge double front door that probably costs more than your truck and just be yourself.* I'm about to cross the road when a vehicle pulls behind my truck. Then I feel every muscle in my body relax. It's Lonnie's pickup.

Lonnie parks, opens the driver's door, and in a flash, he's standing beside me, taking my hand then kissing my cheek. He smiles, tapping the rim of my cap. "Suits you." Then he looks over at the packed driveway and shakes his head. "Dad said a little family get-together, but it looks like all of Hill Country is here."

We walk toward the house, my chest fluttering from the sensation of our shoulders touching. "So, how was your interview?"

He nods. "They offered me the job."

I look up at him. "That's great."

"Yeah. I was impressed with the medical staff there, and it's work where I feel like I could make a difference." He shrugs. "But I can't shake this feeling that there's something else out there for me. A better fit." I nod, and Lonnie continues, "I thanked them for their time and told them I'm not ready to make the commitment."

"Makes sense." I bump my hip against his. "Don't worry. You'll find the perfect fit."

We step onto the stone porch and pause, listening to the cacophony of boisterous chatter, and clinking plates echoing from the other side of the doors. Lonnie faces me. "Ready?"

He's reaching for the knob when the door suddenly swings open. Ming stands there, her barn red lipstick matching her cowgirl boots. "Come on in." She pats Lonnie's shoulder then smiles at me. "Ramona. Great to see you." We step indoors, and I watch Lonnie furrow his brow as he takes in the crowd of guests mingling in the cavernous living room.

Then I take it all in. This house is gorgeous. Forget *Bigger Homes Digest*. This place is straight off the pages of *My Home Is So Much Bigger and Better Than Your Home*. I assumed Butch was financially comfortable, being a retired surgeon from a family of physicians and all. But dang!

I swallow hard as I eye the beamed ceilings, built-in mahogany bookshelves, Persian rugs, and framed artwork that probably cost as much as my trailer. Then I squint toward the group of people holding wineglasses and hors d'oeuvre plates chatting in a circle near the stone fireplace. Where do I know them from? I chew on my knuckle. Cassidy Memorial. Of course. Butch worked there for years before he retired. Looks like his "little family get-together" includes friends and colleagues.

Ming nudges Lonnie then points to an older couple wearing traditional red Chinese Tang suits. They look swallowed up by the mammoth leather sofa. "You remember my brother and his wife." Lonnie nods slowly as Ming turns to me. "Can you believe what they're wearing? They've lived here in Texas for thirty years but dress like they just stepped out of the Qing Dynasty." Then Ming raises her chin and rolls her eyes. "Cousin Cheong just knocked over his wine again." She nods toward the kitchen island where Butch is serving drinks. "You two go grab some sangria. I'll grab some paper towels."

We walk over to Butch standing at the far end of the island cordially pouring wine and chatting with guests. I can't help but smile at the sight of him in khakis and blue shirt looking healthy. He's come a long way since the days when I smuggled candy into his hospital room. I wave, excited for him to see me in my Ranch Z cap. "Hey, Butch."

He looks up and smiles. "Welcome to Ranch Z." Sliding a glass of sangria my way, he nods at Lonnie. "Hello, Son."

"Hey, Dad. What happened to the little get-together? This is more like a Texas-sized shindig."

Butch hands a glass to Lonnie. "Wine, cheese, and dessert. Put it out and they will come." He shoots Lonnie a sheepish look. "Ming and I extended a few invitations, and it took off like wildfire." He gestures to the living room. "Lonnie, why don't you go mingle? A bunch of your colleagues from surgery are here."

Lonnie frowns. "*Former* colleagues."

Butch squints. "I'm sure they'd love to catch up with you."

Ming comes over, wagging her finger at Butch. "If Cousin Cheong comes whining for more sangria, give him lemonade. I've cut him off." She grins at me. "He's a lightweight. And I'm out of paper towels."

I chuckle, and Lonnie smiles my way. Then he wraps his arm around my waist, pulls me close, and all my earlier worries about spilling wine on expensive rugs and feeling like a fish out of water melt away. Grinning up at him, I marvel at how far he and I have come together. We've gone from being saddle burs to road trip companions to confidantes. We've evolved from being intimate friends to rock-my-world lovers. And now I'm standing here, in my Ranch Z cap, with Lonnie's arm snug around me, in his father's house, and we're…a couple. Our romantic relationship might still be young, but my feelings for him are running as deep as the roots of a two-hundred-year-old live oak.

Lonnie kisses my forehead, and I close my eyes, savoring the touch of his warm lips against my skin. We're a couple, and that reality nourishes my heart, soul, mind, and body in a way I never dreamt possible. Dang, I'm in love.

Then I open my eyes to see Butch's and Ming's faces registering confusion, flashing the kind of bewilderment that says, *We didn't see that one coming.*

My breathing pauses, and my mind scrambles. Wait. They didn't know Lonnie and I are dating? When Butch and Ming stopped by my trailer to give me the Ranch Z cap, they didn't know that our road trip took a romantic detour with that kiss? I take a sip of wine. Butch thought Lonnie was bringing me here tonight as…what…a friend?

Butch clears his throat. "Ming, could you take over sangria duty?" He smiles at me. "While Lonnie's mingling with his friends from surgery, I'll give Panda the grand tour of the cheese table."

Lonnie frowns. "Dad, I—"

Just then a gray-bearded man taps his glass with a spoon and calls out, "If everyone could take a seat in the living room, please." I turn my head to see guests pulling chairs around the sofa/love seat area, forming a circle.

Lonnie groans. "Probably some big announcement about a wing of the hospital being named after one of these guys."

Butch puts his hand on Lonnie's shoulder as the man calls out, "Take your seats, please. Then we'll get started."

We move into the living room where most of the seats are already occupied. Butch gestures to an empty chair. "Son, why don't you sit over there? Near the fireplace." Then he grins at me. "Ramona, looks like Ming saved you a spot."

Lonnie shrugs, flashing me an apologetic look. I whisper, "It's okay," then walk over to Ming, who's smiling and patting the chair beside her. Taking a seat, I look around the circle of guests. I've never seen so many designer clothes, expensive watches, and unnaturally white teeth in one room.

"I'm Dr. Lester Hummer," the bearded man in brown corduroy pants, and a buttoned shirt pulled tight at his round belly, says. "We're all here tonight to pay tribute to a very gifted surgeon."

Lonnie shoots me a look like, *See, they're naming a hospital wing after one of these guys.*

Dr. Hummer sits straight. "We're here tonight for Lonnie."

Lonnie jerks his head. "What?"

Hummer goes on, "Lonnie, we want to let you know that this—" He widens his arms. "—is your circle of support."

Lonnie bursts out a sarcastic chuckle. "My circle...I don't get it."

Hummer nods slowly. "Our circle of friends, family, and colleagues is here to help you."

Lonnie grimaces. "Help me—?"

Hummer pipes up, "Help you live your best life."

I shift in my seat, and Lonnie looks over at me, his expression echoing my thoughts exactly: *What the hell is going on here?*

Then I watch Lonnie as he glances around the circle then squints at Hummer. "And you are?"

Hummer pushes his owl glasses up the bridge of his nose. "Sorry. We've never officially met. I'm Chief of Psychiatry at Cassidy Memorial. As we proceed tonight, think of this as a group share."

Ming nudges my elbow and groans. "Group share. That's shrink talk for ya."

I nod and whisper, "I'd like to go back to group sharing the cheese and crackers."

Ming chuckles. "Good one."

Lonnie narrows his eyes at Hummer. "Group share?"

Hummer leans forward. "Yes, as opposed to what some might call…an intervention."

"Intervention?" Lonnie looks at me and mouths, *We're out of here*, then rocks forward to stand.

Butch raises a hand. "Lonnie. You know I like psychobabble about as much as sardines left out in the sun, but let's hear this guy out."

I feel my head snap back slightly. *What the fuck is going on here?*

Hummer gestures to the group. "Lonnie, your friends and family are here to share kind words about you and your work."

A woman with tight blonde curls raises her hand and

grins warmly. "Hey, Lonnie." Her gaze drips with pleasantness. "I've known you since you performed your first surgery at Cassidy Memorial. A ventricular restoration. I recognized your talent immediately. We miss you."

Lonnie slumps back in the chair. "Thanks, Bailey, but—"

A tall man runs a hand over his bald head. "Lonnie, remember when we performed the Thoracic Aortic Dissection Repair? You were brilliant. Our department hasn't been the same since you left. You know there's a vacancy. We'd all love for you to fill it."

Lonnie shrugs. "Cedric, I appreciate that, but the department is just fine without me."

Hummer clasps his hands in his lap. "Allow me to take a moment to reflect on what I'm hearing." He looks Lonnie in the eye. "Your esteemed colleagues are admiring your talent and urging you to fill the vacant position in surgery."

Lonnie shakes his head. "Thanks for the kind words, but the thing is, I don't miss surgery. Over the past year, I've realized that I went into surgery to—" He raises his eyebrows at Butch. "—make Dad happy."

Butch beams. "It worked! Well done."

Lonnie frowns. "But *I* wasn't happy. I worked constantly, always felt stressed, and didn't have time to do the things that really mattered to me."

Butch rolls his eyes. "Welcome to The Big Boy Club. That's what a stiff drink after work is for."

Hummer wags a finger. "I'm feeling the energy in the room becoming less productive. Let's regroup."

Cedric crosses his arms over his chest. "Let's stop beating around the bush. Listen, Lonnie, you're a skilled surgeon who temporarily lost your drive after a…difficult time. It can happen to anyone. But you're wasting your talent, and the department needs you back."

Lonnie purses his lips then opens his mouth to say something, but Bailey pipes up, "Lonnie, you went through a personal rough patch, but that's over now. You can restore your career."

Hummer nods. "Cedric and Bailey touched on something important. Lonnie, we all know you had a tough year."

Lonnie swallows, a pained expression crossing his face, and my heart breaks for him.

Butch shakes his head. "We all had a tough year. But, Son, that doesn't mean you just throw everything away. You were grieving and made hasty decisions. But you can stop chasing chickens and sheep around your yard and go back to your old life, your accomplished life."

Lonnie blinks slowly. "I was grieving, but I did not make hasty decisions. I happen to like my chickens and sheep, but more importantly, I don't want to be a surgeon. I know that's hard for you to accept, but—"

Butch holds up a hand. "It is hard for me to accept. And it would have devastated your mother."

I draw in a breath as I watch Lonnie's shoulders drop, then his jaw clench and unclench. His voice is measured, his eyes locked on Butch. "My seventy-hour work weeks as a surgeon took time away from my mother when she was sick and could have used her son around."

Butch shakes his head. "Your mother understood. She knows what life as a surgeon entails."

Lonnie looks around the circle. "Sorry you all

wasted your evening. I'm not going back to surgery. There's something else out there for me, a better fit. I'll know it when I see it."

There's a hard knock on the front door, and all heads turn that way. The door opens, and at first, my brain feels so foggy that I'm sure I must be imagining things. Then I bring a hand to my mouth, feeling the blood drain from my face as the fog begins to clear and, like a dream, Shi-Yun appears.

Her tall, elegant body is draped in the palest blue silk dress, and her shiny black hair sways with each long, graceful stride through the foyer and toward our circle of guests. She's holding a silk handbag and the gaze of every person in the room.

Did I say a dream? More like a nightmare.

Chapter Thirty-three

Shi-Yun grins over at the older couple wearing Chinese Tang suits. I look across the room at Lonnie, my eyes begging him to meet my gaze. Instead, he stares at the floor, his mouth fallen open, like he can't wrap his mind around everything that's unfolding.

I look at the seated guests. Cassidy Memorial colleagues. Ming's family. I glance at Shi-Yun sitting on the sofa between Ming's brother and sister-in-law, the Tang couple. Then it dawns on me: they're Shi-Yun's parents. No wonder Lonnie flashed them a sheepish expression when we arrived. Lonnie's the former fiancée who called off their daughter's wedding.

I sit straight in my chair, not knowing what to do, then look over at Lonnie again, hoping he'll take action, praying that he'll stand up, walk across the room, grasp my hand, and lead us out of here, away from this bizarre intervention, away from Hummer and Butch, and especially Shi-Yun. But he looks…paralyzed.

Rolling my shoulders back, I try to talk down the tension in my body. Like Lonnie said on our road trip, the situation with Shi-Yun is all too close for comfort. Ming, who's dating Butch, is Shi-Yun's aunt. Lonnie and Shi-Yun share hospital colleagues in common. The bottom line is: with Lonnie in my life, we're all going to cross paths from time to time. I peer over at Lonnie appearing stunned as he draws in deep breaths. *With*

Lonnie in my life. I feel my muscles soften. Coming face-to-face with Shi-Yun, the radiant surgeon who used to be Lonnie's fiancée, does blow royally. But what matters is having Lonnie in my life.

Shi-Yun sits perfectly poised, her hands clasped in her lap, as she addresses the room. "Sorry I'm late. I had no idea this gathering was happening until my parents called and told me all about this group share. Strange that I was not invited, which is rather odd considering that out of all the people here—" She lifts her delicate chin Lonnie's way. "—Lonnie and I have shared the most."

My stomach sinks at the reminder of all that Shi-Yun and Lonnie have shared: an engagement, wedding plans…a bed.

Shi-Yun's words seem to shake Lonnie out of his stupor. Holding up a hand, he rocks forward to stand. "That's it. I've had enough sharing tonight to last a lifetime."

I draw in a hopeful, elated breath as I lean forward, ready to stand, then Hummer puts a hand on Lonnie's arm. "Please. We were talking about your grief, and I believe, making emotional headway on your path forward. Lonnie, you were just saying that you feel there's something out there for you that's a better fit."

Shi-Yun shakes her head slowly. "Better fit? How about a perfect fit?" She narrows her eyes at Lonnie. "Two skilled surgeons with big brains and even bigger 401(k)'s living in that five-thousand square foot house with a fountain, tennis courts, and deer resistant landscape shrubs that we could have bought together."

I stop breathing. Shi-Yun's not trying to convince Lonnie to go back to *surgery*. She's trying to convince him to go back to *her*.

Shi-Yun grins sadly. "We were about to have the perfect, ambitious life together." She reaches into her handbag, pulls out a photograph, and holds it up for everyone to see. "Which was exactly what your mother wanted." She taps a red fingernail against the photo. "Remember this, Lonnie? Our engagement party at The Ritzy Hare. Your mother is beaming. She said it was one of the happiest days of her life."

I peer over at Lonnie now slumped in his chair, a palm pressed to his forehead. "That's so unfair, Shi-Yun."

Shi-Yun sucks air in through her teeth. "Unfair? Unfair was you calling off the wedding. You know our wedding was what your mother wanted more than anything!" She waves her left hand and flaunts her ring finger that flashes a diamond the size of a chestnut. "Your mother gave this ring to you—" She clutches her hand to her chest. "—to give to *me*!"

What? Shi-Yun's still wearing their engagement ring? I lean back against my chair, suddenly dizzy, my head filled with white noise. Breathing out a shaky exhale, I look over at Lonnie, who slowly raises his eyes to meet my gaze, his face appearing stricken.

No. This can't be happening. On our road trip, before that kiss, Lonnie promised me that he and Shi-Yun were over. Absolutely over. They can't still be engaged. There must be some explanation for all this. I gaze over at Shi-Yun, impeccably dressed right down to her designer slingback pumps, looking perfectly at home in Butch's ranch-of-the-rich, clutching her diamond engagement ring to her chest. I stare down at my strappy sandals, the ones I bought on sale for nineteen bucks at Dory's Dress for Less. I don't even come close to fitting into this world.

Butch clears his throat and looks at Lonnie. "Son, it is what your mother wanted. You know that."

I feel my body jerk and notice Ming craning her neck to look over at Butch.

Hummer turns to Butch. "Can you say more about that?"

Butch points to the photo in Shi-Yun's lap. "Priscilla was so happy that night. Her son was engaged to a woman who was his perfect match." He turns his head toward Lonnie. "You and Shi-Yun have fine educations, stellar careers, and you both come from good families."

I swallow hard, fighting back a wave of nausea. *Good families?*

Hummer nods. "And those shared qualities were important?"

Butch sighs. "When Lonnie was younger, we worried about him dating women he didn't have much in common with, women from different lifestyles and backgrounds. Priscilla wanted him to think about lifelong compatibility, to make wise decisions. She was so happy when he started dating Shi-Yun."

My jaw tenses. Lonnie's family worries about him dating women from different backgrounds. I think back to the bewildered expression on Butch's face when Lonnie kissed my forehead this evening. Butch thought that Lonnie brought me here tonight as his friend. I guess, since I'm a woman from a different background, that's the role he thinks I should play. I feel my teeth grind. Butch is my biggest fan when I deliver chocolate to his hospital room, but when I come to his Big Tex house and snuggle up to his son, I guess I'm not in his league.

I want to leave, to bolt the hell out of this intervention circle jerk, and slam the door behind me, but my head is spinning, and I feel as dazed and paralyzed as Lonnie appeared earlier.

Lonnie shoots a defeated look at Butch. "You're right. Mom wanted the wedding. Right down to the harpist and sky-blue bridesmaids' shoes." He stares down at his hands. "Believe me, I've wrestled with this. Of course, I want to honor my mother's wishes, give her what she wanted…" His voice trails off.

My ribs tighten. I bring a hand to my throat, fingering the bluebonnet necklace from Lonnie, my mind swirling with memories of me and him over these past months. Our road trip together, the care package he sent while I was in Snap Peas, the coffees and lunches and lemonades when I returned home to Texas, his steadfast friendship. Then the sex, that mind-blowingly passionate and tender all at once sex that I thought…meant something to him, the way it meant something—everything—to me.

I thought I meant something to him, but the reality is right here in front of me. Lonnie is telling everyone here, including Shi-Yun who's wearing his engagement ring, that he wants to give his late mother what she wanted. And what his mother wanted was for him to marry Shi-Yun.

I shake my head and announce, "I'm fucking out of here."

Finding my bearings, I jump to my feet, then storm through the foyer, ignoring Lonnie's surprised voice tinged with panic. "Ramona?"

When I reach the door, I pause just long enough to yank the Ranch Z cap off my head, hurl it at the coat rack, and hear it thump to the floor, before running out into the clear, night air.

Chapter Thirty-four

I sit on my dinette bench, angrily bouncing my knees up and down because I don't have enough room in this goddamn trailer to pace back and forth. I want to step out the door and run for miles—better yet, for days—until I'm so far away from Lonnie, and the sickening pain in my stomach and ache in my heart, that it's all behind me. So far behind me that I know there's no way in hell it can ever catch up. But it's dark outside, and the long country roads feel lonely and unsafe to run. Besides, I have nowhere to go.

I cross my arms in front of my chest, feeling something big and tight balled up in my heart. I clench my fists as all my childhood insecurities replayed in my adult life come crashing down on me. It's Chester Featherston, captain of the chess team, all over again, pointing out our incompatibilities due to "different backgrounds," which is code for "different leagues."

Tonight, at the intervention, both Lonnie and Shi-Yun tossed around the word, "unfair." Here's what's fucking unfair: Chester, Martin, Lonnie, and those mean, name-calling kids on the school bus grew up with money and the advantages that come with that…and I didn't.

I stare out the kitchen window into the darkness and bring a hand to my roiling stomach. Tonight, being reminded of that unfairness stung, but what doubled me over like a punch to the gut was when Butch said that both Lonnie and Shi-Yun came from "good families." I know what their idea of a "good family" looks like, and that picture does not include a mother with a GED living in a double-wide with a father who burps commercial jingles.

I slump back, rubbing my temple. What an awful evening. No doubt, it was awful for Lonnie, too. The surprise intervention. The pressure from his former colleagues and his own father to go back to surgery. Then Shi-Yun striding in, holding that photo of his late mother beaming at their engagement party, shaming him about calling off the wedding. I'd almost feel sorry for the guy…if he hadn't been toying with me this whole time.

Sitting straight, I slap a hand against the table. Lonnie and Shi-Yun are still engaged. That's why Lonnie didn't tell Butch and Ming that he and I are dating. That's why, months ago, when I saw Lonnie and Shi-Yun arguing in the hospital parking lot, Lonnie didn't pull away when Shi-Yun grasped his hand. My throat burns, but no tears flow. I've been some trailer-park fling on the side while Lonnie sorted things out with his angry fiancée.

I pick up my phone to call Jules, then let out a long exhale. I can't call her, not tonight. Jules, Chase, and the boys are on a well-deserved vacation on the Gulf Coast. The last thing I want to do is interrupt their precious days of family time. Besides, not even Jules's BFF superpowers can change the reality that when I looked at Lonnie, I saw the man I was falling in love with. And when Lonnie looked at me, he saw an opportunity to have fun with some girl from the other side of town.

I'm startled by a hard rap of knuckles against the

door, then jerk my head at the sound of Lonnie's voice. "Hey, Ramona. I'm glad you're home."

I can't pretend I'm not home. My truck's in the driveway. All my lights are on. Hell, he probably saw my silhouette through the kitchen window when he walked across my patio. Straightening my shoulders, I slowly stand, pausing for a moment while my head stops spinning. I walk to the door and place my palm against the cool aluminum, listening to Lonnie say, "It'll be good to talk."

Then I lock the deadbolt, flick off the kitchen lights, and turn away.

Chapter Thirty-five

After a restless night's sleep, it's finally sunrise. I sit on my patio, in shorts and soft T-shirt, my hair pulled into a messy pony, listening to Lonnie's fucking rooster, Mr. Roo, crow its goddamn lungs out.

I lift my face to the fat clouds in the pink sky. Okay, so it's not Mr. Roo's fault that I woke up at five o'clock this morning all brokenhearted. But considering the circumstances, that cock pisses me off.

If I still lived in my sweet town house in downtown Jackalope, I wouldn't have to be within earshot of Lonnie's crowing rooster. But I'm stuck here in Nearly Heaven RV Park just like, as a kid, I was stuck there at Eight Oaks Trailer Park.

Sipping black coffee, I gaze into my backyard where cardinals chatter from tree branches. Despite my brokenheartedness, I can't help but grin, remembering, a few days earlier, when I spotted a painted bunting—his feathers a mosaic of vibrant blues, greens, reds, and yellows. As much as I'd give anything to leave this RV park and move back downtown, I do appreciate my yard here. The redbuds, mountain laurels, and two-hundred-year-old live oaks fill my heart with the magic of nature. Especially those live oaks. I bring a hand to my chest, suddenly aware of what I've had right here in front of me all along.

****

247

Laurie Woodford

I climbed up here two hours ago, my hands holding tight to rough tree bark, my sneakers digging against the sturdy trunk as I hoisted myself from lower to higher limbs, feeling lost and hurt and stuck. Now, perched up here on thick oak branches watching leaves dance in the breeze, birds flit from sprig to sprig, squirrels scramble, and swallowtails flutter, I'm starting to feel like myself again. I run a finger over the worn cover of *Misty of Chincoteague*, that I tucked into the waistband of my shorts as I climbed. I flip through its pages then land on one of my favorite lines. "The ponies were exhausted, and their coats were heavy with water, but they were free, free, *free!*"

Up here, in some strange way, I've found home. I may not have leaves or feathers, fur or antennae, but I don't feel like an outsider sitting cradled in the strong branches of this tree that's been rooted in the earth for hundreds of years. I feel at home. I feel safe. And just like those ponies, I feel free. Free from the petty world down there where people judge others by the clothes they wear and cars they drive and the houses—or trailers—they live in. The world up here is so much bigger, so much better, than all that.

I hear the faint crunching of gravel and peer through the branches to see Lonnie at my door. He knocks, then runs a hand through his hair while he waits for me to answer. I bring a hand to my hardening stomach and watch him knock again. Then watch him wait before he turns and walks away.

****

It's afternoon now. A little while ago, I climbed down to use the bathroom. While I was in my trailer, I packed a Buckeroo Grocer's bag with a sandwich,

248

cookies, and water bottle. Then I climbed back up, higher this time.

Time stands still up here. Sometimes, I watch clouds so fat and fluffy and white that I count them, as they drift by, like sheep jumping over fences. Other times, with my bird's-eye view, I watch the comings and goings of neighborhood life down below. I watch Ugly Jim come by with his Weedy Wack to clear brush from the far end of my lot. Not long after that, Bacon Joe drives his cart past my trailer, parks near the cleared brush, and tinkers with some fencing that needs straightening. Frank and his schnauzer walk by on their way toward the wooded trails.

Then Lonnie comes over again. I watch him knock on my door, wait, then turn away, and disappear. With enough time, I've realized, everyone disappears. I breathe in the sounds of dancing leaves, and fluttering damselflies, and the shattering of my heart.

I climb to a higher branch and tie the handles of my grocer bag to a nearby limb. If I move my head to the left, lift my chin, and peer through the leaves just so, I can see the Nearly Heaven sign in the distance. I bring a hand to my rising and falling chest as my breaths come faster and deeper, remembering the time Lonnie kissed me and said, "Now, this is nearly heaven."

Heaven. Is that where my mom is right now? I never heard her talk about God, but I know she loved living out in the country—the beauty of rolling hills, wooded trails, and wildflowers. Maybe the magic of nature was her church. I lean my head against the tree, press my ear to warm bark, and I swear I hear the echoing of a strong, steady heartbeat. If only I could stay up here for days. Or weeks. Or forever.

****

I startle from voices below. "Ramona. Sweetie. Ugly Jim is getting a ladder." I blink down at Prisha craning her neck to look up at me. She's holding a light blanket. Dazed, I look around. Hours must have passed without me realizing it, because the sun is beginning to set.

Then Bacon Joe steps in view. "We're gonna get you down safe and sound. We gotcha covered."

I catch a glimpse of the wagging of a schnauzer tail then Frank steps into sight and waves. "If the ladder doesn't reach, don't you worry. My friend, Hector, has a bucket truck."

I shake my head, trying to get the fog to lift from my brain, then call out, "I don't want to come down. I want to stay up here."

Frank frowns up at me. "It's going to get dark soon."

Prisha holds out her hands. "We'll bring you down then you'll come to my place for curry and naan. We'll talk, we'll drink tea—"

Joe looks at Prisha and Frank. "Hey, maybe Lonnie's home now. I can go over and get him."

I feel my back stiffen at the sound of his name. They don't know what happened. The last time they all saw Lonnie was two days ago when he and I were dancing under the stars on Prisha's patio. My voice is firm. "No. Don't get Lonnie."

The three of them shrug at each other. Then Prisha asks, "What happened, Sweetie?"

I rub my forehead, trying to clear my brain fog, not knowing where to begin. "Everything," I say. "Butch. Shi-Yun. The intervention."

The four of them huddle, and I can make out the

sound of Prisha saying, "Intervention? And who's Shi-Yun? Maybe she's delirious. When's the last time she ate or drank something?"

I hear the clunk of a tall ladder being set on the ground near my tree. "Miss Ramona. Ugly Jim here to help you down."

I shake my head, my throat burning. "At the intervention I realized they don't think I come from a *good family*."

Jim looks up, confused. "Intervention?"

I nod. "Yep, the intervention on Planet Big Tex where only beings who have money out the wazoo and Ivy League degrees come from good families."

Jim huffs. "Sounds more like Planet Your Anus."

I snort a laugh. "Right?" Then tears sting my eyes. "It's all such fucking bullshit."

Jim nods. "You tell 'em, Sister."

I feel my hands start to shake. "My family is just as good as anyone else's. Okay, maybe weirder. Yeah, they're definitely weirder. But my mom…my mom—"

I peer down to see all four faces looking up at me with expressions of grave concern. Frank clears his throat. "Can you tell us about your mom?"

I cry out, "Her name was Carol. She was a good person. She was hard-working and funny as hell and rough around the edges. She loved nature and bowling and gin and tonics and—" I wipe the hot tears running down my face. "—and her family. She loved us. And I love her."

The group huddles again, whispering and sniffling. Then Jim calls up to me, "Sit tight, Ramona. We'll all be right back."

I watch them disperse, hearing Prisha call over her

shoulder, "Hold on. We'll be back in just a few minutes."

Joe is the first one to return. He sits cross-legged on the ground beneath my tree and sets a square of fabric in front of him.

Frank's back next. He sits beside Joe and places a few things in front of him. From this high branch, I can't make out Frank's and Joe's items, so I untie my bag and start to climb down to the next branch to get a better look.

Jim yells up, "Ramona, drop the bag down to me so you can use both hands climbing."

I do as he says and settle into the V of two thick branches, then squint down to see that Frank has brought a pinecone and leaves. Jim, holding a paper bag, gets situated then Prisha arrives to complete the circle. I peer down, watching Jim remove two bottles from his bag, one that looks like an alcohol bottle and the other, a plastic soda bottle. Then he passes out cups to the others and waves a cup at me before setting it in front of him. "This one's for you, Ramona. When you're ready."

Prisha holds up a gift bag. "We're going to take a moment to remember your mom."

I touch my trembling lips.

Prisha reaches into her bag. "I brought a candle."

I jerk my head.

Prisha looks up at me with an impish grin. "Don't worry. It's lilac scented."

As Prisha sets the candle in the center of the circle and strikes a match, Jim pours the drinks. Then Prisha folds her hands in prayer and says, "To Carol Sadler. Who loved nature." Frank places the pinecone and leaves in the circle's center. "And bowling." Joe unfolds the square of fabric, and I can see now that it's a bowling towel. He places it in the circle.

I call down, "Hey, Joe. What does the towel say?"

Joe shoots me a sheepish look. "It says, 'I use this towel to shine my balls.' "

I burst into laughter, feeling tears stream down my face. "God, Mom would have loved that so much."

Prisha continues, "And gin and tonics." They all raise their cups to me and take a drink. Prisha's voice cracks. "And, most of all, our beloved Carol Sadler loved her family, including her amazing daughter, Ramona, who will always carry her mom with her in her heart."

We're all quiet for a while as the sun sets. Then Prisha says gently, "Are you ready to come down now and toast to your mom?"

I let out a shaky breath. "Yes, please."

Jim stands to get the ladder, and I wave him off. "I'm okay. I can climb down."

Holding up a hand, Jim says, "Only if you feel steady."

Clasping my arms around a limb, I take a step down to the next branch, my legs feeling stiff. Prisha smiles up at me. "You're doing great. You'll be just fine."

Frank nods. "Easy does it." I carefully position my foot on the next branch and continue climbing down as he says, "You've got this. You're gonna be fine."

Then both my feet are on solid ground, and I turn to look into the faces of my neighbors who are now smiling and blinking tears of relief. Prisha wraps the blanket around my shoulders, and I cry, too, tears that are sad and happy and grateful all at once. Because I know they're right: I will, somehow, be just fine.

Chapter Thirty-six

Lonnie called this morning.

I did not answer.

Then he texted. —*Ramona, I'll be home until noon. Please come by anytime to talk.*—

I did not text back.

I head for the hospital early—way before noon—so I won't run into Lonnie during my volunteer shift. I have nothing to say, and no patience for listening, to this man who acted like he cared for *me* while he was still engaged to *her*.

I step through the lobby doors of Cassidy Memorial, walk toward the elevators, and then I remember: mail. Reading whatever Martin sent me is the last thing I feel like dealing with right now, but since I've never checked my mailbox here, I probably should clean it out to make room for any real hospital mail that might be sent my way.

I take a flight of stairs to the basement, then pause in the doorway of the cavernous room, taking in the walls of mail cubbies. Walking past a copier machine and table with office supplies, I scan a block of cubbies labeled— *Part-time, Per Diem, Etc.*—searching for *Sadler*. My gaze darts to a cubby near the top: *Acres, Lonnie*. Just like that, a wave of anger, indignation, and heartache surges through my body so hard and fast that I need to step back to steady myself. I let out a quick breath. *Stay on task. There'll be plenty of time to fall apart later at home.* When I see—*Sadler, Ramona*—I squint in disbelief. For someone whose cubby is listed under *Etc.*, I sure do receive a fuckload of mail. My box is crammed full. I carry the pile of mail over to the table and start sorting through fliers, generic letters from hospital administration about board electees, and policy updates, a postcard reminding me to mark my calendar for Meatloaf Mondays in the hospital cafeteria. And a card and manilla envelope from Martin.

To: Ramona Sadler, Volunteer Patient Panda

From: Martin Smallwood, Distinguished professor, psychologist, and bestselling author

Ripping open the flap, I can't help but burst out laughing when I pull out the copy of *So, The Feeling Wheelhouse Turns.* There's a card attached. On its cover is a drawing of a lily with the words: *With Sympathy.* I open it and read:

Dear Ramona,

I'm sorry to hear about the loss of your mother. My sincere sympathies. Please refer to pages 79–82 to help you process your feelings of grief and move on.

Warmly, Martin

I shake my head. I guess after reading three little pages in Martin's book—like magic—I can "move on" from my grief. Chuckling, I mumble, "How about if I just move on from *you* instead? Oh, wait. I did that months ago."

I pick up the other card, open it, and stare down at the solid blue flap with bold white lettering: *Forgive Me.*

Hmm. Didn't see that one coming. Not that it matters. There's absolutely nothing Dr. Martin Smallwood could ever do or say to move the needle toward me ever wanting to date him again.

Dear Ramona,

Our breakup has brought about many conflicted feelings for me. Remorse for disappointing you, regret for taking you for granted, sadness over losing you...

Wow. That doesn't sound like Martin.

...and compassion and admiration for myself.

Ha! There he is. I keep reading.

More than anything, I feel wrongly dumped.

Yep. He's back in full swing.

But when I expressed these feelings to my mother, she told me to stop whining, grow a pair, and do everything in my power to deliver on my earlier promise to get your job back.

I snap my head. Go, Malvina!

So, I've spoken with Dean Bender. He'd like you to call him ASAP. He's expecting your call. Let's just say...it's important.

Regretfully, Martin

****

I'm greeted at the nurse's station first by Luciana, her brown eyes moist with compassion. She must have talked with James, The King of Gossip. "Ramona, sorry to hear about you and Lonnie. Anytime you need to talk or eat a pint of mint chocolate chip ice cream with friends—"

Meg looks up from her computer then holds a hand heart in front of her chest. "We're here for you, Girlfriend."

Then I look over at James.

Glancing at the wall clock, he says, "Perfect timing. I'm going for my break. I want to hear *everything*." Cupping my wrist, he leads me down the corridor to an unoccupied waiting nook, then points to the vending machine. "Remember, at times like this, candy bars do not have calories."

I take a seat. "Gotta stash of triple-dipped chocolate malt balls at home."

He sits beside me. "Even better. Crunching balls into dust between your teeth." He pats my knee. "Got your text about you and Lonnie." He gives me a sad face. "What happened?"

I sigh. "Shi-Yun showed up at Butch's house wearing their engagement ring."

James jerks back. "No."

"Yes. All this time, they've been engaged."

He shakes his head. "I can't believe this. Lonnie? A cheating bastard? Never would have guessed it."

My chest deflates. "Believe me, me neither."

He throws up his hands. "Remember the time I saw Miguel at the Road Runner Café eating Jalapeno Pie with that well-hung guy in leather pants and a fishnet tank top?"

"How could I forget? You told Miguel to pack his bags and flush the fishnet."

James gives a sheepish grin. "It was a little awkward when the guy introduced himself as Miguel's cousin Tito."

I chuckle. "Yeah, especially since you'd attended Tito's wedding earlier that summer."

"What can I say? One look at fishnet and I jump to the wrong conclusion." He taps his chin. "Which makes me wonder if—"

"If what?"

"I don't know. Maybe with Lonnie and Shi-Yun, things weren't the way they appeared."

I huff. "Shi-Yun was flashing her engagement ring with a diamond the size of a pickleball."

James frowns. "Listen, you know I have zero tolerance for infidelity. But it's mind boggling." He looks me in the eye. "You and Lonnie started out with a rock-solid friendship. That month after your mom died, Lonnie was a genuine, caring friend. Warm and gooey and strong all at once. And all that time while he sat across the table from you at The Yello Armadillo being the perfect gentleman, he had a hard-on the size of Florida in his pants."

I cough a laugh. "How do you know?"

"Because when you showed up at his place and gave him the green light, he was on you like a honey badger on a ground squirrel."

I wrinkle my nose. "Hey, how come Lonnie gets to be the honey badger and I'm the squirrel?"

James rolls his eyes. "I do not have full control over the circle of life. My point is that he's been a stand-up guy."

I sigh. "That's what hurts so much. I thought he was a stand-up guy, too. But as it turns out, he's not. Time for me to accept that sad fact and move on." I shake my head at James. "According to Martin, if I read pages seventy-nine to eighty-two of his stupid book, I can move on from my grief. Maybe it'll work for moving on from Lonnie, too."

James scratches his arm. "I swear just the mention of the M word makes my skin crawl." He snaps his head back. "Hey, why are you talking to Martin?"

"I'm not. He sent me mail. The arrogant ding-a-ling apologized. And he said he talked to Dean Bender."

James's eyes widen. "About your old job?"

"Yep. We'll see if it all pans out, but it sounds like he tried to convince Bender to rehire me." I sigh. "Getting my job back would be my ticket out of Nearly Heaven RV Park."

"It's what you've wanted all along." He winks. "But you're going to miss Prisha and her genitalia-scented candles."

I laugh. "I will miss her. And Ugly Jim and Bacon Joe and Frank and his dog. But I won't miss substitute teaching and living in a twenty-four-foot trailer."

James frowns. "I get that, but I also spent enough Friday nights at Suds and Spurs listening to you complain about Sawyer Pickens University to know it wasn't your dream job." He grins at me. "You know Sawyer's nickname, right?"

I cock my head. "No."

"It's Slim. He's gone by Slim for decades."

I laugh. "Seriously? Slim Pickens University?"

"Yep. You know, instead of going back to slim pickin's, you could take some time to regroup. Shake things up. Make a change." He cocks his head. "If you could do anything, what would it be?"

"I guess I'd want to do something that—" I shake my head.

"What?"

"Ugh. This kills me. My answer is exactly what Lonnie said when I asked him the same question."

He wriggles his fingers my way. "Give it."

"I want to do something where I can help people. You know, make a difference."

He raises his eyebrows. "Hmm," he says, "a helping profession." Then he looks at his watch and sighs. "My break time's up. Let's walk and talk." As we start back toward the nurse's station, James puts a hand on my shoulder. "In the interest of time, I'm going to state the obvious: you help people here."

"Yes, and my Patient Panda pay is amazing."

He ignores me. "You're a natural with patients, a master at putting on compression hose, and you don't toss your cookies when you're faced with poo. I'm just saying, that when it comes to considering a helping profession, keep an open mind about patient care."

We start to pass by Room Five when I pause and say to James, "Hey, I'm gonna stop in here and see—" With a quick knock on the doorframe, I step inside, ready to give a cheerful hello to Malvina. Then I stop in my tracks at the sight of the empty, stripped bed. My chest tightens. "Oh, my God." I thrust a hand onto James's arm. "Malvina."

James jerks his head. "What about her?"

My voice cracks. "She's...gone."

"Discharged this morning."

I blow air through my cheeks.

James glances my way. "I thought you knew. She made a speedier recovery than expected and is on her way back to Houston."

"Oh. That's good news. I'm glad she's feeling better."

He knits his brow. "You look upset."

"For a second, when I saw the empty bed, I thought maybe she'd—"

"Gone to The Big Kielbasa in the sky?"

I nod. "My stomach dropped that same way it did when I walked into the hospital room my mom was supposed to be in and saw the empty bed."

"Malvina is alive and well. She must have pushed

her call button ten times yesterday." He studies me. "Why so glum?"

My chest is heavy with sadness. "I guess I thought she'd say goodbye."

He gently pats my shoulder. "Speaking of goodbyes, I need to head for the nurse's station. You coming or staying?"

"I'll catch up with you later."

Pulling a chair up beside Malvina's old bed, I take a seat and find myself swallowing back tears. I thought Malvina and I had made a connection. Sure, it all started with a few laughs over bunny vibrators and meatpacker's junk, but then it got real when we shared times in our lives when we didn't feel good enough. She talked about her ex-husband. I talked about Martin…sitting straight, I dig through my purse, pull out Martin's card, and reread the part where Malvina told Martin to grow a pair and deliver on his promise to get me my job back.

I grab my phone, search through Contacts then press Call. "Hello, I'd like to speak with Dean Bender, please."

"Whom may I ask is calling?"

"This is Ramona Sadler."

"Oh, yes. He's been expecting your call. One moment, please."

I tap my foot on the floor.

When the dean answers, his voice is firm. "Ramona. I was expecting your call weeks ago."

"Yes, I just received the message from—"

He huffs. "Water under the bridge. Listen, I'm not going to candy coat this. The person we originally rehired to teach philosophy accepted a job at the University of Michigan." He coughs into the phone. "He's choosing Michigan over Texas. Good luck with snow, sucker."

I wince.

Bender goes on, "Fall semester's coming up soon. We're in a pinch. So here I am, talking to you."

"Oh, uh—"

"I'll email you the contract immediately. It's a good offer. Increased salary and benefits. You've got seventy-two hours to sign it, or I'll have to really scrape the bottom of the barrel and hire back Lester Fishstocking."

"Lester—?"

"The professor emeritus who taught Ancient Philosophy. He's old enough to have firsthand knowledge of the subject matter."

I cringe. "So—"

"So sign it. Return it. Then HR will contact you promptly."

I open my mouth to say goodbye, then glance at my phone to see that the screen is already black.

Chapter Thirty-seven

I park in Jules's driveway, taking in the homey feel of her beautiful, rustic farmhouse complete with horse weathervanes and flowery window boxes. As I step from my truck, she bounds down the steps of her wraparound porch. I stretch out my arms for a hug and say, "You deserved every minute of your vacation, but I'm so glad you're back."

She smiles. "Me, too. We had a great time on the Gulf, but I'm always happy to come home." Leading me onto the porch, she gestures to the table set up with breakfast goodies then cringes at the buzzing sound of an electric saw echoing through the screen door from inside the house. She sighs. "But being away from the kitchen remodeling for a few days just might have saved my sanity."

I look at the basket of baked goods and jars of jelly and peanut butter and grin. "Ooh, porch bagels."

Jules hands me a paper plate. "Sorry it's bare bones. With Morris and his giant tool belt in my kitchen, I don't bother to cook anymore."

I spread a heap of peanut butter on my plate, pluck a bagel from the basket, and settle into one of the rocking chairs. "When will the renovations be done?"

Jules slumps into the rocker beside mine. "God only knows." She shoots me a tired look. "We're washing dishes in the bathtub."

263

I grimace. "Ugh."

"Chase started leaving notes for me in the layer of sawdust on the countertops."

"Notes?"

"Yeah, like *I'll be back at eleven am* or *Can you pick up bread at the store?*" She rolls her eyes. "Yesterday I wrote, *How about some afternoon delight while the kids are in science camp?*" I chuckle, but Jules shakes her head. "Morris wrote back, *Sorry, ma'am. I'm a married man.*"

I laugh. "A man with a giant tool belt *and* a code of ethics. Mrs. Morris is one lucky gal." Biting into my bagel, I look out at the horses grazing on acres of pastureland that seem to go on forever. "Dang, it's beautiful here."

She grins. "Can't imagine raising Wyatt and Boone anywhere else."

I tilt my head at her. "What's happening with the bully?"

She blows air through her cheeks. "That's part of the reason we went to the Gulf. Things have escalated. The kids were on lunch break in the cafeteria, and Hawk decided to publicly break up with a girl. When the girl started crying, Wyatt and Boone intervened. They told Hawk, loudly, that a decent man treats women with respect and courtesy. Then they walked the girl to her classroom and told her teacher what happened."

I clutch my chest. "Your boys are so great."

"Chase and I said we were very proud of them for doing the right thing." She gives a wry smile. "Then we got in our truck, drove to the Astor residence, and ripped Hawk and his parents new ones." She slaps her leg. "That's right. Ripped three new assholes in a two-minute visit."

I smile. "Good for you. Did it help?"

She shrugs. "Seemed to for a few days. Then Hawk got back to his old bird shit." Rocking back in her chair, she peers out at her property. "Living here helps. The boys come home from camp, throw down their backpacks, hop on a horse, and ride their little hearts out. It's grounding." Taking a swig of orange juice, she shoots me a compassionate look. "But enough about us. How are you feeling?"

"Angry. Sad. Confused. I mean, I thought I knew him." I gaze out at the big barn and riding trails. "If you'd asked me a few days ago if Lonnie would want to live in a place like this, I would have said, 'Absolutely.' But at the intervention, when Shi-Yun flashed that photo of his late mother's smiling face at their engagement party—" I shrug. "Now I'd bet you anything that he'll be moving back to the city with Shi-Yun just in case his mom is watching from above." I lick peanut butter from my lip. "I should have known. During the road trip, Lonnie told me how much he struggled with lying to his dying mother, assuring her he'd go through with the wedding when he knew he'd call it off." I groan. "I cannot compete with deathbed guilt."

Jules shakes her head. "Guilt. What a wasted emotion. But we all get caught up in it." She waves her half-eaten bagel. "Did I ever tell you about the time, when Chase and I were first married, my mother-in-law invited me to her Kitchen Plastics party?" Biting into her bagel, she rocks back.

"Kitchen party? I don't remember that one."

She holds up a hand. "Now, I have nothing against plastic containers with lids, but I was twenty-one years old at the time and did not love the idea of spending a Saturday evening sitting in a circle with Chase's mama and a dozen middle-aged women with pantyhose bunched at their ankles. So, I lied. Told her I had a funeral to attend."

I widen my eyes and chuckle. "A funeral?"

"Funny. That's exactly what Chase's mama said in a high-pitched voice. 'A funeral? On a Saturday night?'"

I snort a laugh. "What'd you say?"

"I doubled down. Told her the deceased was a DJ, and they were having a Saturday Night Fever disco party in his honor."

I put my hand over my mouth. "Wow. When you lie, you go all in."

She sucks air through her teeth. "It was bad. Guilt City. I couldn't look Chase's mama in the eye for months." She sets down her paper plate and brushes her hands together. "Yet I have no such guilt over calling out Tiffany Dicksteiner's crusty nether regions in the church parking lot and looking her in the eye every Sunday."

I double over laughing. "It's good that your guilt has limits."

She nods. "I sure do wish Lonnie's did."

I slump back in my rocker. "Me, too. God, that night at Butch's ranch was crazy. A total shocker."

"From what you told me, it sounds like Lonnie was as shocked as you were."

"Yeah, he did seem stunned. When he first realized it was an intervention, he tried to stand up and leave, but as things progressed, he seemed almost…paralyzed. He just sat in the chair, staring at the floor."

"So, Butch and Ming were behind the whole thing?"

I tilt my head. "It didn't seem like Ming knew. A lot of her family was there. I think she thought it was just a party. But Butch has been pressuring Lonnie to go back to surgery for a while. I guess he thought if Lonnie's colleagues told him how much they missed having him in the department, it would make the difference."

Jules huffs. "I get that Butch invited Lonnie's colleagues from surgery to try to persuade him, but couldn't he have drawn the line at inviting Shi-Yun?"

"Actually, Butch didn't invite her. Shi-Yun's parents were there, and they called her."

Jules bounces her ankle. "Hmm."

"What?"

"Well, if Butch didn't invite Shi-Yun, how do you know he wants Lonnie to marry her?"

I stretch out my hands. "He started saying all this stuff about how they worried about Lonnie dating women from different backgrounds when he was younger and how happy Lonnie's mom was when he started dating Shi-Yun."

"Okay, but that's how Lonnie's *mom* felt." Jules squints out into the distance then shakes her head. "Something's missing. If Lonnie has been toying with you this whole time, you know I'm happy to go all mama bear on his ass. But you said he was as shocked by the events of that evening as you were. And, I don't know, I saw the guy during that month when you got back from Snap Peas, and he seemed so supportive and genuine. Something doesn't make sense."

I sigh. "I wish it didn't make sense to me. But I know how these things work. Lonnie looks at Shi-Yun, a well-educated surgeon from a 'good family,' and sees a lifelong fit. Then he looks at me, a substitute teacher living in an RV park, and sees a summer fling." I rub my forehead. "The moment I realized that, I was so pissed. I said, 'I'm fucking out of here.' Then I tore off my Ranch Z cap and headed for my truck."

Jules's head jerks. "You didn't ride with Lonnie?"

"No. We drove separately. He had an interview and was afraid he'd run late."

She squints at me. "After you left, he came to your trailer right away?"

"No. He showed up at my place about a half hour later."

Bouncing her foot, she asks, "What do you think he was doing at Butch's ranch all that time?"

"Who knows? Deciding on whether to toss rice or release doves after his and Shi-Yun's wedding ceremony."

Jules shakes her head. "Maybe he was setting everyone straight after you left. Just because Shi-Yun was there trying to lure Lonnie back, doesn't mean he was tempted."

"You haven't *seen* Shi-Yun."

"I've seen you. And not only are you beautiful, but you're smart, funny, and with the strike of a match to a candle wick, your bedroom smells like an heiress's vagina. There's not a red-blooded man within a hundred mile radius who could resist that shit."

I burst a laugh.

Jules leans toward me, her eyes insistent. "Just because Shi-Yun was wearing the engagement ring doesn't necessarily mean she and Lonnie are engaged."

I huff. "Of course they are. If they're not engaged, why didn't Lonnie take his ring back?"

Jules sighs. "Maybe because he's like my Chase.

The type of man who doesn't believe in taking back a gift once it's given."

I cross my arms. "Not buying it. It's his late mother's ring."

"Doesn't matter. Didn't Lonnie say he has a gentleman complex?"

I slump back, trying to take this all in. "That night at the intervention, I know what happened." I remember every detail of that night: Shi-Yun clutching her ring, the look on Lonnie's face when he saw the photo of his smiling mother, the sound of his voice when he said he'd struggled with cancelling the wedding and would do anything to make his mother happy. I remember the clenching of my gut, the pounding in my head, the crushing of my heart. I can't get my hopes up only to be crushed again.

Jules studies me, her gaze turning sad, then she gently pats my knee. "I'm sorry. It's not like Jules's hypothesis is going to take your heartache away. I guess I was hoping it was all some misunderstanding. That there's some magical explanation that would give you a fucking happy ending because that's what my best friend deserves."

"I know you want me to be happy, and I will be someday. But right now, I need to accept the sad reality." I slowly straighten my shoulders and force a grin. "But if it makes you feel any better, I'm getting half a happy ending."

Jules shoots me a quizzical look.

"I talked to Dean Bender. He offered me my job back."

Her jaw drops. "What?"

"Yep. Five-year contract with increased salary and

amazing health and dental benefits. I could buy a town house again or probably even afford a small house near campus."

"That's great!"

I nod, not feeling nearly as excited as Jules sounds.

She knits her brow. "Isn't it great?"

"It is. Except, I mean, it's the same dickhead dean and arrogant philosophy department. But it's what I've wanted all along. Right?"

She speaks slowly. "You've been through a lot over these past few months. Maybe you should take a little time to think about it."

I shrug. "The contract's only good for another forty-eight hours. After that, the dean calls Lester Fishstocking."

"Lester—?"

"It's a great contract. I can't *not* sign it." I force a smile. "I'll get my life back."

Chapter Thirty-eight

Waving a hand out my truck window, I head back down Jules's driveway and turn onto Whispering Hills Road, toward home where I'll sign the university contract and return it to Dickhead Bender. I mean, hell, Lonnie's gone back to his old life. Time for me to go back to mine.

Maybe I'll even call a realtor today. Look at town house listings and check out houses near campus. I tap the steering wheel. That's fucking exciting, right?

I come to a four-way stop, blink a tear, and whisper, "Thank God, I didn't tell him." That evening on Prisha's lawn, when Lonnie held me tight as we danced beneath shining stars and fairy lights, I came so close to saying the words—*I love you*—that had made a home and found a voice in my heart. Luckily, those words didn't pass my lips.

Thank God I managed to keep those feelings to myself as I swayed to the music, wrapped in Lonnie's embrace, my heart practically bursting with love. I rub my temple. I dodged a bullet. It was bad enough growing up in a household where the few times I said, "I love you" were met with silence then an awkward change of subject. But at least with my parents, I knew they loved me even though they couldn't say the words. But now with Lonnie still engaged to Shi-Yun? I know there wasn't a chance in hell that he loved me back.

I'm turning onto Salt Lick Trail when my phone rings. "Hey, Jules."

Her voice sounds urgent. "Hey. I just talked to Chase."

I grin. "Let me guess. He's taking you up on that offer you wrote in the sawdust on your kitchen counter. Tacos and eggplant for lunch?"

I swear I hear her head jerk back. "How'd you know? But that's not what I'm calling about."

"What's up?"

"Well, when you were here, you seemed convinced that Lonnie was going back to Shi-Yun."

"Sad, but true."

Jules speaks slowly. "If that happened, what do you think the chances are of Shi-Yun moving in with Lonnie?"

I cough. "Shi-Yun in a tiny house surrounded by chickens and sheep? Slim to none. At the intervention, she talked about a five-thousand square foot house with tennis courts and some godawful fountain."

"So, Lonnie would sell his property and move into a fancy house with Shi-Yun?"

I scrunch my face. "Well, yeah."

"Hmm. Hard to fit horses in a fountain."

I sit quiet for a moment. "I don't get it."

Jules's voice goes high. "Lonnie and Chase are talking horses."

I jerk my head.

"Chase just told me that Lonnie called this morning while I was taking the boys to science camp."

I lift my chin, looking up ahead at the sign for Nearly Heaven RV Park. "Wait. He called Chase about buying a horse?"

"From the sound of things, probably two. Chase gave him the rundown on price and temperament of a few of our geldings. Said Lonnie sounded *very* interested." She whistles. "He would look mighty good riding one of our quarter horses. Don't you think?"

I bite my lip as I turn into the RV park. "He would. But—"

"Ramona, have you talked with Lonnie?"

"I, uh…no."

"I think a heart-to-heart could clear things up."

I chew a fingernail. "He really called Chase about buying horses?"

There's a smile in her voice. "Yes. Now go talk to Lonnie."

I pull into my driveway and cut the engine, my thoughts spinning with this new information. Lonnie's buying horses? I can't imagine Shi-Yun moving onto his farm. I step from my truck. A wee part of my heart feels like it's drawing in a breath to sing, but I put it on mute. For all I know, they'll move into their city fountain house and keep Lonnie's place for weekend getaways. *Romantic* weekend getaways.

I walk across my patio, and my eye catches something taped to my trailer door. It's a card. Holding a hand to my fluttering belly, I run my finger along *Ramona*, handwritten in blue ballpoint pen. Slowly, I pull it off the door, open the envelope, then stare at the card cover—a night sky filled with shining stars. Then I open it.

Dear Ramona,

I am so very sorry about everything you were subjected to at that shit show of an intervention at Dad's house. No doubt you're angry (You have every right to *be) and confused (Well, no shit. How could you not be?) and, if I were willing to spend $29.95 to buy Martin's Feeling Wheelhouse book (not gonna happen), I'd be able to compile a long list of other feelings you may be experiencing right now. But if you're willing to hear me out, I know I can at least clear up the confusion. And hopefully some of the anger.*

You mean too much to me to let you slip away without doing everything I possibly can to try to make things right between us. So, I'm here, waiting for you. I realize it's slightly obnoxious to show up at your home uninvited (and this time I don't even have wildflowers and a man basket), but I'm here. Up a tree.

Waiting and hoping,
Lonnie

Chapter Thirty-nine

It doesn't take long for me to spot Lonnie sitting way up high in the V of thick branches in the same tree I was in mere days ago. The tree where I lost all notion of time. My leafy refuge away from people down here who sent me messages loud and clear that I'm not good enough because I don't come from a "good family." People like Lonnie. Or at least I thought that was the message he was sending me. Now I don't know what to think. My mind and heart are jumbled messes.

Standing beneath the leafy branches of the live oak, I peer up at Lonnie in khaki shorts and T-shirt. He's reading *The Black Stallion*. I clear my throat, and he raises his hand in a hesitant wave, like he's trying to take the pulse of my emotions. *Well, hell, good luck with that.* I don't even know what my emotions are right now. Part of me wants to cry happy tears over the possibility that Jules is right: that a heart-to-heart talk will clear everything up. And part of me is pissed over the possibility that he's betrayed my trust in a huge way and is engaged to Shi-Yun. In the interest of guarding my heart, I lean in to pissed off.

Planting my feet firmly on the ground, I call up to him, "What? You're waiting for a handwritten invitation to climb down and talk? I'll be at the picnic table."

I sit on top of the picnic table, my sneakers on the bench, and watch Lonnie, his book tucked in his pocket, and arms looped around branches as he digs his sneakers against tree bark and climbs down. Then he sits beside me, his body pivoted toward me, his face flashing an expression that says he's holding his breath.

I search his eyes and swallow hard. "Lonnie, I need the truth. Are you and Shi-Yun engaged?"

He looks so deeply into my eyes that I ache from the memory of the connection we had, or thought we had, the connection that felt so strong and safe and secure that it seemed impossible to break. He shakes his head, a wave of hair flopping onto his forehead. "No. We're not."

I breathe. Okay, that's a good start, but there are more stones to unturn. I narrow my eyes. "Were you and Shi-Yun engaged while we were on the road trip?"

His brow knits. "No."

I place my palms flat on the table to steady myself, my chin trembling in anticipation of my next question. "Were you dating Shi-Yun while I was in Snap Peas with my mom?"

Lonnie must sense the level of heartbreak a "yes" to that question would bring with it because his face appears suddenly stricken. "Absolutely not."

I blink up at the sky, my eyes stinging with tears. "If what you're saying is true, then what the hell was all that at the intervention?" He opens his mouth to say something, but I go on, "Shi-Yun wearing the engagement ring? You saying you'd do anything to give your mother what she wanted, when what she wanted was for you to marry Shi-Yun?"

Lonnie reaches for my hand, but I pull it away. I want to trust him again. I want to…love him again. But I need to understand what happened that night first.

He swallows hard. "The intervention was surreal. I was in shock until the moment I saw you run out that door. Then I finally shook off my paralysis and grew some cajónes. I was furious at my dad, colleagues, and Shi-Yun. They don't get to tell me what to do with my life. More importantly, when it comes to you, they don't get to mess up a good thing, a wonderful thing." He holds out his hands. "After you left, I told my former colleagues to bug the fuck off. I told my father to butt the hell out." His eyes turn fiery. "Then I told Shi-Yun that just because I'm the kind of man who doesn't believe in taking back a gift once it's given—"

I draw in a sharp breath. *Dang, that Jules.*

He huffs. "—does *not* mean we're engaged."

I'm quiet for a moment, listening to the pounding of my chest. "Then what happened?"

"Then I stormed out. The way I should have at the very beginning."

I slowly nod as I look into his eyes then take in his handsome face: the stubble on his square jaw, his full lips, and that ridiculous dimple on his right cheek. I want to wrap my arms around his muscular shoulders, press my face into his warm neck, and cry those happy tears that a heart-to-heart talk has cleared everything up. But I can't. Not yet. I draw in a breath. "There's something else I don't understand. When Butch and Ming brought me the Ranch Z cap, I assumed they knew about what happened on the road trip. I mean, not that anything really happened, it was just a kiss. But then at Butch's house, when you put your arm around me, they looked surprised, like they didn't know we were dating."

He nods. "You're right. They didn't know."

My chest caves. "That night, when I realized you

hadn't even told them we were seeing each other, and Shi-Yun showed up 'engaged,' I thought I was some little secret on the side."

He slumps forward. "God, Ramona. It never occurred to me you'd think that." He looks at me with sad eyes. "I didn't tell Dad about what happened on the road trip because I felt awkward about the timing. I mean, it sounds kind of bad—me putting the moves on you during a trip to visit your sick mom. Then when you came back to Texas, we were friends for a while."

"Until things heated up." I cock my head. "But you kept that under wraps, too."

He chuckles. "I wasn't about to pick up the phone and say, 'Hey, Dad. Ramona and I have romantic feelings for one another.' No offense, but guys don't do that."

A grin sweeps across my face.

Lonnie's eyes flash tenderness. "Besides, I figured, on some level, they already knew by the way I talked about you all the time."

I arch an eyebrow. "Really?"

"Oh, yeah. And I knew it would be obvious when they saw us together, which it was. I wasn't hiding anything."

It's true. That night, Lonnie didn't hesitate to hold my hand or put his arm around me. He wasn't hiding us as a couple.

He arches an eyebrow. "Have I cleared up the confusion yet?"

I gaze out into my backyard. "You're sure you were absolutely clear with Shi-Yun? You know, sometimes people hear what they want to hear."

"Oh, I was clear. I took the ring back."

"Really?"

"Yep. It's in my nightstand drawer. My gentleman complex protested, but I told it to go to Hell." He reaches for my hand again, and this time, I slide my hand into his. He sighs. "Good. The confusion's cleared up. But I bet you're still angry. Here, I told you we were going to my dad's house for an intimate gathering, and you made the effort to put on those sexy jeans and cute camisole and shave your legs and—"

I squint at him. "How do you know I shaved my legs?"

He gives me a look like, *please.* "Of course you shaved your legs. You knew what we'd be doing after we left Dad's house."

I chuckle, feeling exhausted and relieved all at once. "Anger's cleared up, too. I mean, how could I stay mad when I found you in my tree reading *The Black Stallion*?"

He cocks an eyebrow. "Nice touch?"

I cup both of my hands around his, practically shuddering from his warmth. "Nice touch."

His eyes plead. "Ramona, I'm sorry. When I thought about that night, how you must have felt seeing all that transpire…I'm just so sorry."

"I'm sorry you had to go through all that, too. All that pressure from your dad and colleagues and Shi-Yun."

He nods. "Thanks, but I'm not." I shoot him a quizzical look, and he explains, "I mean, it sucked. But this entire year, I've known that people at work were talking. I could feel the judgment from coworkers. Not to mention my father's disappointment. Then when Shi-Yun showed up—" He shakes his head, looking

279

suddenly exhausted. "The shock of it all helped me finally say what I needed to say to everyone."

I place my hand on his jaw and bring my lips to his so softly, it's like a whisper. He whispers back with the tender touch of his lips, and, in an instant, my heart feels strong and safe and full enough to soften into a gooey, sugary mess, like a Valentine's box of chocolates in the warm sunshine. We linger in that kiss, a kiss so gentle and loving and healing that I know I should cry happy tears, but instead I'm suddenly sad.

Lonnie wipes the fat tear rolling down my cheek. "Hey, what's the matter?"

"The only part that still stings for me about that night is—" My voice cracks. "I thought Butch liked me."

Lonnie knits his brow. "He does like you."

"To an extent. When you kissed my forehead that night, let's just say, he did not look thrilled. I think he likes me as long as I know my place."

Lonnie sighs. "Ramona, he was surprised. That's all."

I shake my head. "I don't know. I remember Butch saying it was one thing for you to date women from different backgrounds when you were younger, but now that you're older, you need to make smart decisions. I think he was talking about you choosing Shi-Yun over me."

He snaps his head back. "What? No. I'm sorry you thought that, but Dad was talking about Candy Hamms."

I shoot him a look like, *Who the fuck is Candy Hamms?* Then I say, "Who the fuck is Candy Hamms?"

Lonnie sighs. "I was a nineteen-year-old college sophomore home from Stanford for summer break. Candy was a twenty-eight-year-old barber who drank tequila three shots at a time and lived in the studio apartment over Teddy's Shoe Repair." He shrugs. "I was head over heels for Candy, and her tequila. Dad thought I was going to drop out of college and move in with Candy. He was worried she'd derail my ambitions."

I grin. "Candy Hamms."

He widens his eyes. "And the joke's on Dad. Candy's done well for herself. Turned out she has quite the entrepreneurial spirit. Owns a Texas chain of hair styling salons."

My jaw drops. "Wait. Candy Cuts?"

"Yep. Candy Cuts. One Cut Above the Rest. And she owns Hamms Bone Bar-B-Que."

"Oh, my God! The Best Bone Money Can Buy."

"That's the one."

I flash him a mischievous smile. "You could have been a hair and ham bone mogul."

"Lonnie Hamms. Somehow not tempting."

"Or Candy Acres. Could have had a theme park with your names on it."

He chuckles then brushes his thumb along my jaw. "I don't want Candy Hamms. Or Shi-Yun Wang. I want you, Ramona Sadler."

My chest warms then my brow furrows. "I'm afraid your dad may never approve of the two of us. He also talked about you dating women from 'good families.' I have the sneaky suspicion that, in his eyes, my family doesn't fit the mold." Lonnie winces, and I sigh. "That one burned me to the core."

Lonnie takes my hands in his. "Sometimes my dad says shit. I'm sorry. He'd better not have meant that." He kisses my forehead. "Listen, that night was confusing on so many levels. The surprise number of guests, the intervention, Dr. Hummer wearing corduroys in ninety-degree weather." I chuckle, and he searches my eyes. "And quite frankly, something you said a little while ago."

I tilt my chin. "What?"

"You said that on the road trip, nothing really happened."

"I just meant, you know, we didn't—"

"We may not have had to put up the sign, 'If the trailer's a rockin', don't come a knockin'.' But that doesn't mean nothing happened." He pulls me into him, his smell of pine, honey, and leather making my knees feel weak, and says, "For me, that kiss? It was like *everything* happened."

Chapter Forty

"Where's that sign when we need it?" Lonnie murmurs, his hand skating along my bare thigh as he presses his warm mouth against my neck.

I roll my body up on top of his, straddling him as I dig my hands into my bed sheet. "The one that says, 'If the trailer's a rockin'—?' "

He looks up at me, his gaze sweeping from my eyes to my lips, down my throat then lingering on my breasts, causing every cell in my body to tingle. "That's the one." Sliding his hands along my waist and ribcage, he then firmly cups my breasts, making my nipples squeeze beneath the fabric of my bra. He shakes his head slightly. "This won't do." His eyes are dark with passion as he unhooks my bra then lets out a soft groan as the straps fall from my shoulders. Then he devours me. One breast at a time. Instinctively, my thighs tighten around his hips, and I gasp at the feel of the length of him between my legs growing ever harder. Rocking my hips against him, I'm suddenly desperate to tear off my panties, to remove any barrier between his body and mine.

As if he read my mind, he rolls me to the side and slides my panties down over my hips and down my legs, taking a moment to tug his briefs free from his body. As he kneels between my legs, I look at him, taking in his form, his angles and contours, marveling over my visceral excitement at the mere sight of him. Yet sight's not enough. I want to experience Lonnie with every one of my senses, breathing in his manly scent, tasting his salty skin, hearing his heart pound in his chest, feeling his skin against mine. I'm about to reach for him, to pull his hips toward me, to take him in my mouth, but Lonnie's lowering his face to my parted legs, teasing me with his tongue, raking his stubbled jaw against the insides of my thighs higher and higher. When his mouth lands in the center of my being, my back arching in response to heavenly pleasure, he takes me higher still.

At some point, as my body pulses with desire teetering on the edge of bursting into all the stars and planets in the universe, I hear the faint snap of a condom wrapper being torn, the slick swoosh of it being rolled on from head to base. I moan as Lonnie enters me so tortuously slowly that I swear time has no beginning or end. He cups a hand on the back of my neck gently, moving carefully inside of me as he looks into my eyes. His gaze smiles and softens into mine with each rock of his hips, each unhurried, attentive push of his hardness deeper inside of me, then deeper still until, like flashes of lightning before a good steady rain, we both come undone and together all at once.

We sit on my bed, our backs propped against pillows, as Lonnie traces a finger over my bare shoulder. "The last few days without you have felt like a lifetime."

I nod his way. "I suppose we have some catching up to do."

He grins. "I think we just did that. But…what's new?"

I glance up at the ceiling. "Hmm. Let me see. Yesterday at the hospital, I thought Malvina had gone to the big stuffed schnitzel in the sky, but it turns out she only went back to Houston." I sigh. "I kind of miss her." I think about Malvina. Her matted house slippers and tripe stew. Her surprise visit and excitement over Martin's and my "engagement." Her telling me not to let anyone ever imply I'm not good enough. Her being there one day and gone the next. "You know, as much as Malvina freaked me out when I first met her, she turned out to be really cool. Long story short, she helped me get my job back."

Lonnie blinks. "Really?"

"Yep. Dean Bender sent me the contract to sign. It's a great offer. Higher salary. Awesome benefits. Hell, Bender even threw in upgraded faculty parking and free gym membership." I look around my tiny bedroom. "My trailer was someplace to stay when my life unraveled, but I can't wait to have a real place in downtown Jackalope again." I shoot him an earnest look. "It's not like Jackalope is far from here."

He pffts. "Like a fifteen-minute drive in my truck is going to keep me from seeing you every day. Good luck with that."

I startle at my phone's ringtone and wince at the screen. Dean Bender. "God, speak of the devil."

I pick up on the third ring. Bender's voice is tense. "The clock is ticking, Sadler." I glance at Lonnie who's narrowing his eyes at the sound of Bender's tone.

"But, I thought I had seventy-two hours to sign the contract. And it's only been, like, a day and a half."

Bender clears his throat. "Last fall, you were fired. A day and a half ago, I offered you your job back with better pay and benefits. What's there to think about?"

"I, uh—"

"You, uh, have a degree from Idaho *State*." I bristle

at his sarcasm, and he adds, "I thought you'd jump at the chance to sign my offer."

I sit straight and push my shoulders back. *He thought I'd jump at the chance to sign his contract? Just like Martin thought I'd jump at the chance to marry him.* "Dean Bender, according to the offer, I have until tomorrow evening at ten o'clock to sign."

"Like I said, tempus fugit. If I don't have the signed contract tomorrow night, Lester Fishstocking wins the prize."

I hang up, roll my eyes, and grumble to Lonnie, "Dickhead Bender."

He rubs a hand on my arm. "Do you really want to work for that guy again?"

"He's definitely not my dream boss, but it's such a good offer."

"Yet, you haven't signed it. Wanna talk about why?"

"I was going to sign it this morning, but I got kind of…busy." I cock an eyebrow. "Hey, what about you? Any news on the job hunt front?"

He smiles. "I interviewed for a position in Cassidy Memorial's hospice wing."

I bring a hand to my lips. "You'd help hospice patients?"

His eyes deepen in thought. "During the interview, I spoke with staff members and spent time with the patients, and it clicked. This is where my heart is: supporting patients at end of life. Then, when they offered me the position—"

I clasp my hands in front of my chest. "That's great! I mean, I'm not surprised. They're lucky to have you, but—" I take his hand. "It's such meaningful work. It's just…wonderful."

"Thank you. It feels like the right fit."

I bite my lip. "Maybe I shouldn't ask, but how does Butch feel about you being a hospice doctor?"

He shrugs. "Don't know. We haven't talked since the intervention." I sigh, and Lonnie shoots me a reassuring look. "He sent me a text asking if we could get together. I said it's a good idea, but I need a little time. We'll figure it out. Somehow, we always do. My dad and I have a long history of butting heads. Sometimes over the most ridiculous things."

"Like—?"

"Like, a while ago I mentioned to him that I was thinking about getting horses."

"Oh, yeah! Jules told me you talked to Chase. That's so exciting."

He grins. "That's the reaction of a normal person, especially considering that I already have twenty acres of fenced pastureland." He rolls his eyes. "Dad told me I should get my head examined." He shakes his head. "That's my dad. But I'm excited about the horses. Chase has a couple of geldings for sale that sound amazing. Steady, affectionate temperaments. Athletic. Gorgeous." He leans close to me. "Hmm. Just like you."

I inch my body toward him. "Well, if you want to get some riding practice in, just let me know." Tangling my hand in his hair, I nibble his lips. "I'm a big fan of the way you never giddyup until I'm satisfied with your sit trot."

Chapter Forty-one

Lonnie and I sit cross-legged on a thick blanket in front of the firepit in my backyard. It's evening. The sun is beginning to set. Lonnie's got a fire going, and we stare into the red flames, listening to the wood crackle and pop. I draw in a deep breath. "Okay. Time to do this."

Lonnie gestures to the notebook in my lap. "You first?"

I write in my notebook, its pages illuminated by the glow of the fire, then rip out the page, and look at Lonnie for reassurance before reading the sentence aloud. "I wish I had visited my mom more."

He gently rubs my back then gazes into my eyes. "It's okay to have regrets. Are you ready to let that one go?"

Nodding, I fold the paper, then lean forward and set it in the firepit, watching its edges catch then burn until it's engulfed in flames.

Lonnie grins warmly. "Goodbye, guilt?"

"Goodbye, guilt. Or as Jules calls it, the wasted emotion." I reach over and place my hand on his leg. "Your turn."

He picks up his notebook and takes a minute or two to scroll words on the page. Tearing off the paper, he looks at me, then reads what he wrote. "I wish I'd been strong enough to be honest with my mom when she asked me to promise that the wedding would go on. Being honest with her would have been the respectful thing to do. And she deserved that respect." He folds the paper in two, sets it in the firepit, and quietly watches it burn until there's nothing left but ash.

I ask softly, "Goodbye, guilt?"

He nods, audibly exhaling. "Yeah. In fact, that felt good."

I write a note, rip off the page, and read it. "I wish I'd been more involved in Mom's medical care after her heart attack. I should have—"

Lonnie lifts his finger. "Remember the rules: no shoulds."

I cross out "should have" then recite the edited version. "If I had to do it over again, I would have taken her to some of her doctors' appointments." I pause, allowing myself space to imagine what that might have been like. Driving my mom to the appointment, being with her in the waiting area and exam room. Having the opportunity to ask the doctor questions and clarify any confusion. On the way home, I would have treated Mom to lunch anywhere she wanted to eat. I look Lonnie in the eye. "I really wish I'd done that." A sad smile sweeps across my face. "It would have been nice. I think Mom would have appreciated it." I crumple the paper into a ball, toss it into the flames, and sigh. "Goodbye, guilt."

Lonnie writes for a bit then holds up his paper. "I wish—" He closes his eyes. "I *really* wish I'd taken a break from work to spend time with my mom after she was diagnosed with cancer." His voice cracks. "If only I'd given her more of my time."

"It's okay to have regrets. I know I'm not supposed to add comforting sentiments because this exercise is about burning our guilt to the ground, but—" I search his eyes. "—I have no doubt that every minute you were at work, your mom still knew how very much you loved her."

He kisses my cheek, then balls up the paper, tosses it into the flames, and whispers, "Letting go of my guilt. I love you, Mom."

Holding up my final note, I feel tears sting my eyes. "I wish I'd spent less time being embarrassed by my mom." I choke out a sob. "And more time being proud of her."

Lonnie pulls me into him, and I bury my head against his warm chest. Then he says softly, "What did you tell me you told your mom in her final days?"

I wipe my face with my hand. "That I love her."

He holds me closer. "And?"

"And that I hit the jackpot having her as my mom."

He kisses my hair. "And when you told her at the end that she was brave, what else did you say?"

"That I'm so proud of her." I'm quiet for a moment, listening to Lonnie's heartbeat, then I slowly sit straight, and place the paper in the firepit, watching it catch, the flames burning bright. I look at Lonnie. "You know, it was funny. Near the end, when Mom and I were talking, she told me she'd always wanted to visit me in Texas. Then she got all excited about packing up and going on the trip." I look up at the sky. "I was surprised because she was always such a homebody, and at that point, she was too sick to travel to Texas, but she said she was ready to pack her bags and go."

Lonnie smooths my hair. "Yeah, my mom talked about getting ready to go on a trip, too. At the time, we thought she was disoriented, but now that I'm delving into hospice care, I realize it's a common theme." He grins sadly, and I notice a tear trickling down his face. "They're ready to go on their journey."

"Yes. That makes sense." I write one final note then hold it up to read. "Happy travels, Mommy."

Smiling, Lonnie writes a note, then waves it toward the sky. "Happy travels, Mom."

It's a cloudy night, but I make out a few stars sparkling, reminding me of the Eskimo proverb that Wyatt and Boone wrote in their card to me: *Perhaps they are not stars in the sky, but rather openings where our loved ones shine down to let us know they are happy*. I point to the stars and nod Lonnie's way. "They're twinkling. Our moms are happy."

He turns to me, gently kisses my lips, and murmurs, "I'm happy, too."

Car tires crunch on gravel, and we both turn to look. Lonnie frowns toward the Prairie Pizza sign. "They weren't supposed to deliver until eight-thirty." He stands, walks over, and I watch him chat with the delivery fellow. Then Lonnie bursts into laughter. He returns carrying six extra-large pizza boxes. Nodding at the surprised look on my face, he says, "There was a mix-up with our order. They called the delivery guy on his way over here, but since the frat house that was supposed to receive these is on the other side of town, we're getting these for free."

My jaw drops. "That's a lot of pizza." I stand up and nod at Lonnie. "Well, there's only one thing to do. I'll be right back."

When I knock on Prisha's door, she opens it and smiles. "Ramona, to what do I owe the pleasure?"

"It's Saturday night. Lonnie and I have enough

Prairie Pizza to feed an army. Time to party. Spread the word."

"Will do. Anything I can bring?" I crane my neck to see Frank sitting on her sofa, his dog curled on the rug next to his feet. "Patio chairs. Drinks if you've got them." I wink. "And don't forget your handsome schnauzer owner."

Chapter Forty-two

My outdoor space may not have fairy lights and potted hibiscus. Hell, it doesn't even have patio furniture. But tonight, the mood outside my trailer is bright and colorful. My neighbors brought over lawn chairs and folding tables, potluck appetizers and desserts, and coolers crammed with soda and beer. Prisha spread the word fast, and now a couple dozen people are chatting, laughing, and lining up at my picnic table for pizza slices.

Lonnie and I are handing a plate of food to Bacon Joe, who's playing country music through the portable speakers he set up on my patio, when I look over to see Jules and her family walk toward us. I run over, spreading my arms out wide. Jules and Chase set down their six-packs of soda and wine coolers, and I give them big hugs, then smile. "Hey, glad you guys could make it." Then I wave at Wyatt carrying folding chairs, and Boone, holding a big package of store-bought cupcakes.

Jules smiles at Lonnie before pulling him into an embrace. "So good to see you again."

Chase and Lonnie are giving each other bro hugs, when Prisha and Myra join our group. Prisha beams, wrapping an arm around Myra, then says to me and Lonnie, "You remember my granddaughter."

I introduce Prisha to Jules and Chase. Then Myra waves at Wyatt and Boone. They grin, their faces turning red. Wyatt sets down his chairs and gives a quick wave. "Hey, Myra."

I look up. "Oh, that's right. Y'all know each other from science camp."

Jules nods sudden recognition. "Yes. Hi, Myra."

Myra smiles then asks the boys, "Are you guys learning about bubble cell membranes with Mr. Gupta?"

Shaking his head, Boone says, "No, we're extracting DNA from onions with Mrs. Jackson."

Prisha grins. "Bubble cell membranes and onion DNA. You kids are making me hungry. So, you're in different classes?"

Wyatt pipes up, "Yes, ma'am. But everyone has recess and lunch together."

Myra sticks her hands into her jean pockets and huffs. "Which would be fun if we didn't all have to deal with stupid Hawk Astor. He's the worst."

I look at Jules, who nods and says, "Hawk? Yeah, he is the worst."

Prisha shakes her head. "Yep, that kid's a real dickwad."

Myra winces, then bursts a laugh. "Nani! You're lucky Mom's not here. She'd make you put a quarter in the cuss jar."

We all laugh. Prisha shrugs. "I call it like it is. Hawk's a bully." She looks at the boys. "You two gentlemen know that bullies are just trying to overcompensate for their shortcomings, right?" The boys look a bit confused, but nod anyway. Prisha raises her eyebrows. "It's like my meatpacker's candle. You know, short wick."

Myra drags a hand over her face and giggles as the boys laugh. Then Myra pinches her chin. "Nani, can we take a few eggs from your refrigerator?" Then Myra says to the boys, "Wanna start the eggshell experiment?"

Boone's eyes widen. "Yeah, we can grab some plastic cups and sodas."

Wyatt looks at his mom. "It's the experiment where you see what affect sugary drinks have on eggshells, which is similar to tooth enamel."

Jules nods. "Sounds good. After that, start the experiment where you see what affect brushing your teeth after every meal has on our dental bills."

Chase laughs. "I'll second that one."

Wyatt and Boone roll their eyes.

Prisha pats Myra's shoulder. "Help yourself to eggs." She gestures toward the pizza line at the picnic table. "And get something to eat."

Boone hands his mom the cupcakes, then grabs two sodas from the six-pack before the three of them run off. Then Prisha quickly turns toward the patio at the sound of the song, "Bom Diggity Diggy" playing, and we all look over to see Frank waving at her. She bursts into laughter. "Well, I guess I'm off to diggy."

Ten minutes later, Jules, Chase, Lonnie, and I are settled in lawn chairs, balancing paper plates on our laps and drinking beer from the can. Lonnie and Chase have paired off and are deep in conversation. They're talking horses.

Jules and I are talking boys.

Taking a bite of pizza, Jules eyes me. "So, things are good?" She wipes a string of mozzarella from the corner of her mouth.

I swig some beer. "Very good. Tomorrow night Lonnie's taking me to Bowl-a-Roll."

She chokes a laugh. "Seriously?"

"Yep. Says he wants to get some bowling practice in so he doesn't make a complete fool of himself when we're in Snap Peas next week."

She winks. "He'll be the first man on the planet who actually looks good in those stupid, rented shoes."

I chuckle. "What about Chase?"

Jules jokes, "Are you kidding? My cowboy only wears boots." Looking over at Chase and Lonnie drinking beer and talking up a storm, she asks, "You'll both stay with Earl?"

"Yeah, a week on his new sleeper sofa." I take a big bite of pizza.

She raises her eyebrows. "Hope it's got good springs."

I groan. "There's no way in hell I can have sex on that sofa with Earl snoring in the next room."

"You got a point there."

"It's going to be torture. I'll be a frothy mess hanging around Lonnie for a week, watching him eat cube steak and bowling strikes in those stupid striped shoes. I mean, how much can a girl take?"

She laughs. "I'm sure you'll make up for lost time when you get back home." She tilts her head. "Actually, school will be in session soon after you come back. Have you made a decision about jobs?"

I bolt straight so fast that my beer splashes from the can. "Oh, shit. I forgot to call Dean Bender."

"Last time you talked with Bender, didn't he tell you to sign the offer soon or Lester Fishstocking wins the prize?"

Pulling my phone from my pocket, I nod. "Yep. Sure did." I scroll to Bender and type a message. Then I sit back, cross my legs, and take a long swig of beer.

Jules cocks her head. "What'd you tell him?"

I smile as I read the message aloud. "And the mule's ass trophy goes to…Lester Fishstocking."

Her jaw drops into a big smile. "Good for you!"

"Thanks. I'm still not sure what I want to do professionally, but while I'm figuring that out, my substitute teaching job gives me the flexibility to explore options and to move on when I find something. Lonnie says that whatever's in store for me will reveal itself the way the hospice doctor opportunity revealed itself to him. And I think he's right."

She nods. "I'll miss having you around at Slim Pickens, but I think he's right, too." Her eyes shine mischievously. "Now you need to text Martin. Tell him thanks for nothing and that he can stick the Dean Bender contract up his—"

I laugh. "Thanks for the reminder." I pick up my phone again, unblock Martin, then type him a message.

Jules shoots me a curious look. "Come on, show me."

I hold out my phone, and she reads aloud, "Thank you for talking to Bender. I'm not taking the job, but the offer brought closure." Jules looks at me and frowns. "Seriously?"

I grin. "Keep reading."

She squints at the message. "Thanks, and good luck." She snorts a laugh. "The signature line on the sympathy card Wyatt and Boone gave you."

"It's a classic."

She sits back. "Well, I was hoping for something more vindictive, but at least you can finally close that chapter. No more Smallwood. No more Mama Malvina."

I grin. "Actually, about Malvina…she sent me a

card. Mailed it here, to the RV park. The cover has two hedgehogs clinking champagne glasses. It says, 'Sending hedgehugs.' "

Jules slaps her knee. "Well, dang. That's kind of cute."

"Yeah, she said she was thinking about me." I feel suddenly verklempt. "Said she always wanted a daughter. Gave me an open invitation to Houston for a girls' weekend with plenty of booze and candles and the best part: no Martin allowed. It'll be kind of nice to have a mother figure in my life. I mean, Malvina's a really unconventional mother figure, but my mom wasn't exactly traditional."

We turn toward the sounds of laughter in the distance coming from the boys and Myra as they sit on the grass eating pizza and drinking sugary sodas. Jules looks around, her eyes appearing starry. "You know there are worse things than living in Nearly Heaven."

I clink her beer can to mine. "I just might be starting to get used to that idea."

"Sometimes life comes with surprises."

"Yeah. Like the other day. You know how Earl and I are pen pals? Well, in his last letter, he sent me a check." She jerks her head back, and I explain, "Turns out Mom had life insurance. I mean, it wasn't a huge amount, and, of course, most of her insurance goes to Earl for living expenses. But she designated a chunk to me and Ricky." My throat thickens. "Here, my mom never had squat financially, yet she makes sure she leaves money to her grown kids."

Jules looks over at her boys then back at me and smiles. "Of course she did. She's your mom." She places her hand on my knee. "Giving to you and Ricky is what makes her happy. Even now."

I sit back, my eyes intuitively blinking up at the night sky. The clouds have cleared, and the stars are shining bright. *I'm glad you're happy, Mommy. And just so you know, I may not have a twinkling star to tell you, but I'm happy, too.*

Chapter Forty-three

I sit on Lonnie's deck, looking out at the barn and fenced pastureland where, soon, two American quarter horses will be grazing, running, and kicking up their hooves. I clap my hands in front of my chest. "Tell me all about the horses. I wanna know everything."

Lonnie sets his coffee mug under his chair. "Sage is a buckskin. He's a good barrel racer, great on trails, and isn't barn or buddy sour."

I bite my bottom lip. "You sound so…horsey."

He grins. "Then there's Spirit. He's a big boy, a sixteen-hand bay. Only four years old, but real levelheaded. Good ranch horse, and he's shown well at reining and versatility classes."

"Sage and Spirit." I let out a long exhale. "Can't wait 'til they're here."

"Glad to hear that because I'm planning on putting you to work." He winks. "Mucking stalls, stacking hay bales."

I chew on my knuckle, feeling so excited that I'm practically jumping out of my skin. My childhood dream is about to come true. Lonnie's getting horses, and he told me I'm welcome to ride them anytime I want. "I'll do anything. Pick hooves, comb manes. Hell, I'll even clean tack if you want me to."

He reaches over and strokes my arm. "It's a plan. But before you go all farmhand on me, we have a very busy week ahead of us."

Tomorrow, Lonnie and I fly off to Snap Peas for a week.

He grins. "I'm stoked for bowling, meat raffles, and belching contests with Earl and Ricky."

"Don't forget corn bag tossing and bingo." I smile. "Then the day after we get back, Chase delivers Sage and Spirit."

He tilts his head. "I'm excited about the horses, but I'm really looking forward to getting to know your family."

"Just remember not to pull anyone's thumb."

"Oh, I'm beating them to the punch. I've been practicing farting on command. Got the thumb and finger pulls down solid."

I cough a laugh.

He raises an eyebrow. "How are you feeling about the visit?"

I draw in a breath. "Good. It'll be nice to spend time with Earl, see how he's managing without Mom, and look for ways to be helpful. And it'll be good to see Ricky and Tina."

He grins. "Sounds like you've warmed up to Tina."

"Yeah, I realized I've been unfair to her. She loved Mom, too. Ricky and Tina are having us all over to their house for dinner." I wink. "Get ready for an evening of defrosted burger patties and jalapeno mashers."

"Yum."

I lift my face to the breeze. "Earl and Ricky said we should go through some of Mom's stuff together. That'll be hard, but…you know, good." I exhale. "I mean, I'll cry. A lot. But that's fine. It kind of keeps her with me, you know?"

He leans over and gives my cheek a gentle kiss. "Yes, I do. I still think about my mom a lot, but there are times I go about my life for a few days and don't think about her once. Most people would probably say that's progress, like the goal is to move on and be grief-free. But I usually feel a little sad when I realize my mom didn't visit my thoughts that day."

"I like the way you said that. My mom's still visiting."

He turns his chair to face me. "I wish I'd had time to get to know your mom better. I know I would have loved her because she was your mom." He looks so deeply into my eyes that I swear he could describe every detail of my heart and soul. "And I love you." I bring a hand to my mouth, and Lonnie shakes his head ever so slightly, a grin sweeping across his face. "Confession time: I know you think my feelings for you developed on the road trip, but I fell for you way before tofu dogs."

I chuckle. "No way."

"Oh, yeah. Why do you think I gave you such a hard time about your volunteer paperwork? I was like some lovesick schoolboy socking the girl of his dreams in the arm at recess." I smile, feeling tears sting my eyes as he goes on, "But it all makes some kind of crazy sense. Because the question for me has never been whether or not I love you. The question has always been: how could I not love you, Ramona?"

I gaze into Lonnie's eyes, my heart—hell, my world—brimming with warmth and passion, bliss and knowing. "Lonnie, I love you." I pull his face near mine, touch my lips to his, then I hear a vehicle pull into the driveway.

Lonnie lets out a long exhale at the sight of Butch's

SUV. "Guess I needed to talk to Dad one of these days. But, dang, the man's timing sucks."

I squint toward the vehicle, at Butch sitting stiffly in front of the steering wheel and Ming perched in the passenger seat, the memories from that godawful intervention suddenly flooding in, drowning me in shock and hurt and anger. Butch was the one who set the whole night from hell in motion. I try to breathe through the tightness in my chest then I look at Lonnie. "I should give y'all time to yourselves. You know, to talk things through."

He shakes his head. "There's nothing that can't be said in front of you."

I bite my knuckle. "Here's the thing: Butch is your father and you two have stuff to mend. That should be the top priority."

"It's not just about me and him. That night was no picnic for you either."

"Which is why I should leave. Because I'm pissed off all over again." My jaw tightens. "I know you explained the whole Candy Hamms thing, but the bottom line is, Butch doled out the phrase 'good family' like he was serving up slow cooker wieners at a church potluck. And I know his criteria for a 'good family' excludes families like mine." I shake out my arms, trying to relax the tension in my body. "Yep, I'm mighty pissed."

Lonnie nods. "You should be. I'm pissed, too."

I hear the SUV doors close and suck in my cheeks. "You're sure I should stay? Gotta warn you, I'm feeling scrappy."

Lonnie stands and reaches for my hand. "I'm sure. Have at it."

Butch walks toward the deck, his elbow linked with

303

Ming, who carries a huge red handbag. Lonnie and I walk down the wooden steps and meet them on the stone patio. I study the two—Butch in pressed jeans and white shirt, looking tan and healthy, Ming in white skinny jeans and blue blouse, her hair teased to new volumes. Neither is smiling, but I can't tell whether that's due to anger or nervousness.

Butch squarely faces Lonnie. "Son, the last time I saw you, you were telling me to butt the hell out of your life."

Lonnie lifts his chin. "Considering the evening, sounds about right."

Butch turns to me. "And, Ramona, you were throwing your Ranch Z cap on the floor and storming out of my house without so much as a goodbye."

I nod. "And I'd do it all over again."

His head jerks back the slightest bit, and I take a step toward him. "You know, Butch. I know you and Lonnie have a lot to talk about, but first, I have something I need to get off my chest."

Squinting, he tilts his head. "Go on."

I feel my gaze grow fiery. "That night, you seemed to be equating education, wealth, and career status with the definition of a 'good family.' "

Butch flashes a confused look then opens his mouth to say something.

I hold up my hand. "I'm here to tell you that your definition of a 'good family' is more than just limited. It's asinine. My parents have GED's, are poor as shit, and retired from entry-level jobs." I lift my chin. "It's taken me a while to get here, but I'm proud as hell of them." Bringing a fist to my chest, I say slowly, articulating each word, "I come from a good family."

Butch blinks. "Ramona, when I said that, I never intended to insult you or your family. I had no idea—"

I raise my eyebrows. "Well, now you do, Butch. So, choose your words more carefully next time."

Ming smacks her handbag against Butch's arm. "She's right. If I had a Chinese Yuan for every time I told this old bean goose the same thing—"

"I…uh." Butch suddenly sounds tired. "Can we sit down?"

We all move to the table and take seats—Lonnie and I on one side and Butch and Ming on the other.

Butch clears his throat. "I guess I should have led with this, but I came here to apologize to you both." He looks at Lonnie. "Son, I was a stubborn fool."

I glance up at Lonnie, who cocks his head at Butch and says, "That's a start."

Butch nods. "I convinced myself that all I was doing was inviting a few of your former colleagues over to tell you how much they want you back in the department. I justified it by assuring myself that your mother wouldn't have wanted you to leave surgery because you were grieving her loss." He shakes his head. "But the truth is, I had a vision for you and your life, and I did everything in my power to push that vision on you." He looks at Ming. "After everyone left, Ming read me The Riot Act."

Ming purses her lips. "I read him Acts One, Two, and Three. Let's just say it was not his favorite play."

Butch nods. "Drama City." Crossing his arms on the table, he leans toward Lonnie. "Son, I was wrong. It's your life. Your career. Your choice. I'm sorry. I hope someday you can forgive me."

Lonnie draws in a deep breath and swallows hard. "I appreciate your apology, Dad." He gently rubs my shoulder. "But it wasn't just me you hurt that night."

Butch blows air through his cheeks then looks at me. "Now for you, Panda. I'm sorry you got stuck in the middle of that mess. When you left, I wasn't sure exactly what I'd done to tick you off. I figured it was the whole ugly situation that evening, which I was responsible for. But I knew I owed you an apology." Butch nudges Ming, and she holds out her handbag. He reaches in and pulls out a box of chocolate-covered caramels and sets them on the table in front of me. "And I know that every sincere apology starts with chewy chocolaty goodness."

I can't help but chuckle. I roll my eyes at Butch, my shoulders softening. That's the old Butch I know and, God help me, have a soft spot the size of Texas in my heart for. But his words that night about family cut deep which is why a tinge of coolness lingers in my voice when I say, "Thank you, Butch."

He locks his gray eyes on mine. "And my hurtful remarks about coming from a 'good family'—" He shakes his head. "—Panda, I'm so sorry. There's not enough candy in the world to make up for that one."

My throat thickens, and I see Ming bring a hand to her mouth.

Butch sighs. "All I know is, whatever stock you came from must be Grade A Premium because you are a cut above the rest." I hear Lonnie swallow hard, and suddenly tears sting my eyes when Butch says, "I know I don't deserve it, but I hope you can forgive me, too."

My voice cracks. "Well, jeez, Butch. You're killing me."

Ming wipes a tear from her cheek. "Stupid bean goose."

I look into Butch's sad, remorseful eyes and feel a

tear roll down my cheek. "Yes, I forgive you. I mean, you're my favorite patient ever."

Butch's chin trembles, his eyes fill with tears, and that's when we all lose it. Ming and I wipe our wet faces with our fingertips. Lonnie starts sniffling. I pat my pockets for tissues with no luck.

Ming digs in her purse. "I know I have tissues in here somewhere."

I gaze up at Lonnie, then say to Butch, "Plus, not only are you my favorite patient and stubborn old man, but you're the father of the man I love. So, you know, there's that."

Lonnie clears his throat, and his voice cracks when he says, "Ming, did you say you have tissues in that army rucksack you call a purse?"

She digs up to her elbows then pulls out two wadded cocktail napkins from Suds and Spurs, and we dive for them. Butch nabs one, rips it in two, and gives the halves to me and Ming, then rips the other one for him and Lonnie.

Lonnie looks at Butch. "Dad, before things get too kumbaya, you should know that I was offered a nonsurgical position at Cassidy Memorial, and I accepted it."

Ming looks up, her black mascara running down her cheeks. "That's great, Lonnie."

He nods. "Thanks. I'll be a hospice physician. I start in a few weeks."

Butch lets out a long sigh. "You'll be a hospice doc." He stares down at the table for a while, then looks at Lonnie. "I'm real proud of you, Son." I hear Lonnie draw in a breath. "You know, when your mom was nearing the end of her life, I was at a complete loss for what to do. I couldn't fix it. Couldn't make her healthy. Couldn't keep her alive." Ming puts her hand on his shoulder, and I feel my eyes well up again as Butch goes on, "I wanted to support her, but I didn't know how." He grins sadly at Lonnie. "Then you'd come in the room and just hold her hand, say something softly to her, and she'd immediately seem at peace. You're going to help so many people in hospice. You're going to make a difference at a time when they're most vulnerable. Just like you did for your mom."

Then we're all sniffling and choking back sobs and wiping tears with our hands when Lonnie leans back and says, "Okay, Dad. You're forgiven, and you don't even need to buy me chocolate."

Ming dabs her face with the crumpled napkin as Butch digs through her handbag. Then he pulls out my Ranch Z cap. "Ramona, I was hoping you'd want this back. There's nothing that would make me happier than you being part of the team."

I press my lips together to keep my chin from trembling then say to Ming, "Anymore napkins in there?"

She digs through her purse then tosses two mini pads on the table. "They're clean. I keep a steady supply because sometimes that old bean goose makes me laugh so hard I dribble in my pants."

I grab the mini pad, notice Lonnie looking at me like I'm crazy, then say, "What? It's absorbent." I wipe my cheek, then pull on my cap.

Then Butch reaches over to hold Ming's hand. He looks at Lonnie. "You know, Son, Ming and I were talking. We realize that things between us happened fast."

Ming nods. "I'm sure that was difficult for you." She pats Lonnie's hand. "I want you to know that, for some insane reason, I love your father." She looks into Lonnie's eyes. "But I think about your mom every day. I miss her so much."

Lonnie swallows back tears. "Me, too."

Butch puts his arm around Ming's shoulder. "Call me crazy, but I'm head over heels in love with Ming. But, Son, not a day goes by—" His voice cracks. "Well, you know how much I miss your mother."

Nodding, Lonnie grabs the other mini pad and wipes his face. "I know, Dad."

Butch sighs. "And about that photo Shi-Yun brought to the intervention. The one of your mother looking happy at the engagement party…I've given it some thought. It's true she was happy that night, but here's what I also know to be true. She was happy because she wanted you to have a partner in life, someone who'd always be there beside you when she was no longer around." Butch searches my eyes then grins at Lonnie. "And your mother would have loved Ramona. Hell, she would have hand-knitted the Ranch Z cap for her if she'd had the chance."

Lonnie leans over and kisses my cheek. "I know. Mom would have loved everything about Ramona." He brushes his hand along my cheek. "You're right. Mom just wanted me to be happy. And nothing makes me happier than having Ramona in my life."

Chapter Forty-four

Three weeks later

Jules practically pirouettes in the center of my patio. "You've transformed this place!" She points to the sitting area I've created with a wicker sofa and coffee table that's shaded by a huge festive umbrella and surrounded by large ceramic pots with planted hibiscus and cascading vinca.

I smile. "Out back, Lonnie helped me hang fairy lights over the picnic table, and we put stone mulch and Adirondack chairs around the firepit." I raise my eyebrows. "And just wait until you go indoors. Got some cheerful throw pillows on the dinette bench and fun artwork on the walls."

Jules bounces on her toes. "So cute!"

I gaze over at the welcome mat I placed at the foot of my trailer steps. It reads: *Ramona Sadler, Happy Camper.* "I figured it was about time I started making this place feel like home."

We sit on the wicker sofa and cross our ankles on top of the coffee table.

Jules lets out a long exhale. "This is so nice. After running around with the boys all summer, I finally get to sit back and put my feet up."

"Livin' the dream." My lips curl into a grin. Three months ago, moving into this trailer at Nearly Heaven was my worst nightmare. Today, it may not be my dream come true, but living here is…good. Really good. I don't have to worry about making ends meet on my substitute teacher's pay while I figure out what I want to do professionally. I have Prisha and Frank here, offering curry and tea and laundromat quarters. And Ugly Jim and Bacon Joe a few lots down to lend a helping hand with weed whacking and pest control. More than that, they all offer the promise of friendship and laughter, and a warm blanket around my shoulders if I ever need it again.

And I have Lonnie right next door cooking me omelets, giving me closet and dresser space, reminding me every day that his house is my house. Talk about livin' the dream.

I look at Jules. "Do you think the guys are waiting for us in the barn?"

Lonnie invited Chase and the boys over to ride Sage and Spirit. The day Chase delivered those two amazing horses, Lonnie issued me an open barn invitation. I'm there all the time, brushing manes, picking hooves, hand-feeding carrots, and mucking out stalls. And Lonnie's giving me riding lessons. I've gone from being a little girl reading about horses to being a grown woman riding off into the sunset with the man of her dreams.

She flicks her wrist. "Are you kidding? Chase and the boys are probably talking Lonnie's ears off about barrel racing and neck reining." She pats my knee. "Speaking of riding wild ponies, how was the pullout sofa in Snap Peas?"

I snort a laugh. "Considering the close quarters, we had to keep the stallion tethered. But I swear after we got home, we couldn't keep our hands off each other. We were ravenous."

She nods. "Like sugar addicts on Choconutters."

"You got it." I grin. "We couldn't even control ourselves in the barn. Lonnie still has straw burn." I shift in my seat. "And I think I have a few oats hiding in an undisclosed location."

She laughs then arches an eyebrow. "So, things are going really well with you two."

"Yeah, I was kind of nervous about Lonnie staying in Snap Peas with me for a whole week. But he made himself at home. He played horseshoes with Earl and Ricky and helped me cook dinners and go through Mom's stuff. It was like…God, I don't even know what."

Jules brings a finger to her chin. "Hmm. Doing family things with your partner. Maybe it was like…being a couple."

I jerk my head back in surprise. "Yes! And the weird thing is that being a couple with Lonnie is just so easy. If we get tired or hangry and have a disagreement, we just talk it through. Then it's gone. There's no lingering resentment or, God forbid, some feeling wheelhouse marathon to process. It's just…nice."

She squints at me. "That's how it's supposed to be, you know."

I look into the distance, my eye catching the Nearly Heaven sign. "I didn't know. But I do now."

Jules and I walk along the path to Lonnie's place.

I lift my chin toward the sound of voices. "They're still in the barn." Stepping through the wide-open doors, I breathe in the smell of fresh hay, oats, and leather, then I stop in my tracks at the sight of a shirtless Lonnie, in boots and jeans, leading Spirit out of his stall. I grasp Jules's wrist. "Got any Choconutters? I'm dying here."

She shakes her head and nods toward the far end of

the barn where Chase, in jeans and leather chaps, is mounting Sage. "Did you say something? I was distracted by that Almond Bliss in spurs over there."

Wyatt and Boone run over to Jules. Wyatt points to Spirit. "Lonnie had me tack him up. I chose the Ranch Saddle and put a Western D Ring bit on him."

Boone waves toward Sage. "I put a Hound Bone Snaffle on him. Lonnie says he rides him bareback a lot, but today I put on his Barrel Saddle."

Jules side-eyes me. "Told ya the guys weren't waiting on us."

Chase presses his bootheels against Sage's belly, cueing him to walk toward the barn door. Then he calls to the boys, "Come on, gentlemen. We're ready to ride."

I listen to the soothing clip-clop of hooves as Lonnie leads Spirit out of the barn, mounts up, and then we all head for the riding ring.

Jules and I stand outside the fence, watching Lonnie and Chase trot then lope the horses around the ring for a while before bringing them to a halt and dismounting, so the boys can mount up.

I turn to Jules, whose blonde highlights look like they're dancing in the sunshine. "How are the boys liking seventh grade?"

She beams. "They love it."

"Really? That's great. So, Hawk Asshole, I mean, Astor—?"

She wriggles her eyebrows. "Hasn't bothered them once. I guess that night Chase and I went to his parents' house and ripped them all new ones has finally sunk in."

I hear the sound of footsteps on gravel and turn to see Prisha, Myra, and another girl approaching the riding ring. Prisha waves and says, "You know Myra, of course.

313

And this is her friend, Heather. The boys texted them and—"

Jules's head snaps back. "My boys? Texted...girls?"

Myra stretches her hands out. "We're in Mr. Durkee's homeroom class together. We were talking yesterday, and they told us Lonnie—"

Prisha clears her throat loudly.

Myra says, "I mean, Dr. Acres invited them over to ride his horses today. They said they'd text us if it was okay for us to come over, too."

Heather nods. "Myra and I ride at Windsong Farm." She looks out at the ring where Boone trots Spirit and says, "Nice working trot. He's maintaining a proper frame." She holds her hands to the sides of her mouth and calls out, "Hey, Boone. Try easing his rhythm down a bit and doing a slow extension."

Chase and Lonnie look over and wave.

Myra calls out to Wyatt, "That gelding looks great. Have him do a loping square."

We all watch the boys ride for a while then Jules turns to Myra and says, "Hey, remember at Ramona's pizza party a while back, we were all talking about Hawk Astor being a big pain in the butt?"

Prisha pipes up, "Big bully, short wick."

Myra and Heather face each other and bust out laughing.

Jules asks, "Is he still bothering y'all?"

Myra shakes her head. "Nope. Hawk's not a pain anymore."

Jules nods, looking satisfied that she and Chase helped Hawk turn a new leaf. "Glad to hear that."

Heather smiles. "The first day of school, we were all

eating lunch in the cafeteria and Hawk started picking on a kid with wraparound orthodontic braces."

Myra leans forward. "A bunch of us girls decided we weren't going to put up with that kind of bull for one more minute."

Heather drums her fingertips together. "We started a food war, and Hawk was our target enemy."

Myra snorts a laugh. "There were, like, twenty of us girls plastering Hawk with mashed potatoes and peas."

Prisha wags her finger at Myra then tries to bury a smile. "Your mother told me all about it."

Myra looks down at her boots. "We all got suspended for a day."

Heather sighs. "My parents were not happy." She bites her lip. "But it was worth it! We explained everything, and the principal talked to the teachers."

Myra beams. "The principal put a note in our records saying—" She holds up a finger, reciting the note. "—our infraction was to lessen the negative impact that a bully was having on the seventh-grade student body."

Heather stands straight. "Hawk hasn't bothered anyone since."

Jules smiles. "Well done, mares. You chased the horse's ass out of the barn."

The boys dismount from their horses, hand the reins to Chase and Lonnie, and walk over.

Wyatt wipes his sweaty forehead with the back of his hand. "Spirit's young, but he's got a nice gait and listens well to cues. Lonnie might have to work with him on transitions."

Myra squints at him. "It looked like he was almost starting to get the flying lead change."

315

Wyatt nods. "Yeah, it might have been that my alignment was off."

Boone looks at Jules. "Mom, did you bring something to eat?"

She shoots him The Mom look. "Yep. Corn casserole. Extra corn."

Boone rolls his eyes. "Mom—"

Jules smiles. "There's a bag of snacks in the barn. Your father said he set it on the hay bales."

Wyatt looks at Myra then at Heather. "Hey, y'all wanna see the sheep? They're really cool."

Boone pipes up, "Don't forget the chickens. Lonnie said whatever eggs we collect, we can bring home." He grins at Prisha. "Nani Prisha, you can come, too."

They all head off, and Jules and I watch Chase and Lonnie trot and lope the horses around the ring.

Jules glances at me. "You and Lonnie should come over for dinner this weekend. There are steaks on the grill with your names on 'em."

"I'd love that, and I know Lonnie would, too. But how about next weekend?"

"That'll work." She eyes me. "Let me guess. This weekend you're staying in to eat Choconutters."

I shake my head. "Nope. I'm going to Houston. Girls' weekend with Malvina."

Jules snorts a laugh. "In a million years, would you ever have guessed that things would turn out this way?"

I smile. "You mean, me getting pedicures and drinking shots of palinka with Martin's mother?"

Jules wrinkles her nose. "Yeah. That."

"Nope. Didn't see it coming." I pinch my chin. "And I never would have guessed that I'd *choose* to keep working as Miss Mona at Liberty Trail School District where I specialize in dodging spit wads in sixth-grade math class and wiping up first graders' nose bleeds." I hold up my hand. "For now."

Studying me, she tilts her head and says, "But you look…happy."

Tears sting my eyes. "Amazing, right? To think I'd be living in my little trailer feeling so ridiculously fucking happy."

Jules's eyes grow moist, and she sniffles. "Do you remember the day you moved into Nearly Heaven, and I told you that you deserve to be head over heels with a man who's head over heels about you?"

I laugh. "Yes, and I told you that's a tall order."

I look out at the ring, watching Lonnie ride, the golden-brown skin on his muscular arms and chest glistening in the sun as he holds the reins steadily in his strong, sure hands. "I don't know who's more athletic, the equine gelding or the human stallion." I grin. "And they both have big hearts and soft mouths."

Jules bursts a laugh. "Oh, you are head over heels."

I throw up my hands. "Guilty." I watch Lonnie halt Sage, then close his spurs to prompt the horse to back up, then release Sage forward again. They lope around the ring, and as he nears the rail where I stand, Lonnie lowers his chin and tips his hat. My breath catches and body tingles exactly the way it did that day I moved into the RV park, and he walked by my trailer cradling a lamb against his bare chest.

Jules nudges my elbow. "Do you remember the other thing I told you that day you moved in?"

I chuckle. "Yep. You told me to dump Martin and jump a cowboy."

Jules gestures to the riding ring and flashes her

317

trademark smile that's as broad as the San Gabriel River. "Looks like you got your cowboy."

Epilogue
Six months later

Breathing in the scent of sweet grass and earthy leather, I reach down and pat Spirit's muscular neck, watching his long, black mane flap in the warm February breeze. I smile over at Lonnie, seated atop Sage, looking like that magical mix of warmhearted doctor and strong-bodied cowboy that, I swear, every single day still turns my insides into a big, swoony, wondrous mess.

I call out to Lonnie, "Ready to ride?"

He answers with the tip of his hat.

Gathering my reins, I look out at the vast expanse of meadow ahead that, just a few days earlier, we rode over on our way to the field of Texas bluebonnets that had bloomed in all their glory.

That was on Valentine's Day. I'd spent the morning drinking coffee, eating frosted cinnamon rolls, and snuggling with Lonnie. After we cleared the breakfast dishes, he gave me the biggest heart-shaped box of chocolates I'd ever seen, along with a candle that somehow smelled like champagne bubbles and angel wings and love so enduring it couldn't possibly have a beginning or end.

Then we tacked up the horses and rode them along shady, wooded trails until the terrain opened into sunny, wide-open fields that we loped across until we reached our destination—the stretch of bluebonnets. We dismounted, then stood gazing at the brilliant blue flowers for a good long time before Lonnie turned to me and said softly, "Are you ready?"

Placing a hand on my heart, I offered a bittersweet smile. "Yes. It's time."

Lonnie stood patiently as I waded into the field of blue until I felt deeply surrounded by beauty. Then I cradled the baggy of my mom's ashes in my hands and tearfully told her, "You made the trip, Mommy. You've been here with me, in my heart all along, but now you're here in body, too."

Taking her ashes in my hand and stretching my arm as far as I could reach, I began twirling faster and faster, just like I had as a little girl in Snap Peas, whirling and watching the world blur around me. Twirling knee-deep in bluebonnets, and easing my grip, I let go and watched my mom's ashes fly free over the vast bed of blooms, then softly land in the field of blue as she came to rest.

When I finally stopped spinning, my head dizzy and body weak with grief, Lonnie was there to catch me, just as he had been that day at Rivermore Cemetery when my legs could no longer carry the weight of mourning and sorrow. Just like that day at Rivermore in Snap Peas, he was here in the bluebonnets in Jackalope, his strong arms around me, his steady heartbeat assuring me that I was not in this alone, and I breathed.

Lonnie clears his throat, and I glance over to see his mischievous grin. "So, when you asked if I was ready to ride, and I tipped my hat? I was answering 'yes' in Texan. Looks like some horse riding New Yorker needs to brush up on her Texas language skills."

Chuckling, I squeeze my bootheels against Spirit's belly to move him forward at a walk, then cue him to trot, then lope, my face stretching into a full-on smile at the sounds of Spirit's heaving breaths beneath me and the stomping of Sage's hooves behind me.

It's these moments on horseback, when my pulse races with excitement, and my heart bursts with gratitude, that those years of being bullied as a trailer-park kid, all those days of feeling small and stuck, just blows right off my shoulders with each mile I ride out in the open. Because as I race Spirit across this grassy terrain, my heart pounding and lungs filling with sweet fresh air, I'm free. Just like those wild ponies in *Misty of Chincoteague.* The ones that, thanks to my mom's encouragement, I read about over and over again. I'm free. And I know my mom is free, too.

Urging Spirit faster, we move into a gallop, and I call out to the wind, "Got those riding lessons you always wanted me to have, Mommy!" Heels down in my stirrups and my legs closed around Spirit like a hinge, I feel his mighty chest expand and contract with each powerful breath and stride as we cover more ground. When I see the flowers up ahead, I ease my leg pressure and relax my seat in the saddle to slow Spirit to a lope, then a trot, and, finally, a walk as we approach the far end of Hill Country Park where the bluebonnets seem to go on forever.

I halt Spirit in the shade, dismount, then pull his reins over his neck and look into his huge, soulful brown eyes. "Good boy, Spirit. When we get back to the barn, there's a big scoop of oats with your name on it." I run my hand over the white blaze on his face, and he lets out a happy snort. "Don't tell Sage, but I'm giving you extra sugar cubes."

I hear the clop of hooves slowing to a halt then grin at the sound of Lonnie saying, "Dang, you two were going strong. Sage and I could barely keep up."

I watch Lonnie dismount, his leg swinging over the saddle, his boots hitting solid ground, and my breath catches in my throat the way it does every time I look at this man—this doctor, farmer, cowboy man. The man I love.

Lonnie pats Sage's neck, then moves to his rear and opens the leather saddlebags, pulling out halters and lead ropes, then tethering Sage then Spirit to nearby tree limbs. Then, as if some enchanted wind blew him to me, in an instant it seems, Lonnie's by my side, his arm wrapped around my waist, and just like that, I'm giddy from his scent of bee balm and salty, musky goodness.

We walk to the park bench overlooking the bluebonnet field, and Lonnie stops and faces me. "Yep, that Spirit is too much horse for me. I'm more Sage's speed." I grin, and he kisses my cheek. "So, what do you say we make it official?"

I look up at him. "Make what official?"

He tilts his head. "Spirit being your horse."

My jaw drops into a smile.

He winks. "I mean, if you want him."

Throwing my arms around Lonnie's neck, I let out a joyous laugh. "Oh, I want him all right." Then I kiss Lonnie, because I want him, too, and, for a moment, the only things in this world that exist are Lonnie, love, happiness, and…my horse. I burst into another laugh. "Oh, my God. Not only did I get my dream man, but now I got my dream horse."

He kisses my forehead. "Let's face it, Spirit's been your horse from day one. I've given him how many bags of apples and carrots? But he follows you around with cartoon hearts over his big equine head, then looks at me like, 'Who are you?' "

We turn to the park bench that was donated a few months back by Butch and Ming. Before sitting down, Lonnie and I kiss our fingertips then touch the engraved plaque. *In loving memory of Carol Sadler and Priscilla Acres.*

Taking a seat, I look out at the field of wildflowers and sigh. "Gosh, I never tire of seeing these bluebonnets." They bloomed early this year, thanks to warm winter rains, and I'm soaking them in knowing that, just as the moon waxes full then wanes, soon enough these brilliant blue flowers will wither, brown, and go to seed, just as it's all meant to be.

Lonnie turns toward me on the bench, our knees touching. "Funny. I never tire of seeing you." He blinks at me. "I swear every time I look into your eyes, I feel like my heart is going to burst."

"Aw, right back atcha."

"I'm just saying, it's a good thing you know CPR, Nurse Sadler."

"Well, I'd hate for your heart to literally burst—" I wink. "—but I do need to brush up on my practical nursing skills before the next exam."

I've started nursing school. I decided to use my mom's insurance money to help pay the tuition. I think she would have liked that. Even Earl thought it was a great idea. The nursing program is grueling, but luckily, I have the best mentor ever: Nurse James. He quizzes me on protocol, tests me with flash cards, and, after every round of exams, he meets me at Suds and Spurs for a round of Texas Hurricanes. He also tells me that, after I graduate from this program, I should set my sights on becoming a nurse practitioner or teaching nursing at the University of Texas. And I may very well do that. Someday. The possibilities, for the first time in my life, feel endless. But right now, I'm happy studying and learning in a career field where I know I'll make a difference, where it feels like the right fit.

Lonnie sits straight, then pats my leg over my black leather chaps. "Almost forgot something. I'll be right back." I watch him walk toward Spirit and Sage, who are contentedly grazing. Then he unlatches one of the saddlebags and digs around. He returns, holding something in his hand, then takes a seat beside me, and grins. "Scored some after Christmas clearance." He holds out his hand revealing an ornament—a red and white camping trailer with a cute little door and windows with checkered curtains and a sign that reads, *Home is where the heart is.*

I bring a hand to my mouth. "That is so fucking adorable I can hardly contain myself."

"That's how I feel every time I look at you." He sets the ornament on the bench, then runs his thumb along my jawline. "You know, our road trip was my trip of a lifetime. The laughter, the heart-to-heart talks, the…vegan bacon."

I chuckle.

"That day you backed up your trailer in that crowded gas station parking lot being all I love my big-ass truck Ramona, I just knew." He places a hand over mine. "That even when we hit a pothole here and there, as long as you're beside me, it's the journey I want to be on, with the destination of who-the-hell-cares because I'm with you."

I let out a shaky breath. "Oh, Lonnie."

He sits straight and smiles. "I also scored some after Valentine's Day clearance." He reaches into his shirt pocket and holds out a miniature box of heart-shaped candies.

"Oh! These are like the ones we had at parties in

elementary school." I open the box, pluck out a candy heart, and read its message, "Hug Me." I pull out another one and chuckle. "Wink Wink. These are so cute."

Lonnie leans forward, peering into the box. "Where's the one that says—?" He holds out his hand. "May I?" I pass him the box, and he gently dumps the remainder of its contents into his palm. "Oh, there it is."

He places the heart that reads, "Be Mine" in my hand. I look at it, then blink at the pile of sweets in his hand, feeling suddenly stunned. "Is that a—?"

I look at Lonnie's handsome face flashing an expressive mix of nervousness, hopefulness, and endless sincerity. Then I look back down at the pile of candy hearts in his hand, and the diamond ring nestled in them.

He says in a gentle voice, "I'd planned to give you this on Valentine's Day, but when the weather was so nice and you mentioned riding to the bluebonnets to spread the ashes, well, I thought the day should be devoted to your love for your mom."

My chin trembles. "Thank you."

Lonnie picks up the ring—a gorgeous, crystal-clear diamond bookended by blue topaz. "This isn't my mother's ring. I'd like to have that gemstone put into a necklace for you to wear on our wedding day." He bites his lip. "I mean, if you say 'yes.' " He searches my eyes. "I wanted to choose a ring just for you. The two blue topaz remind me of shining stars in the night sky."

I'm not sure I'm even breathing as he puts the candy hearts in his shirt pocket then takes my left hand and gently slides the ring onto my finger.

"And the diamond reminds me of your beauty and my clarity in knowing that you are the love of my life. Ramona, how about we make it official? Will you—?"

He nods at the candy heart in my palm. "—be mine?"

I open my mouth, trying to push that simple, one-syllable word past the bottleneck of happy tears in my throat. I swallow hard. "Yes." Then I say it again, louder this time. "Yes!"

We both look at one another, wide-eyed, for a moment. Then we're in each other's arms—hugging, laughing, nuzzling, kissing—knowing that this day is devoted to our love for one another. And that tomorrow will be, too. And the day after that...and the day after that...

A word about the author…

Laurie Woodford is a novelist, memoirist, and educator who taught college English in the U.S. and Asia for over twenty years. When she's not writing, teaching, or spending time with her amazing husband, Bruce, and wonder dog, Journey, she volunteers for hospice as a certified end-of-life doula. For more, please visit www.lauriewoodford.com.

www.lauriewoodford.com